The Twisted Vine

Jeanne Vaughn

Knoxville, Tennessee, USA
crippledbeaglepublishing.com

Cover design by Maria Loysa-Bel Nueve – de los Angeles

Paperback ISBN 978-1-965334-16-4, 978-1-965334-18-8
Hardcover ISBN 978-1-965334-19-5
Ebook ISBN 978-1-965334-20-1
Library of Congress Control Number: 2024922470

Printed in the United States of America

"Ballade of True Wisdom"
by Andrew Lang

...I'd leave all the hurry,
The noise, and the fray,
For a house full of books,
And a garden of flowers.

Chapter 1

The bright morning sun streamed through Addie Kent's lace curtains, casting fragments of light about her room like thousands of twinkling fireflies. Her wide-open eyes gazed blankly into the dazzling display, causing them to tear and her lids to flutter. Forcing her eyes closed, she drew in a long, deep breath, exhaling a frosty vapor that lingered in the chilly air.

It had been an agonizingly long and sleepless night, but she wasn't ready to face the day, not yet. She snuggled deeper under the pile of warm quilts and pulled them over her head. Here, she took refuge from the frigid air and the pesky light that beckoned her from her cozy nest.

Her twin, Lizzie, had been the source of her unease, haunting her dreams and leaving her restless all through the night. Her thoughts drifted back to the day Lizzie left—they had just celebrated their seventeenth birthdays when she walked out of their lives. Her hateful last words still rang clear: "I never want to see any of you ever again, and you can take this to the bank—hell will freeze over before I set foot in Beau Ridge, South Carolina, again."

Following her stinging vow, she stomped out of the room and slammed the door behind her. Without so much as a backward glance, Lizzie strode down the walk to the waiting car, to the boy behind the wheel, who then pulled onto the street, burning rubber on the asphalt as they sped away. She and her parents stood at the door in a state of shock, mouths gaping open, sad and wounded by Lizzie's hurtful words, watching as the car retreated until it was no longer visible. Just like that, Lizzie had gone out of their lives—to who knows where.

Addie and her parents were heartbroken. Life without her had never been the same for any of them—the first year was the hardest of all. A gloom had settled over their home. That gloom ran straight to the very core of their souls. In public they put on a good show but proved to be poor actors, for their attempts fooled no one; sadness swirled around them like bees on a honeycomb.

Addie placed a hand over her heart, feeling that old familiar ache, a longing for her twin so deep it hurt. She remembered how Lizzie's absence had affected each of them—in different ways.

Her mother, to Addie's and her father's astonishment, abandoned her garden for an entire season, choosing instead to sit for hours making far too many crocheted doilies for the church bazaar. All were made from black thread, which no proper Southern lady would be caught dead displaying in her home; white for sure, or ecru is always a nice choice, but never black. Addie didn't have the heart to tell her mother what a waste of time it was and that her efforts wouldn't financially benefit the cause at all.

But in her heart of hearts, she knew they were all coping the best way they could, and if making black doilies gave her comfort, then so be it. It was only when she needed more thread, that busybody Miss White at the five-and-dime would go on and on saying she couldn't imagine why on earth anybody needed that much black thread, stating that it was just plain morbid. Her mother would simply smile, pay her bill, and place her order for more. But it was at night that her mother let down her hair, exposing her raw, anguished emotions—when, through her bedroom wall, Addie could hear her mother's mournful sobbing, ceasing only when her tears ran dry.

As for her father, his usual kindness had all but walked out the door with Lizzie. He had become quick-tempered and critical and, worst of all, he forbade Addie or her mother to speak Lizzie's name or allow anyone else to do so under his roof. This put the two of them on constant guard, and they found themselves shushing visitors just before her name was spoken. She recalled the time when his good friend Burt Stone dropped by for a visit. Burt's family lived just two houses down from them, and his daughter, Abigale, often came to their house to play. Burt, bless his heart, was known for putting his foot in his mouth, so most of the time he chose to stick his red head in the sand to avoid a misstep. It would have served him well to have stuck with that plan, but on this occasion, he threw caution to the wind. Thinking he was doing a good deed by adding a little levity to this good friend's dismal frame of mind, he started in on a tale about the time when Abigale was pulled into one of Lizzie's wild adventures. Just as his mouth was about to utter Lizzie's name, Addie faked a coughing spell followed by her mother asking for Burt's forgiveness, and that Addie had caught a virus at school and had been throwing up all day. Burt stopped mid-sentence and made a hasty departure.

A smile crossed Addie's face. It wasn't a bit funny at the time, for she and her mother dreaded every knock at the door, but looking back she saw the humor in the extreme measures they took to keep Lizzie's name from being spoken.

As for herself, she would awaken at the slightest sound, rolling over expecting to see Lizzie in her bed, only to find it tidily made and no one there. Her ears would listen for the slamming of the screen door that announced Lizzie's return from a long day of doing who knows what. Sometimes, when she closed her eyes, she could visualize the two of them lined up, side by side in the long hallway, and on the count of three, racing to be first to the bathroom—a game she lost every time because Lizzie could outrun her any day of the week.

The sorrowful memories brought tears to her eyes, and she wiped them with the palms of her hands. They had all wanted to believe that, in time, Lizzie would come to her senses and come back to the family who loved her so much.

Addie grimaced. She knew Lizzie would never come back to them. She would rather cut off an arm than be proven wrong—she was just that dad-burned stubborn.

Buried beneath the covers, the face that had plagued her through the night came into view—clear as crystal. The face was definitely Lizzie's, but it lacked the vivacious spark, the twinkle in her eyes, and the mischievous grin she knew so well. Instead, it was a face that revealed years of sadness and something else, something that she dares not think could be true. One thing was certain: the past ten years had taken a heavy toll on Lizzie.

She rubbed her temples. The feeling that something was going on with her sister continued to nag her. She shook it off—it was just a feeling—nothing more.

Ever since Lizzie's departure, Addie had been left with mixed emotions. She could have such good memories that caused her to miss her badly one minute and be mad as hell the next because of the cruel and heartless way she had deserted them. The rollercoaster effect left her wondering how she would react if one day Lizzie showed up on her doorstep. Would she open her arms to her or slam the door in her face? She didn't think she'd ever know the answer to that question.

Lying in bed was only making matters worse. Her mind kept swirling around Lizzie. She resolved to get out of bed, make a strong cup of coffee to clear her thoughts, and do something more productive than worrying herself silly over seemingly nothing.

She crawled out of bed and slid her feet into her old fuzzy slippers. Slipping into her robe she shuffled to the bathroom.

Standing in front of the misty mirror she shrieked at the shocking image staring back at her. She leaned in for a closer look; the whites of her eyes were riddled with wavy red lines and under them were dark puffy circles. Her usual peaches and cream complexion was instead rosy red. Worst of all, her long strawberry blond hair, unruly on any day, was wound tight like old mattress springs.

She picked up her brush and tugged it through a section of wiry hair, grimacing as it caught in the tangles and pulled at her scalp. Throwing up her hands, she laid the brush aside. She gathered it up at the base of her neck and tied a satin ribbon around it.

Gazing again into the mirror, she released a long, exasperated breath that fogged the cold glass. She shivered and wrapped her robe tighter around her, bewildered that, in all these years, she had never gotten used to the cold that made its way into the oversized rooms, lingering far too long like guests who overstayed their welcome.

Her mind wandered off to her decision to keep the drafty old house after Reggie passed. It had the townsfolk wondering if she'd lost her mind, and they'd felt it was their duty to put in their two cents.

Her neighbor, Joe Cox, said, "Sell the place." Of course, she knew he had wanted her land for years. Minnie Ray had said, "Move to town and rent a place, let the landlord take care of the upkeep." Then, there was Sue Biggs, who insisted, "Just buy a little place, lay down some roots somewhere other than out in the boonies all by yourself."

She could have taken any of their suggestions—they all made perfect sense. It was not that she's not practical, she had assured herself. It's just that the land and the house are the only familiar things she had left, now that everyone was gone. She had made it work; the money from her share of the crops paid the taxes with a little left over, not much, but she'd been surprised that she didn't need much. To her amazement, the changes she'd implemented had come easy—even fulfilling.

She shivered, and made her way to the kitchen, straight to the coffee pot. She filled the pot with cold water, measured two heaping tablespoons of grounds into the basket and set it on the stove eye. While the coffee brewed, she settled into her chair at the table, picked up her notebook and turned it to a blank page.

Subconsciously, she thumped her pen on the page and stared out the window into her garden. Whenever she was troubled, she turned her thoughts to her beloved sanctuary, and like snowflakes touched by the warm sun—they melted into nothingness. But today, her garden had failed to work its magic. Her thoughts of Lizzie were all-consuming, swirling around in her mind like a song you can't get out of your head. *What's going on with you, Lizzie?*

Her eyes settled on a framed photograph that hung on the wall by the window. It was a picture their mother had taken of her and Lizzie on their first day of school. Hand in hand, they stood on the broad steps, smiling brightly in front of the building's double doors. Addie sat transfixed, her eyes studied their young faces. She loved this photograph; the memory it brought to mind never ceased to bring a smile to her face.

It was on the very day that the picture was taken that their first-grade teacher, *Miss Dingaling*, as Lizzie called her, of course not to her face, had discovered they were twins.

In front of the whole class with her hands on her hips, her snooty attitude on full display, she had pointed to the two of them and said, "I find it hard to believe the two of you are twins. You bear no resemblance whatsoever. Why, you're just as different as daylight and dark."

Lizzie stood up, straightened her back, and in an equally snooty la-de-da way said, "You don't have to look alike to be twins, Miss Ding," she caught her words before they came falling out, "uh, Miss Moore. Addie and I share something you obviously know nothing about, we share our hearts." After her little speech Lizzie sat, lifted her chin, and reached across the aisle for Addie's hand.

To this day she could still see the look on Miss Moore's dumbstruck face. She smiled at the fond memory of her feisty twin, who always said exactly what was on her mind, never minding the consequences—it's one of the things she loved and missed most about Lizzie.

Addie touched her heart, and it actually ached in the spot where she held Lizzie close. *What happened to us? How did we drift so far apart?* But she knew what had happened, and it had a name—*Jim Bob Thornhill*.

Addie ran her hand over her forehead, and an overwhelming sadness swept over her as she recalled the negative effect Jim Bob had on Lizzie. From the very first day he came into her life—everything changed.

Jim Bob was eighteen and wilder than a buck. Everyone in town knew he was totally lacking discipline, being raised by his no-account drunken father, who knew the jailhouse better than he knew his own. Maybe because Jim Bob had to raise himself, he had lived by his own rules. He drove too fast, partied too hard, drank too much, and was as bull-headed as the day is long. Problem was, Lizzie didn't fall too far from that tree herself. When you put the two of them together, the result was a surefire recipe for disaster.

Poor Lizzie just couldn't see the forest for the trees even though they all begged and pleaded with her, tried to talk some sense into her, anything to keep her from running away with Jim Bob. *If she had just listened to Mama's warnings.*

Mama had seen Lizzie's life play out in a vision, and she pleaded with Lizzie, telling her just how miserable her life with Jim Bob would be. But, her warnings went in one ear and out the other. Lizzie was headstrong and in love. No amount of pleading, begging, or fortune-telling would ever change her mind.

The familiar perking sound drew Addie's attention to the coffee pot, with its dark contents bubbling up into the glass top. Into her favorite china cup, she dropped in two lumps of sugar and poured in the steaming liquid, stirring until the sugar dissolved. Settling back in her chair, she sighed deeply, cradling the warm cup between her hands. She took a slow sip, eyes drifting over the walls then up to ceiling. The house, and all it holds within its walls, came rushing back to her in a flood of memory.

Her heart had been set on Magnolia Place from the moment she first laid eyes on it. She'd even convinced herself that one day it would be hers and once her mind was set, neither hell nor high water would get in her way.

She sighed heavily as the truth of her former self washed over her. She had been greedy—she had wanted it all: the mansion, the rich husband, the fancy clothes, the servants, and the prestige that went hand in hand with wealth. But, to be truthful, money was at the root of it all. The Kents, owners of Magnolia Place, had everything she desired—they also had a son.

She'd known the Kents' only son, Reggie, all her life, they had been classmates forever—she, the top in her class, Reggie, the class clown. When becoming teenagers, it wasn't that she couldn't have had any boy she wanted, it was that she wanted him—the rich boy. She'd made up her mind to have him—by hook or by crook.

Given that Reggie was spoiled rotten and allowed to do just as he pleased, he could have been arrogant and obnoxious. To the contrary, he was actually kind to a fault and possessed a boyish charm. School didn't interest him in the least, and making good grades interested him even less. By the time they were in the eighth grade, he was mere inches from failing and having to repeat the grade. That was when she had begun to set her hook by stepping in and offering herself as a tutor. She found out quickly that Reggie, bless his heart, was not only lazy, but he was incapable of learning—plain and simple. This, too, had worked in her favor. He couldn't pass on his own accord, so she did all his work for him—keeping him from failing. The hook was set, he'd become totally dependent on her; he could hardly make a move without first consulting her.

She grimaced, recalling how she'd made poor, unsuspecting Reggie the target of her scheme. In the long run though—he got what he needed—she got what she wanted. After all, hadn't she always heard—all's fair in love and war?

For generations Magnolia Plantation and the Kent family had prospered from their thousand-acre cotton operation. As a matter of fact, the Kents were the richest family in all of Clayton County. They had accumulated so much wealth that they didn't know what to do with it all, spending it lavishly on anything and everything their hearts desired. Through the years the families thrived on what the land produced, enabling them to maintain the enormous house and grounds with plenty left over—of which little was saved. By the time Reggie's father inherited the house and the land, hard economic times had hit, and the endless flow of money came to a screeching halt. But, compelled as his parents were to keep up appearances, they began to sell one valuable item after another, enabling them to continue throwing their lavish parties and purchasing expensive clothes while downright neglecting the upkeep of the house.

Their marriage was inevitable and like everything else the Kents did, their wedding was spectacular—the social event of the season. As a wedding gift, Reggie's parents had signed over Magnolia Place—lock stock and barrel. Two days later, they boarded a ship bound for Italy—never to return to South Carolina.

She was only eighteen, and the house and husband she had so desperately wanted were hers at last, but what now? She had expected her in-laws to help out, but instead they had abandoned them—left them with a huge house that was falling apart before their very eyes. The roof leaked, the floors creaked, the paint was peeling, the doors were warped, and that was just a start. Her husband, seemingly allergic to work and lacking any useful skills, offered little help—she was just as helpless. Even if they had been capable of fixing what needed fixing, there was no money. Instead of the prestige she had so desired, they were what people called land poor, meaning they had land but were poor as dirt.

Reggie had no attachment to the house or the land, he cared only about the money they could have from selling it. But Addie loved it, shabby as it was. She knew it was all they had of lasting value. She also knew that the money they would get from selling out would be gone in a New York minute. Reggie's gambling addiction, and the fact that he was known to lose more than he ever won, would see to that.

Up to this point, Addie had been oblivious to matters concerning money, but for their survival, she had no choice but to get involved. The land made enough money to pay the taxes and provide for necessities. Everything else, she realized, would have to be done by themselves. The two of them, spoiled and inept as they were, would have to make adjustments. So, she mended the holes that kept appearing in their clothes, cooked their meals, and grew the food they ate. Reggie was hopeless when it came to even the most trivial repairs, and needless to say, the house fell into further ruin. Yes, it was all about money. Money had made them kings—the lack of it had made them paupers.

When, at first, finding herself thrown into the unfamiliar waters of domestic chores, Addie was overwhelmed—to say the least. The kitchen and all the goings on between the sterile white walls had been the job of others. Everything in the room was new to her, full of things she had no idea how to use. Reading a cookbook was like understanding a foreign language, neither of which made sense to her.

With no one to help her in learning the functions of a kitchen, she began with one appliance at a time, discovering the workings of each and jotting down notes as she determined what knobs did what and the function of each. The cabinets were filled with gadgets for which she found uses that may or may not have been their intended purpose.

The kitchen had everything a cook could possibly desire and more, but every time Addie entered it, goose bumps popped up on her arms from the impersonal coldness it exuded. Since this was now her space—that would have to change.

Color was what it lacked: warm, appealing, inviting color. It needed curtains on the windows and cushions on the chairs, and herbs on the windowsills. The thought of redoing the space and making it her own gave her new purpose, and she eagerly began the transformation. And just as the kitchen transformed, her own personal transformation began.

A satisfied smile crossed Addie's face as her gaze surveyed the space around her. A familiar sense of tranquility surged through her. It was the same feeling she had whenever she was within these walls.

Even when gray clouds loomed outside, Addie's kitchen with its walls of bright yellow, warmed the soul like a sunny summer day. The crisp white eyelet curtains, pulled to each side, allowed her a clear view of the outdoors. Clay pots filled with various herbs sat side by side on the windowsills, infusing the air with their fragrant scents. Delicate white lace topped the kitchen table, and cushions of pale yellow sat atop the painted white chairs that encircled it. On the walls were beautiful framed flowers in an array of vibrant colors that Addie embroidered herself.

A painted white cabinet with glass doors holding a variety of china plates, bowls and dainty tea cups sitting atop mismatched saucers stood against one wall. Addie loved discovering that mixing and matching made for such an appealing display.

She was amazed how quickly she had taken to her new circumstances, even finding it fun and rewarding. She'd discovered that she had a real knack for making all kinds of things work together. She'd made friends with the owner of Frugal Freda's, the thrift shop on Main Street, that had become her favorite place to shop.

Freda frequented auctions, bringing in boxes of various items, that she allowed Addie to go through before putting anything out on the shelves. Like a kid in a candy store, Addie relished finding treasures she prized far more than the expensive things that had once filled the house.

She stretched her arms over her head and for the first time this morning, she turned to look at the clock. She stared in disbelief—*it couldn't be ten o'clock.* She walked to the window and peered into the bright blue sky. Through the glass, she felt the warm sun on her skin. She turned to walk away, but her eyes caught a glimpse of something. Spinning back around she stepped close to the glass; her gaze fixed on the little green shoots in her garden—the first sign of spring. Like flipping on a switch, she instantly felt her melancholy mood lift. Her beloved garden was summoning her.

Addie moved about the kitchen like a buzz saw. She hastily ate part of a bran muffin, washed it down with a few sips of coffee, and then tidied up, humming gaily. Her feet danced down the hall and into the bathroom. Not wasting precious time, she didn't bother looking into the mirror again but washed her face and gave her teeth a quick brushing. In her room she changed into a flannel shirt and duck cotton pants and scurried to her storeroom.

The room, though relatively small, was amazingly organized from floor to ceiling and held everything Addie needed for indoor and outdoor tasks, all of which were finds from Frugal Freda's. On one wall was her sewing cabinet, and above it were shelves that held spools of thread, neatly folded fabric and glass jars filled with buttons and pins. Next to that her coats, coveralls and overalls hung in a neat row. On the floor, a line of boots stood at attention like toy soldiers ready to trudge through mud, rain, or snow. On the opposite wall stood a sturdy washing machine and beside it was a bench over which scarves, hats, and caps hung from hooks of varying heights. Everything had its place, even under the bench, where wooden crates held various useful items tucked tidily out of sight.

Addie took down her warm coveralls and slipped them on over her clothes, then wrapped a woolen scarf around her neck. Sitting on the bench, she tugged on her tall, insulated boots and groaned. Lately, she'd been noticing tiny aches and pains that she attributed to her winter inactivity.

Stepping out onto the porch, she stood there a moment, breathing in the fresh morning air. Her heartbeat quickened at the thought of returning to her garden—her sanctuary— the only place where her loneliness was left outside the gate. Quickening her pace, she made her way across the stepping stones. At the gate she lifted the cold iron latch and stepped inside. At that very moment, as always, she felt her mother's presence. A tingling sensation ran through her, as she anticipated the two of them working side by side, just as they had done when she was a child.

The corners of her mouth lifted as she took in the scene before her. She had read that British people love their winter gardens. Although colorless, they were lovely just the same—where English ivy twines around stone statues that stand hither and yon among the meandering paths.

She loved the concept so much that she patterned hers after it.

She'd been surprised to discover that not everyone shared her opinion, recalling the time when uppity Charlotte Vandergriff, remarked that her winter garden resembled a graveyard with its dead vines and cold grey stones. Addie had bit her tongue almost in two to keep her bad thoughts from pouring out. Remembering her Southern manners and in her sweetest Southern drawl, she plastered a sappy grin on her face and replied, "Charlotte honey, how you do go on about things you know so little about." It was a cutting remark, she'd known, but not half as cutting as the tongue lashing she held back.

Shaking thoughts of Lizzy and silly Charlotte from her mind, she eagerly made her way to the sprouting buttercups. Bending over the tender shoots, with her fingers, she carefully raked aside the dried leaves and twigs, discovering more and more as she worked.

Addie connected to the earth like a duck to water. Like a sixth sense she could evaluate the condition of the soil by rubbing it between her fingers; it was the reason she preferred to work with her hands whenever possible. However, some jobs were made more efficient with the right tool—this was a such a job. Rising to her feet, she brushed her hands on her coveralls and made her way down the path to the small building near the back of the garden. A hand-printed sign in a lovely script hung on the door that read "The Shed"; like everything else, it had Addie's signature touch on it.

The small building was made of wood with a gable roof. On either side of a dutch door were two windows under which were wooden boxes that would soon overflow with showy flowers and trailing vines. Inside was an assortment of various gardening implements, large and small, that hung from hooks and lined one wall. Against the opposite wall stood a long table and atop it were glass jars labeled with curious names and containing strange ingredients. A large container, used specifically for mixing, sat in the center of the table surrounded by a scale and measuring devices of all shapes and sizes.

From their specified place, Addie gathered the tools she needed: a leaf rake, a shovel, a spade, and a pair of hand clippers. From behind the shed she retrieved a wheelbarrow and placed the tools inside it. She pushed the wheelbarrow to the area where she'd been working. Starting with the rake, she carefully dragged its metal teeth across the tender shoots. Humming happily, she worked until all the sprouting leaves had been exposed to the bright sunlight.

Addie cupped her hands over top of the rake handle and rested her chin. A pleased look settled on her face. The exposed pointy green leaves would soon produce a sea of her favorite yellow flower: the buttercup—the first flower of spring and known to represent joy, happiness and friendship. This was the sign she'd longed for—the end of winter—the renewal of life.

Nothing in Addie's garden was done willy-nilly. In her shed she kept a notebook with a master plan for every season, every plant, and every task. She valued it like her life and followed it to the letter. On the cover, in her beautiful flowing script was the simple title: Addie's Garden Handbook. And, just in case—heaven forbid—something caused her to forget, on the first page, in big, bold capital letters were the words: **DON'T MESS WITH WHAT WORKS!**

Retrieving the book, Addie turned to the first section, titled *Spring,* to see what chore she would tackle next. Item one read: remove last season's dead foliage by using hand clippers. Below it were specific instructions for each flower and plant. Closing the book, she slipped the pair hand clippers into the pocket of her coveralls and retrieved a five-gallon bucket to discard the clippings.

She made her way to her perennial beds and began clipping away the dead and damaged foliage and placing the cuttings in the bucket. When the bucket became full, she emptied the contents into the wheelbarrow and proceeded on in the same manner from plant to plant.

Hours had passed before Addie looked to the sky, noting the low position of the sun—an indication that the sun would soon be setting and there would be no light left to work by. Like everything else, there was a process to quitting a day's work; everything had to be put back in its place. The contents of the wheelbarrow were dumped into a pile that she'd later separate to either compost or burn. The wheelbarrow was returned to its place at the back of the shed, and the tools were back on their designated hooks inside the shed.

As a final step, she studied her workbook, making a mental note of what her next tasks would be. Taking a last look around, she double-checked that everything was in its place. She stepped out of the building that had already grown dark and into the bright golden glow that illuminated the western sky.

Addie had thoughtfully designed every aspect of her garden down to the perfect placement of her stone benches where sunsets and sunrises could be best viewed. At the end of a full and rewarding day, it had become her ritual to retreat to her evening bench where the warm golden tones filled the sky and warmed her soul, leaving her with a feeling of complete contentment.

Seated contentedly on the stone bench, she fixed her gaze on the dazzling display of rich golden tones that grew brighter with every passing minute. As the sun melted into the horizon and its colors faded, a quiet peace settled over her.

She sighed deeply. Something about this day had put her in a reflective mood, her thoughts continually pulling her into the past. Reflectively, she stared into the colorless sky and thoughts of her mother returned. Addie had been her little clone. From the time she could walk, she could be found at her mother's side, mimicking her every move from morning to night. Their mornings were spent together in her mother's garden with her soft voice, ever so patiently, filling her with her wisdom. She taught her things like how to prepare the soil for planting, how deep to plant the seeds, how to care for the plants and flowers, so many aspects, so much to learn. She remembered clinging to her every word, soaking in her knowledge like a thirsty sponge. Her mother had so freely and lovingly passed on all her gardening secrets, even her most sacred one—The Formula, as she fittingly called it.

The Formula was a fertilizer of her mother's own creation. Applied in just the right proportions, the results were astounding: enormous blooms, vibrant colors, the greenest foliage, and extraordinary fruits and vegetables. Year after year, her mother had gracefully accepted first-place ribbons in every category at the county fair.

The Formula had been years in the making, having a series of failures and successes, trials and errors until her mother came up with just the right ingredients measured in the precise portions. It consisted of things most people would consider smelly and disgusting; things like bat guano, fish emulsion, blood meal, worm castings, and other ingredients so secretive that she literally made Addie cross her heart and hope to die—never ever to divulge.

Her mother's recipe for The Formula was perfect; Addie followed it to the letter—until the day she didn't.

It was a day she'd never forget as long as she lived. She'd been adding ingredients for The Formula into the mixing pot. From out of nowhere a bird appeared and hovered directly over it and dropped two tiny seeds on top of the mixture—then immediately flew out. Her shocked reaction had been a long, drawn out sheeeeeit—the word her fiesty Aunt Ida Lou famously uttered whenever anything went wrong. The incident sent her into a frenzy—the mixture would have to be thrown out, she'd have to start over—unless—she could extract them. Reaching in with her fingers, ever so carefully, she successfully removed them before they had a chance to settle into the mixture.

On a whim, she had taken her magnifying glass and scavenged through her garden on hands and knees, scratching with her fingers through the dirt, plucking up every seed she found, comparing them for an exact match. She'd known this could be a waste of time—but what if it wasn't? She believed in fate, and she had a strong feeling that this was meant to be. She had searched until she thought she was going cross-eyed. Just when she didn't think her strained eyes could bear another minute—she found the match. Clutching the seeds in her hand, she rushed back to the shed, closed her eyes and tossed them into the batch.

She had immediately regretted her impulsive action and went to retrieve them—it was too late—they had disappeared out of sight. The Formula had been altered and she feared the worst. Later, when it came time to fertilize her garden, she proceeded with her normal routine. Carefully, measuring the precise amounts of The Formula and working it into the soil around her plants and flowers, then giving everything a good dousing of water. Upon returning to her garden the following morning, she couldn't believe her eyes. To her astonishment, overnight, phenomenal growth had taken place—exceeding any previous results. The only explanation had to be the addition of the two tiny seeds. Needless to say, after that, the seeds became a permanent ingredient and because she had now had a hand in its development, she renamed it— The Formula 2—giving proper credit to the two miraculous seeds. Soon after, she discovered what made the tiny seeds so beneficial—but like the other secret ingredients, that also, would remain undisclosed.

The sudden drop in temperature caused Addie to return her thoughts to the present. She shivered and wrapped her arms around her. Rising from the bench she took one last look though the dim light, then started walking back to the house. As she approached the gate, her heart grew heavy. It happened every time she had to leave her mother and return to her solitary existence. She whispered, "I love you

Mother," blew her a kiss, and walked slowly through the gate, latching it behind her.

Back in her storeroom, she put away her outdoor garments and made her way to the kitchen. While washing the dirt from her hands, a dizzy feeling came over her, and she realized she hadn't taken the time for lunch. She rummaged through the refrigerator and found a slice of leftover meatloaf, and some raw broccoli and carrots. Pouring a tall glass of water, she settled into her chair at the table.

Her appetite and meals had changed drastically since her husband, Reggie, passed away—barely more than two years ago. She gazed out the window into the pitch blackness, her most dreaded part of the day. Her days, she filled with various activities, but when darkness fell, her mood fell with it, making way for loneliness to swoop in and consume her.

She sighed heavily. The excitement of the day had vanished, returning was the tension she'd felt earlier, building in her shoulders and neck. She ran her hand over the back of her neck. *A good night's sleep will make everything seem better.*

Gathering her dirty dishes, she hastily washed them, then flipped the switch, leaving the room in darkness. With heavy steps she made her way to her bedroom.

Prepared for a repeat performance of the previous night, Addie took a book from her nightstand and climbed into bed. At least she could pass the hours doing something rather than lying awake all night. She opened the book to the first page and began to read, her eyelids drooping, her head nodding. Realizing she had no idea what she had just read, she started over, her lids growing heavier and heavier. Her body became limp, the book fell to the floor—she drifted off into a sound sleep.

At precisely six o'clock, Addie awoke with a jolt. She sat bolt upright in bed. Like a movie playing in her mind, she saw Lizzie, a baby and a young girl. They were in grave danger. Lizzie, her body being kicked, bright red blood staining her white nightgown, her baby wailing in a man's clutches, the young girl running, a long iron stick in her hands. Alarm bells sounded in Addie's head. She knew this was no dream—not even a nightmare—it was the sight. She had to get to them now! Something terrible was happening!

Her mind kept replaying the scene she had witnessed as her instincts guided her through the motions of preparing to leave. Throwing off her gown, she put on the clothes she had worn the previous day. Making a quick stop in her bathroom, she splashed icy cold water on her face and tied back her hair. Hastily, she made her way to the storeroom for her coat and boots. She stopped abruptly.

A defiant look spread across her face. *What are you doing? Lizzie left you, and for what? That good-for-nothing, lowlife Jim Bob—that's what. She chose him, not you, or mother or father. She made her bed—let her lie in it.*

A battle played in her head. Part of her wanted to ignore it, it was none of her business. The other part was urging her to go to her sister and her children, do what she could to help. She trusted her visions. What she saw was real. She could never live with herself if she didn't act, knowing that even now—it could be too late.

Hurriedly, she threw on her coat and pulled on her boots, and within mere minutes she was in her truck, her foot to the floor, loose gravel and dirt flying out in all directions. Her whole body was in overdrive with one objective—get to her family as fast as her old truck could take her there.

Addie reached over, opened the glove box, and retrieved the map and directions that had been there for years. She knew in her heart of hearts that sooner or later, the day would come when she would need them. That was why years earlier, she asked her oldest and dearest friend, Lester, to play detective and find where Jim Bob had taken Lizzie.

Lester was an attorney with a nose like a bloodhound, but even with his keen instincts it hadn't been easy. There was a time when he began to think they had dropped off the face of the earth, but it turned out they had just dropped down to LA—Lower Alabama. At the time, all she wanted was to know where Lizzie was living. She had stored the map where she knew it would be most needed when the time came. The time was now.

Out on the highway she glanced at the map. Five hours and fifty minutes would take her to the town of Little Hope, located in the southernmost part of the state. Checking the fuel gauge, the needle indicated a full tank. She sighed in relief. She hoped she could make the six-hour trip without stopping. Putting her foot to the floor, she threw caution to the wind, speeding along the highway like a woman possessed. With every mile her urgency grew stronger—she found it hard to stay focused.

As she drove her thoughts returned to Lizzie and the sight. Knowing her sister like the back of her hand, she knew she would never have reached out to her for help. And, due to their estrangement, she wouldn't be driving like a maniac to get to her if it hadn't been for what she'd seen.

The sight ran in her mother's family, passed down through the generations from mother to only one daughter. She loved hearing her mother tell the story of how she had watched her twin daughters like a hawk, anxious to see which one of them would inherit her treasured gift. As she told it, Addie had been only three when she was watching her from the kitchen window. There had been a loud cracking sound, then she saw the branch falling. Addie hadn't looked up but had walked casually away seconds before the branch fell in the exact spot where she'd been standing. With her heart pounding in her ears, she ran to her and checked for injuries. Unshaken, Addie told her that she'd seen the branch falling in her mind—that was why she'd walked away. It was then that she knew Addie was the one.

The sight could have varying levels of strength. Some who possessed it had strong, accurate visions, while others had weak, undependable ones. Addie recalled her mother boasting that both the Richardson females had very strong traits, which was a source of great pride for her mother whenever she was in the company of her relatives—never missing an opportunity to flaunt it.

Lizzie had made all manner of fun of their mother, mocking her behind her back whenever she touted some dire prediction. The memory made Addie chuckle. Stubborn as Lizzie was, she paid no heed to her mother's visions and went around with two fingers stuck in her ears whenever her mother warned her of some bad thing that was sure to happen. She even had a name for the sight, calling it fortune-telling, for she didn't believe a word of it. Addie wiped the tears falling down her cheeks—how she missed Lizzie's spunk.

The tender memory had only briefly relieved Addie's anxiety. Her body tensed as her mind was drawn back to the horror that awaited her in Alabama.

Chapter 2

With the cold, pitch blackness of the moonless night came an unusual quiet, an eerie stillness in the house that had Lizzie's nerves on edge. She was accustomed to the sounds, the creaks and groans the house made at night, but tonight, there was only silence.

Lizzie shivered and drew her children close to her body as they lay in her bed, buried beneath piles of heavy blankets. February temperatures in lower Alabama rarely dipped below thirty, but the tin thermometer that hung from a single nail on the kitchen wall showed a rare twelve degrees. With no working heat source in the house and no wood for the unsightly potbelly stove that sat useless in the front room, the pile of coverings and their body heat was their only defense against the bitter cold.

The air seemed relentless, unwilling to release its frigid grip. Lizzie briskly rubbed her children's arms and legs in a desperate attempt to keep their blood circulating. Softly, she hummed a soothing tune as she drew her daughters' bodies in close to her. Meshed as one, the heat from their bodies finally warmed the bedding, lulling them into a deep, comatose sleep.

Lizzie didn't stir when the door was forced open nor when it slammed shut. She didn't hear the heavy footsteps approaching her bed, or feel the presence of someone hovering over their sleeping bodies. She didn't flinch when hands pulled back the covers and snatched the baby who slept peacefully beside her.

Only when she heard Lillie's startled cry did she awaken. Instinctively, she reached out to comfort her infant child, only to feel a warm, empty place where her body had been. Her eyes flew open. She tried to focus in the dark, seeing only a shadowy figure retreating from the room, her baby dangling like a rag doll in the intruder's careless clutch.

With a blood-curdling scream, Lizzie clambered out of the cumbersome bedding. With long, purposeful strides, she caught up with the intruder, forcefully striking him in the back with her fists. He stopped and turned to face her. She froze. Those eyes. There was no mistaking them, even the absence of light. "Jim Bob!" she gasped, clasping her hand over her mouth.

He glared at her with blazing hate in his eyes and struck her across the face with a powerful blow from his free arm. The horrible sound of shattering bones and tearing flesh filled the air. Lizzie's slight frame collapsed in a heap on the floor. Blood gushed down her face from where he struck her. She tried to stand but collapsed to her knees. Determinedly she tried again, only for her feet to become entangled in her nightgown—again falling to the floor.

Helplessly, with outstretched arms, she pleaded, "Jim Bob, please! Give me my baby!" Her words fell on deaf ears.

Jim Bob showed her no mercy. He thrust his heavy boot into her side over and over and over until her cries went silent. Excruciating pain shot through her. Everything around her went black, her body lay limp.

Jessie ran to her mother, unsure if she was dead or alive. She knelt at her side, gently tapping her still body, "Mama, Mama," she cried. There was no response. Jessie's attention turned to her father, who was making his way to the door with Lillie. She ran at him, kicking and punching him with all the might she could muster.

With no regard whatsoever for his little daughter, he turned and violently kicked her leg, her small body crumpled to the floor, blood dripping from the broken skin below her knee.

Jessie attempted to stand—pain surged through her body. She didn't know how, but she knew she had to save Lillie.

Jim Bob was back on his mission. At the door he pulled on the knob with his one free hand. It was stuck as always. "Darn that stupid door," he hissed. Only now did he regret that he'd never taken the time to fix it. Mumbling inaudible foul words, he sat the screaming baby on the floor away from the door, took the knob in both hands and jerked with all his might.

Adrenaline pumped through Jessie's entire body—she reacted quickly. Her gaze went to the fire poker propped beside the potbelly stove. She picked it up and ran toward her father. The strike was fast and hard at the back of his legs. He fell to his knees.

With fire blazing in his dark eyes, he glared at Jessie, and between clenched teeth, he spat out, "You worthless, pathetic, pitiful brat. Get your ugly face out of my sight."

Unfazed by his heartless remarks, Jessie refused to back down. In a shaky but confident voice, she uttered the first words she had ever spoken to him. "You will not be taking my baby sister anywhere!"

Jim Bob got to his feet and laid back his head, laughter of the evilest sort escaped his mouth.

Jessie gave it no heed. She raised the metal iron. Jim Bob lunged toward her, but his knees buckled under him. He fell forward, his head hitting squarely on the sharp edge of the metal potbelly stove. His body sank motionless to the floor, blood pooling around his head.

Jessie limped around her father's lifeless form, gathered Lillie into her arms, and hobbled to where her mother lay crumpled on the floor, her white nightgown a deep, wet crimson.

Jessie prayed. "Jesus, please don't let my Mama die. Please don't let her die—please, Jesus, please." In her arms, Lillie's fitful cries quieted. Taking the blankets from the bed, she covered her mother and Lillie, and nestled in beside them. On the cold, hard floor, huddled close to their mother's side, Jessie and Lillie's ragged breaths eased into a steady rhythm. Their exhausted bodies drifted into a deep sleep—in the house where evil could no longer harm them.

Chapter 3

Looking for something to occupy her mind and fill the hours that lay ahead, Addie reached over and switched on the radio. She gritted her teeth at the shrill, irritating noise as she turned the dial to one staticky station after another. With a quick flip of her wrist, she switched it off.

Dismissing the fact that she couldn't carry a tune in a bucket, she decided to make a little music of her own. With no passengers to object to her off-tune crooning, she cleared her throat and began to sing a beloved tune from her childhood. She tapped her left foot on the floorboard and drummed her fingers on the steering wheel as she belted out the words of the catchy folk song, "Coming 'Round the Mountain".

The confined space became filled with such off-tune caterwauling that it would surely cause wild animals to howl. Bobbing her head to the lively beat, she belted out all five verses. After four full renditions ending with "We'll sing hallelujah when she comes," she had grown tired of the tune.

She tapped her temple to bring another song to mind. Recalling a favorite, "The Wheels on the Bus", she sang several rounds then made up her own words to the tune: "The wheels on the truck go round and round, I'm on my way to Ala-bam. The wheels on the truck go round and round, on my way to Al-a-bama". Her funky rendition brought a smile to her face. Finding it a fun way to pass the time, she put her words to other tunes and sang until her throat became as scratchy as sandpaper. She reached across the seat for the thermos of water she had thrown in at the last minute. She twisted off the cap, took a sip and let the cool liquid linger for a few seconds in her throat, then replaced the cap. She had to keep trucking. There was no time for a bathroom stop.

Her singing had created a much-needed distraction, but the silence that followed allowed her to concentrate on the scenery drifting by the windows. She passed by vast fields awaiting the spring crops, and pine forests that seemed to go on forever. Here and there a lone house appeared. As she neared a town, the houses multiplied, crowding close together on small narrow lots.

She noted how the character of a town revealed itself at first glance. Some charming and inviting, others grim and depressing. Each town seemed to set the tone for everything in it—the homes and the people mirroring its mood.

With miles of road and many towns behind her, Addie picked up the map and studied her course. Lester had meticulously detailed every road to follow and every town she was to pass through. With a heavy black line, he had charted the route, beginning at her house and ending at Lizzie's. At every dot on the map that indicated a town, Lester had noted the remaining miles to her destination.

The directions were clear and precise, leaving no room for error. That was Lester—her faithful guardian angel.

A sign appeared ahead: Goldwater, Established 1903. She peered across the seat at Lester's map. Fifteen miles to go. Suddenly stricken with panic, her eyes widened. She hadn't seen or heard from her sister in ten long years, and now she was just going to show up, unannounced, and waltz into her tragic life. What had seemed so right—now felt wrong.

Her heartbeat quickened. She never gave a thought to how Lizzie would react to her showing up so suddenly, and at a time when she couldn't deny her miserable life, the life she had chosen, the life she obviously didn't want exposed. The question hit her hard—*what am I doing here?*

For all these years, Lizzie had remained true to her vow, obviously she had erased her twin from the pages of her life. In her heart Addie knew that Lizzie would never retract those words, not even if she now regretted them. No, she would carry them to her grave. Most of all, she feared her interference could be met with Lizzie's fury—if that was the case, she wasn't sure how she'd react.

The situation called for further thought. She pulled to the side of the road and got out, taking the map with her. Leaning against the truck she drew in long, deep breaths of fresh air to calm her worried mind. With the map on the hood of the truck, she ran a finger along the charted line to the town she had just passed noting that the next town she'd come to would be Little Hope—fifteen miles ahead.

Back inside the truck, she sat motionless behind the wheel, gazing at the road that stretched before her. She had a choice to make: carry on or turn back—the clock was ticking.

In a small, childlike voice she said, "Father, Mother, what should I do?" The answer came quick and direct. She turned the key, grasped the steering wheel tightly, and put the pedal to the floor. With a gleam in her eye, she said, "Next stop, Little Hope."

****

Fifteen miles later she squinted to read the faded lettering on the leaning rusty sign: Little Hope, Established 1915. She slowed her speed and squinted harder to read the additional information: Population 1,302. Noticing that the numeral "1" had been scratched out, her brow furrowed. *Had the town really lost a thousand residents, or was someone being funny?* She'd know the answer soon enough.

As she drove onto the main street, she frowned. *Oh, poor, poor Lizzie. How have you survived in this dreadful place?*

Her frown deepened as she drove through the shabby little town. The potholed street was lined on both sides with abandoned buildings—graffiti covering every surface. An overturned trash container rolled hither and thither as it spilled out bottles, cans, and paper that littered the dirty, crumbling sidewalks.

Addie's mood lifted a bit when she came to an old but attractive two-story building with actual glass in the windows and potted trees that graced both sides of double front doors. A plaque mounted on an iron bracket read Sloan's General Store. Addie shook her head and sighed. "I don't know who Sloan is, but for sure—he's Little Hope's only hope."

On the edge of town was a two-pump gas station with a mechanic bay attached. A weathered, grime-streaked sign read Adler's Service Station, below, in smaller letters: Service with a Smile.

She scratched her head, the whole town appeared deserted. She hadn't passed another car, nor had she seen anyone milling about. *Odd.* Little Hope and her beloved Beau Ridge were worlds apart. Beau Ridge, where everything was picture perfect and businesses thrived, where the residents gathered leisurely on the sidewalks, discussing the weather, the local sports teams, or the latest town gossip. *Where are the people?*

Pushing aside her critical views, she turned her attention back to the map and slowly followed the route. To her dismay, the house numbers were inconsistent in their placement. Some appeared on mailboxes, some on the left or right side of the front door, and all appeared to have been spray painted on their random surfaces. She noted how the houses here were a mixture of shabby and downright disgraceful, a true reflection of what Little Hope had become. *No doubt, somebody had a crystal ball when they named this place.*

"302 Front Street," she said, as if saying it aloud would make it appear. She assumed Front Street would be close to town, but each number took her further away—away from anything—away from everything.

The farther from town she drove, the fewer the houses became until there were only foundations where a house or trailer had once sat. Left behind were tin cans, discarded tires, and abandoned vehicles. Obviously, the residents had moved on due to lack of work, that would account for the decline in the town's population, she deduced.

The rough two-lane road became filled with potholes, so deep they appeared bottomless. Overgrown tree limbs scraped against the truck's sides as she struggled to steer away from the larger ones. Towering pines, so thick that no daylight penetrated through them, obscured her vision as she searched for the house. She slowed the truck to an almost crawl.

Almost invisible in the darkness of the pine thicket, the outline of a house came into view. Addie stopped the truck in the middle of the road and narrowed her eyes to read the barely visible number 302 that had been painted on a piece of wood and nailed by the door. Deep tracks buried beneath pine needles lead the way to the house that appeared dark and deserted.

She eased the truck into the tracks and drove slowly, eyeing her surroundings. A black car came into view, which she hadn't seen in the dark of the pines, but assumed it belonged to Jim Bob.

Parking her truck beside the car, she turned off the motor. Before opening the door, she sat in the stillness—gathering her courage. "You're doing the right thing." She prayed she was right.

Standing in front of the porch steps, she eyed them suspiciously. The wood handrail that ran along one side leaned outward, the second step bowed in the center, and the landing leaned inward. Carefully, she moved up the steps to the uneven landing where she found it impossible to stand upright. Her body fell forward into the door—it moved, ever so slightly. Something heavy was keeping the door from opening further. Repositioning her weight, she planted her feet firmly, and with both hands pushed hard against it; again, It moved only inches. Putting her shoulder into it, she shoved with all her might. A space, just big enough for her to slip inside, gave way. Stepping through the opening, her eyes went at once to the obstruction: Jim Bob's motionless body lay in a pool of blood at the base of the door.

Her eyes went cold. She didn't bother to check his body for signs of life—she knew he was dead. For one fleeting second, the thought crossed her mind to kick his worthless carcass. She pushed the thought aside—he'd gotten what he deserved.

She sidestepped the body and moved on. From another room, light filtered through threadbare curtains with fingerlike rays that fell on the three bodies lying on the bare floor. "Oh, dear God," she said, dread rising up in her voice. Kneeling beside them, she checked each one for signs of life. *Thank goodness—they're alive.* Relieved tears welled in her eyes.

Ever so lightly, she rubbed her niece's arm. "Sweetie, wake up."

With her eyes still closed, the child turned her head toward the unfamiliar voice.

"Sweetie, wake up. Please, wake up."

In a daze and with half-opened eyes, she stared into the face of the person calling her name. The way she looked at her let Addie know she recognized her—somehow, someway—she knew her.

"Honey, you don't know me, but I'm Addie."

Jessie blinked, then blinked again. "Mama's sister," she said, mater of factly, tears forming in her eyes.

"Yes, honey. I'm your mama's sister, your Aunt Addie."

Her tears began to stream like water from a faucet. In a trembling voice, she said, "I think I killed my daddy—he was trying to take Lillie away from us."

That revelation answered a big piece of the puzzle, but she couldn't let this child bear that burden. "No, sweetie, you didn't. He's just unconscious—that's just a big word for sleeping. He'll be fine, I'm sure of it," she lied. *Fine, when I get his disgusting carcass in the grave.*

She watched as relief flooded her niece's face. Falling into her arms, she sobbed uncontrollably. Addie held her tightly until her cries subsided.

She examined Jessie's injuries—her leg being the worst of them. The open gash made her stomach lurch. Dried blood covered her leg, and an ugly black bruise had already formed around it. She couldn't be certain it wouldn't need stitches, but she would see to that later. With Jessie still in her arms, Addie turned her gaze to Lizzie and the baby.

"Lillie cried herself to sleep, and Mama hasn't moved at all. She isn't dead, is she?" Jessie asked, her tiny voice trembling.

"No, sweetie. Now don't you worry—your mama's going to be alright." Addie prayed she was speaking the truth.

Jessie turned her woeful eyes to her aunt, causing Addie's heart to pulse in her chest. She saw misery in those eyes that went well beyond this tragedy—it broke her heart.

Lillie awakened, her eyes wide with apprehension, kicking her tiny feet, her fingers twitching before going into her mouth, and a fretful cry began to form. Addie reached over, picked her up, pulled her into her arms, and whispered soothing words in her ear. "Shush, sweet baby girl. I'm here— everything will be okay. Shush."

Within minutes Lillie had quieted. Addie placed her in Jessie's arms and turned her attention to Lizzie, who still hadn't twitched a muscle. She tenderly placed a hand on Lizzie's arm and tapped it gently.

"Lizzie, it's me. It's Addie, wake up, honey".

At first there was no movement, but Addie continued to coax. "Sweetheart, your children are safe. We're all right here; we need you to wake up. Wake up, sweetie, wake up."

Lizzie opened her eyes ever so slightly and gazed deeply into Addie's face. Her eyes closed again, pulling her back into the deep realms of sleep.

Addie pleaded again and again, each time louder, urging Lizzie closer and closer to consciousness. "Lizzie, honey, wake up. Lizzie, you need to wake up."

Lizzie turned her head slightly toward the voice calling her name. "Addie?"

The words came out so faint that she barely heard them. Taking Lizzie's hand in hers, she said, "Yes, yes, honey, it's me. Your children and I are here," she repeated, "please wake up, your little girls need you—I need you."

Tears streamed down Lizzie's face. Weakly, she squeezed Addie's hand, groaning from the pain caused by the simple gesture.

"Don't try to talk, honey. Right now, it's just important that you stay awake—I'll take care of the rest. I'm taking the three of you home with me. You'll need rest and someone to take care of you and the girls. Don't worry—I'll take care of everything."

Addie turned back to Jessie. "I need your help, ok? I need you to take care of your baby sister and stay here by your mother while I take care of some things. Can you do that for me, honey?" Addie said.

Jessie nodded and drew Lillie closer. Addie gave her niece a tender hug and went back to the room where she had encountered Jim Bob's body.

Staring down at the body, Addie was suddenly overwhelmed by the enormity of the task ahead of her. Beads of sweat popped out on her brow—she wiped them away with the back of her hand. She had never been one to shirk responsibility, but this...well, this was a nightmare on so many levels. She was faced with what to do with two very injured people, a baby, and a dead body. "What in heaven's name am I going to do?" she said despairingly.

Her mother had always said to take ten deep breaths to calm down. She didn't have time for ten—she took three. Three was better than nothing, she reasoned.

****

Standing over Jim Bob's body, she considered the possibilities. Involving the police was out. Anyway, who would believe that his death was an accident? No doubt about it, Jim Bob was a lowlife, wife beater, and child abuser, among other despicable traits, but the police might take his side in the matter. She couldn't risk any suspicions that would put them in jeopardy.

She was certain that no one had seen her drive through town, and she hadn't passed a single vehicle, nor had she seen anyone along the way. That could change. Someone could drive by, see her truck, and get curious. She couldn't risk it. There was no time to devise the perfect plan. She had to do something and do it now!

Right or wrong, she quickly hatched a plan. Jim Bob was going with them to South Carolina. The four of them would get out of town before anybody even knew they were gone. Besides, who would come looking for Jim Bob—nobody would miss him, she assured herself.

Mindlessly, she went to work; she grabbed up all the sheets she could find and laid them out on the floor beside Jim Bob's body. Kneeling beside him, she began rolling his body onto them. He was a big man, almost twice her size, making her work slow and tedious. She pushed his body over and over and over until it was encased like a mummy.

Now, somehow, someway, she had to get his body into the bed of the truck. *Think Addie*, she told herself.

Her first idea was to pull on the end of the sheet and drag him toward the door. She got a grip and pulled; his body moved only inches. She tried again, but still, she hardly moved him. This wasn't working. She had to find another way. Time wasn't on her side. She needed a faster, better plan. Then it occurred to her: *A fire! I'll set a fire and burn the house with his dead body inside.*

But just as fast as that idea took form she had worries. Little Hope, didn't seem like a place where a woman's word would be believed. It seemed more like a place where men stood up for one another. There would be an investigation. His bones would be found in the ashes—they always find the bones. The police would come for Lizzie. *No, bad idea— think again.*

Fresh out of ideas, she went back to work with the only plan she had. She began to pull on the sheets again, this time putting more muscle into it. To keep herself motivated, she kept repeating to herself, *you can do this, you must do this, there's no other way.* Inch by inch, she managed to move the body closer to the door, stopping only briefly to wipe the sweat that dripped from her brow. Then, gripping the sheet tighter and through gritted teeth, she gave one mighty tug—and at last, the body was on the porch landing. Breathing heavily, she looked at the body and said, "Now, how do I get you into the truck?" She snapped her fingers as a plan came to mind. "That will work," she said.

She hurried to the truck, let down the tailgate, and backed up to the side of the landing. Climbing out of the truck, she returned to the landing. Standing behind the body, she pushed it forward until it landed on the tailgate with a loud thud. Hopping down into the truck bed, she rolled the body over and over until it was positioned at the front of the bed.

Exhausted from the exertion, she collapsed in a heap over the body. "That's one mission accomplished," she said, brushing her hair from her eyes.

Back inside, she began going through drawers, gathering up clothing that Lizzie and the girls would need, as well as food for the trip and bottles for Lillie.

When all the collected items had been loaded into the truck, she went back inside for her passengers. It was difficult getting Lizzie to her feet. Her body was as limp as a dishrag. She urged Lizzie to stand, and from somewhere— probably her stubborn nature, she gained the strength to pull herself up. Arm in arm, Addie supporting Lizzie's weight, they made their way to the waiting truck. She positioned Lizzy in the seat and covered her with a quilt. Returning to the house, she gathered the children in her arms and carried them to the truck, laying them beside their mother.

Addie heard a tiny voice whisper, "Aunt Addie, could you get my diary, please? It's beside our bed. It's white with gold writing on the front".

"Of course, I will, sweetie. I'll be right back."

Addie went back into the house, retrieved the diary, and started out the door. She turned for one last look around the room. It was then that she saw it, the pool of blood where Jim Bob's body had lain. She'd forgotten all about it. Anyone would instantly deduce that something bad had happened here. There was too much blood. She couldn't take the time to clean it up. There had to be a better solution.

Seeing the box of matches on top of the potbelly stove, the container of kerosene, and the stack of newspapers, she instantly knew what she had to do. Without a second thought, she placed the papers in a pile, gave them a good dousing of kerosene, then took a match from the box, struck it, and threw it onto the pile. At once a large blaze shot upward. She poured more kerosene onto the angry flames and watched as it reached its fingers higher and at the same time, creeping out across the tattered rug.

Addie continued pouring the igniter over the floor as she made her way to the door. Behind her she could hear the crackle of the fire as it grew hotter and hotter. She exited the house, got in the truck, and sped away, leaving behind them a world of misery. Little Hope was in her rearview mirror—she wasn't looking back.

Lizzie touched Addie's hand and whispered weakly, "Jim Bob came for Lillie. I can't make any sense of it—he despised his children."

Addie's eyes filled with tears. "Sweetie, I wish I had an answer for you; I can only say that your problem has been taken care of. You need to rest and try not to think about it; we have a long drive ahead of us. There will be plenty of time for us to talk once you're feeling up to it."

"You have no idea what it means to me to leave that dreadful place. You burned it, didn't you?" Lizzie didn't wait for a response, she simply said, "I'm glad you did." She laid her head back on the pillow, pulled her two children close, and lay in silence for the remainder of the trip.

Addie frowned. *Yes, I think I have a pretty good idea—* as she drove the road toward home.

****

Addie had driven like a mad woman to Alabama, but on the way back home, she was careful to obey every traffic law. She didn't want to be pulled over by the police, who would surely discover the body rolled up like a mummy in the bed of her truck.

When they had been on the road for almost two hours, the gas gauge read less than a quarter. Soon she'd need to stop and fill the tank. The backroads she was traveling would have very few stations—it would be best to stop at the first one she came to.

Traveling with a dead body in the bed of a pickup in broad daylight was a very risky thing to do. Warning signals were going off in Addie's head: *What if, while she was pumping gas, a police car pulled into the space beside them? What if the sheets had blown off, exposing their cargo? What if someone had seen them leave the scene of the burning house and reported them to the police, and they were being tailed?* She eyed every passing vehicle with suspicion. *Negative thoughts aren't helping—stay on task.* She rolled down the window just a crack to let in some cool air to clear her head.

A few miles farther, a sign towering above the building gave advance notice of the station ahead. As she approached, she realized it had only two pumps attainable from either side—she chose the side furthest from the building.

The station was small, the kind that had an attendant whose job was to pump gas for the customer. Through the window of the small building, Addie could see the attendant and noted his clear lack of energy. His legs were propped on the desk in front of him, and he showed no interest in the fact that he had a customer. She preferred that he stay just as he was. She had pumped her own gas plenty of times and today, found it especially to her advantage to do so.

She had just put the nozzle into the tank when the attendant lazily shuffled toward the truck. She walked forward to meet him, thinking it best that he didn't get too close.

"How much you need?" he asked in a slow drawl, a welcome greeting not forthcoming.

Having read the name on the plastic pin attached to his shirt pocket, she turned on the charm and replied in a thick Southern drawl. "Thank you kindly, Donnie, but I don't mind one little bit pumping my own gas." She batted her long lashes and gave him a sweet smile.

He eyed her suspiciously. Apparently, he wasn't accustomed to a woman wanting to pump her own gas.

"Well," he said lazily, "if you're sure."

"Oh, yes sir. I get fidgety driving; it'll give me a chance to burn some energy, and the cold air will do me good, but thank you kindly just the same," Addie said.

The man seemed relieved. Hands in his pockets, he ambled back into the building. Addie watched as he went back to his chair, resuming his earlier position with his boots propped on top of the desk.

Addie released a heavy sigh, lifted her head skyward, and said, "Thank you, Lord, for lazy men."

Back on the road her mind returned to her cargo in the bed of the truck. What in heaven's name was she going to do about that? *The what* wasn't the problem, it was *the how* that perplexed her. She had been fortunate to load ole Jim

Bob in the truck by herself, but the place she intended for his remains would require some help, help that she knew would not come from her three passengers, one being so terribly injured she was lucky to be alive, the two others not even an option.

There was only one person she trusted more than anyone on the face of the earth: her long-time friend and attorney—Lester P. Cobb. Their lifelong friendship began in grade school, and they had remained close as thieves through the years. Truth is, Lester had always wanted their relationship to go beyond friendship, but as much as Addie loved him—and she loved him with her whole heart—she wouldn't allow anything to jeopardize what they had. She knew, though, that there was nothing Lester wouldn't do for her. *I have no other choice—tomorrow, I'll pay Lester a visit.*

****

The low hum of the truck's motor had worked like a sleeping pill for Addie's three exhausted passengers, who had hardly twitched a muscle since leaving their home in Alabama. Having no children of her own, she was of the opinion that babies needed constant attention. They either needed a bottle, or a diaper change, or would just fret for no clear reason at all. This baby hadn't uttered a sound. *Astounding.*

Addie's gaze went to Jessie as she lay sleeping, and a loving smile crossed her face. She was in awe of this child, of her endearing sweetness and her impressive strength. Jessie had touched her heart in a way that defied explanation.

She rubbed her forehead as she thought about her passengers and her next course of action. Her top priority would be to get Lizzie and the children settled in, tend to their injuries, and get some food in their empty stomachs. She knew it would be dark when they arrived at her house. A plan formulated in her mind about the other passenger: she'd park the truck in the old shed where his body would be well hidden. She'd deal with him tomorrow.

Addie wasn't one to go looking for trouble, but somehow, she managed to get into very messy predicaments. A few years ago, she had to face the same dilemma: what to do with a dead body. Through no fault of her own, she had found herself in the middle of a big old mess and handled it the best way she knew how. The solution worked so well she didn't have to think twice about where to put Jim Bob. With Lester's help—he'd be laid to rest beside the other one.

Chapter 4

The impressive sign that read Welcome to Beau Ridge, South Carolina, came into view and sent a comforting sensation coursing through Addie's veins. She was well aware that It was purely by the grace of God that they had made it without incident—injured and exhausted, to be sure, but in one piece. Her grateful sobs broke the silence.

Lizzie raised her head ever so slightly, groaning from the sharp pain it caused. "Anything wrong?" she said in a weak, strained voice.

"No, sweetie, everything is as right as rain. We're home. We've just come to the city limits of Beau Ridge. If you feel like sitting up, you can see if the town still looks as you remember it."

Lizzie slowly eased herself upright, as low moans emerged with every movement. Gathering her now awake children around her, she peered out the windows at the buildings illuminated by the bright streetlights.

Addie watched her sister intently as her head turned slowly left and right, taking in the sights of the home she once knew. For several minutes she was silent, lost in her thoughts.

Her voice, barely a whisper. "It's more beautiful than I remember—it's glorious. Best of all—it's not Little Hope."

They both laughed. Lizzie held her sides in agony and gritted her teeth through the pain. Their laughter was good medicine, a temporary release from the many troubles facing them.

As the truck took them closer to Addie's home on the southernmost end of Claymore County, Lizzie stared silently out the windows.

Addie wished she could read her thoughts. *Was her return home met with regret and sorrow for abandoning her family? Would she ever know the answer to that question?* She scolded herself for her judgmental attitude. Heaven knows she has plenty of regrets of her own. She hoped she and Lizzie could get over the past and mend their fences. They needed each other, and Lizzie's children needed a stable environment—they could have that here with her— if the two of them had matured enough to forgive and forget.

****

Twenty minutes later, they arrived at Addie's property. Stately stone columns flanked the entrance, each proudly bearing bronze plaques engraved with the letter K. The columns supported a wrought iron arch with swirling scrolls and intricate curls. Suspended from its center hung an elegant wooden sign, hand-painted in graceful, flowing script, announcing the name: Magnolia Place. The sign, with its peeling paint and faded letters and the wrought iron, tinged a reddish-brown were the first indication that the place wasn't the grand estate it had once been.

Addie stopped the truck and gazed up at the sign that loomed overhead. She was about to announce, "We're home," but before she could get the words out, she felt Lizzie's light touch on her arm.

"Oh, Addie! It's absolutely breathtaking, and just as I remember it," she said, managing an enthusiastic tone that caused her to cough hoarsely.

"Obviously, things look better in the dark," Addie said, chuckling. "In the daylight you'll be putting aside those images of grandeur; it's not the glorious place it once was."

"Oh, Addie, I have no expectations whatsoever. After where I've been, anything would be grand. Coming back home is the dream I never thought would come true. You came to my rescue and saved my life," Lizzie said, her weak voice trembling.

Saved my life. The words echoed in Addie's ears as she realized just how close she had come to losing her twin. *Darn you, Jim Bob!* This was a sentiment Addie would find herself repeating again and again.

****

On either side of the long lane magnificent live oaks stood in a row, their branches creating a canopy from which

Jeanne Vaughn

silvery moss shimmered in the moonlit night. Addie glanced over to see Jessie sitting forward in the seat, her eyes wide open as if she'd been transported into another world. She spoke for the first time since leaving Alabama.

"Oh, Aunt Addie, I've never seen anything so beautiful! Thank you for bringing us here." Her voice became almost a whisper. "I feel like I've come home."

Addie blinked back tears. She didn't expect this. She didn't know this child, but just those few words told her so much. This is a grateful child, a loving child, a child who had already begun to steal her heart.

"Oh, sweetheart, I hope you will always feel that way; I want you to call it home for as long as you want." Addie wanted to add that one day it would all be hers, but that seemed like a lot for a child of seven to take in, so she put it on the back burner—for now.

Emerging from the covered lane, the house came into view—bathed in the light of the full moon that rested just above the roofline. Addie heard the gasps of amazement from Lizzie and Jessie, and she had to admit it was a magnificent sight to behold, looming immense and awe-inspiring before them.

The house was a two-story Neo-Classical Palladian with Doric columns and an immense front porch that spanned the entire width. A line of rocking chairs along with a slatted wood swing hanging from the high ceiling were a welcoming invitation to guests. The front door stood twelve feet tall and was flanked by sidelights with images of lovely magnolia blooms etched in the glass. On the second level, double doors were set behind an intricate wrought iron balcony with the letter K embossed into the center. Magnolia Place—back in its heyday—had been truly spectacular. It still held an irresistible charm.

Lizzie reached over and took Addie's hand. "Could you stop here? I want to take in this moment. Everything seems so surreal—this house, this night, you—it's all so unbelievable."

They sat in silence, staring out into the night. Feeling something wet drop onto her hand, Addie turned to see tears cascading down Lizzie's cheeks. For now, no words were needed—there would be time for that later; it was enough to have her home again.

Addie put the truck in gear and slowly drove to the front of the house, where she parked close to the steps. She made her way to the front door and quickly went through the house turning on lights, then returning, she helped them one by one out of the truck. Understandably, the porch steps brought painful wincing from Lizzie and Jessie as Addie guided them inside.

There was a time when the house bustled with overnight guests—that was years ago. It wasn't in Addie's nature to be unprepared, so her guest room stayed fresh and ready at all times—just in case. The room would be Lizzie's and the children's for as long as they wanted.

Holding Lillie in her arms, Addie led the way down the hallway while Lizzie and Jessie followed slowly.

"This will be your room as long as you want," Addie said. She opened the door and stood back, allowing Lizzie and Jessie to enter. Although the furnishings were sparse, the room had a lovely feminine flair. Dainty lace doilies covered the dresser and the broad chest of drawers. On the bed was a lovely, crocheted bedspread with crisp white cotton sheets and pillowcases embroidered with pink rosebuds. White lace curtains covered the tall windows, and the fresh scent of lavender filled the air.

"Exquisite!" Lizzie said in a soft voice, her eyes wide with wonder. "Addie, you have a knack for making everything so lovely and inviting; I'm simply overwhelmed. I can't thank you enough for all you've done for us."

"Believe me, it's my pleasure. I'm just so happy you're here. I want you all to feel completely at home." She sighed, wiped away a stray tear and quickly changed the subject. "Let's find some food, I'm famished. After we've had something to eat, I'll get you all settled in."

Addie prepared a simple supper of scrambled eggs, bacon, and her homemade blackberry jam spread on toasted bread. With the four of them gathered around the table, the years seemed to have melted away—once more they were a family.

Having children in the house seemed so right, but it was a new experience for Addie. She turned her attention to

Lillie, so tiny now, but it made her wonder: *when do children need a highchair, and solid food?* She lived mostly off the land: vegetables and herbs from her garden, fruit from her orchard and eggs from her chickens. A baby's needs went beyond what she had on hand. She made a mental note of the items to pick up on her run into town.

The conversation around the table was minimal. Each seemed deep in their own thoughts. The last two days had been grueling. Addie studied their faces. Lizzie's eyelids were mere slits, Jessie's face was set in a blank stare, and Lillie, cradled in her mother's arms, was fast asleep.

We're all exhausted beyond words, and for good reason, but it's more than that for them. She sensed a sadness that tore at her heart, a sadness that came from one source. She made a silent vow to do everything in her power to bring some happiness back into their lives. *Darn you, Jim Bob Thornhill—if you weren't already dead ....*

"I've got an idea. Let's call it a night," Addie said. "Everything will look better after a good night's sleep."

Addie led the zombie-like bodies from the kitchen down the hall and into Lizzie's room, where she tended to their wounds and helped them into clean nightgowns. Tucking the children into bed around Lizzie, Addie gave each a kiss and whispered, "Sweet dreams, dear ones."

As Addie turned to leave the room, she felt Lizzie's soft touch on her shoulder.

In a faint whisper, Lizzy said, "I know we're all exhausted, but could we have just a few minutes together before turning in?"

It was the first time they'd had a chance to be alone. They sat side by side on the soft couch. There was so much Addie wanted to know, but she couldn't bombard Lizzie with questions in her current fragile condition, and to be truthful, her heart couldn't take any more upsets tonight. She told herself that later, there would be plenty of time for serious discussion. Right now, she just wanted to plant some words of comfort to make her sister feel at home and safe.

Not waiting for Lizzie to speak first, Addie started the conversation. "I hope you'll come to love it here, Lizzie. I know this house is a disaster and falling down around me, but I think we can be so happy here together. You may find this hard to believe, but even though my house is in shambles, and I'm living like a pauper, I have never been so happy."

"I have to admit, it's quite contrary to the Addie I remember," Lizzie said with a sly grin. "That Addie was dead set on having a big house, prestige, and lots and lots of money," Lizzie said. There was no judgment in her voice, only familiarity.

"I can't hide from the truth. I made no bones about it; I was dead set on having it all," Addie said.

Lizzie shrugged. "Well, look at me, the wild child who did exactly as I pleased, and look how that turned out."

Addie laughed. "We're a pair, you and me; hell bent on having our way with little regard for the road it would take us down. Well, hon, we could sit and reminisce for days on end, and I'd like nothing better, but you need your rest, and I'm fading, too. We'll have lots of time to catch up; I don't think you'll be going anywhere for a good while."

"Yes, we'll talk more tomorrow, but I can't rest until I tell you how grateful I am for all you've done for us. You came to us like an angel from heaven just when we needed you most. I love you more than you'll ever know; I yearned for you every single day," Lizzie said. Tears gushed down her cheeks.

"I love you, too, sweetheart. You know it was the sight that brought me to you."

"Yes, that darn sight! I would never have thought in a million years I would say this, but I'm so grateful for it." She placed a kiss on Addie's cheek and held her in a warm embrace. Starting toward her room, she turned back to face Addie. Her voice cracked as she said, "Please hold Jessie near to your heart. It saddens me to say it, but she's had a pretty miserable childhood. She is the sweetest, kindest child I've ever known, but her tender nature has left her vulnerable. She needs all the love we can give her."

After Lizzie left the room, Addie dropped her head. Lizzie's words weighed heavy on her heart. Silent tears fell like rain as she wept sorrowfully for them.

****

Before turning in, Addie washed the dishes and tidied up the kitchen. Flipping off the light, she made her way to her room where she changed into her nightgown. Feeling the effects from the day's events, every muscle in her body ached as she climbed into bed. She lay still, hoping sleep would come, but her mind wouldn't shut down. Seeing her twin again after so many years, she was reminded how different the two of them are—different in almost every way imaginable. Thoughts of their childhood came rushing back.

Lizzie was never content to work in the garden or sit on the porch knitting or reading like Addie and their mother. She sought adventure. In the morning after she had woofed down the last bite of breakfast, she was out and gone. There was the sound of the screen door slamming that told of her departure, and it wasn't until the ringing of the dinner bell that the screen door slammed again announcing her return. A blissful smile crossed Addie's face as she recalled the times when the family was gathered around the dinner table, and Lizzie held them spellbound with her outlandish tales of her day's adventures. Her parents would laugh hysterically, believing them to be mere figments of her wild imagination. But Addie knew better, having been with her on one of her wild adventures when they came close to being seriously injured. Frightened to death, Addie had sworn never to go adventuring with her ever again. The terrifying event had a lasting effect on her, causing her to worry constantly whenever her sister left the house.

Addie's reflections were interrupted by a sound coming from her sister's room. She got out of bed and padded quietly down the hall. Peeking into the room she found Lizzie murmuring in her sleep; no doubt—having a nightmare. *Poor little thing, there's no telling what kind of hell she has had to endure. Darn you, Jim Bob!*

Back in her own room, she climbed back into bed and was asleep as soon as her head hit the pillow.

Chapter 5

A persistent tapping on Addie's bedroom window pulled her from her comatose slumber. She rolled over and gazed through squinted eyes to see a cardinal fluttering its wings against the glass. Still groggy, she turned to look at the clock on the bedside table. Her eyes shot open. "Noon?" she said in disbelief as she flung herself out of bed.

Hastily, she slipped on her robe and made her way to the bathroom where she gathered her tangled hair into a loose bun and quickly brushed her teeth. Then, with long, purposeful strides she marched to the kitchen, chastising herself all the way.

"Mercy sakes, what must they think of me—and with them unable to do for themselves? Never in my life have I slept till noon, and to do so today of all days," she grumbled.

With her expression set in an irritated scowl, she burst into the kitchen. Six sets of eyes turned in her direction, obviously startled by her frantic behavior. Her gaze took in the serene scene before her. Her three guests were peacefully seated at the table having breakfast—appearing to be very much at home.

The scowl didn't leave her face. "Why didn't you wake me? I should have been up early making your breakfast and letting you sleep in, not the other way around. What must you think of me?"

"Mercy sakes, Addie," Lizzie shot back in a weak voice that barely carried across the room. "After what we put you through, you have every right to sleep in," she said, as she reached over to wipe strawberry jam from Jessie's chin. "You missed a spot, Jess."

Jessie giggled—the sound was like a breath of fresh air. Lizzie turned her attention back to Addie. "Besides, we haven't been up that long ourselves—only about an hour. As you can see, we've made ourselves at home."

Hearing the strain in Lizzie's weak voice, Addie started to chide her again for taking on so much in her frail condition. She studied the group gathered around the table and realized no harm had been done—their faces glowed. Gone was the misery they had shown only hours earlier. At the sight, the corners of her mouth turned upward. Her love for this group was growing stronger with every passing moment.

"I know we Richardson gals are tough, and it takes a lot to keep us down, but after breakfast it's back to bed with the three of you, and I mean business." She looked at Jessie and winked.

Jessie grinned revealing red stained teeth.

"I'm surprised you were able to find anything to eat. I can't remember the last time I went to the store. Later, while you're resting, I'll run to town for groceries and a few things we need—like a crib and a highchair," Addie said.

"We didn't have any trouble at all, and you can see how much Jessie loves your homemade jam," Lizzie said.

Jessie grinned and took another bite of toast slathered with jam as Lillie looked on longingly. She dabbed a bit on her lips, and Lillie smacked with delight.

Lizzie smiled at her daughters' interaction. Wagging her finger at Addie, she said, "Don't even think about buying those things. You're looking at a group who have learned to make do with practically nothing," Lizzie said.

"Hogwash," Addie said, her hands on her hips, indicating that the subject wasn't up for debate. "Lillie needs them, and she'll have them."

Lizzie responded by putting her fingers in her ears. "You haven't changed a bit. You're still as bossy as ever," Lizzie said, in her old teasing tone.

Addie plastered a playful smirk on her face and said, "Some things never change."

"Obviously," Lizzie said, laughing. She tapped Addie on the shoulder and gestured toward Jessie and Lillie whose mouths were rimmed with her homemade jam.

A smile spread across Addie's face and a warm sensation spread through body replacing the tension she had carried in with her.

Outwardly, Lizzie and her children seemed to be adjusting well to their new surroundings, it was their inward scars that troubled Addie. Her overwhelming urge to pamper and comfort them caused her to ask, "Was your room okay? Did you have enough blankets?"

"We slept like logs. You've made your home so comfortable and inviting, just as a home should be. I have to say, Sis—I'm impressed," Lizzie said.

"Thank you, but it took losing everything we had for me to realize that a house isn't a home. There's a lot more I could say about that, but for now, making you feel at home here is my main concern," Addie said, her voice a mixture of regret and hope.

Addie lifted Lillie from Lizzie's arms and sat beside her at the table. Lillie's hand went straight to her hair, pulling out a long strand and twisting it around her tiny fingers. Jessie came and stood at her side, and Addie lifted her onto her lap. The three of them snuggled silently, soaking in the pure joy of the moment. Life had taken on new meaning for Addie—it was a new beginning for all of them.

****

After breakfast Addie dressed for town. She slipped into her pink floral dress and pulled on a loose wool cardigan over it. At the mirror she brushed her hair and fixed it into a neat bun, then added some blush to her cheekbones. Standing back, she gazed at her reflection and nodded approvingly. Makeup and fancy clothes no longer held any appeal for her; this was her new down-to-earth style. She'd never felt more true to herself.

Their need for supplies was only part of the reason she was going into town. Most important was her visit to Lester's office, but first she had to unload her cargo. Letting down the truck's tailgate, she climbed into the bed. In the same way she had rolled Jim Bob in, she rolled him out onto the floor and covered his body with burlap bags. She then backed the truck out of the shed, closed the door, and locked the latch.

Before leaving, she took one last look toward the house. All was quiet. Putting the truck in gear, she started toward town.

At the town square, cars and trucks filled the streets. Groups of people gathered about on the sidewalks. The sight of her familiar truck drew waves as Addie passed by. On the north side of the square, she pulled the truck into an empty space in front of Lester's law office and took a quick glance in the mirror before getting out.

As always, a warm, familiar feeling came over Addie as she stepped into the charmingly masculine office. The room exuded Lester's strong, steady, and reassuring presence. The rich scent of leather and the serene scene depicted on the exquisite oriental rug wrapped around her like a comforting embrace. Leather bound books with gold embossed lettering were arranged neatly atop an oval coffee table situated between two leather sofas. Side tables flanked the sofas, each topped with a bronze horse head lamp that gave off a soft amber glow. Everything in the room worked together to create a pleasing and inviting ambiance.

Upon seeing Addie enter the room, Lester's long-time secretary, LeeAnn, greeted her with the familiarity born of a life-long relationship. She and Addie had grown up together and had been close friends through the years. Addie's frequent visits to Lester's office had kept them close, and their easy friendship was filled with playful banter.

"Well, look what the dogs drug in—long time no see," she said as she came around her desk to give Addie a hug.

"Yep, I look the part, too, I'm afraid," Addie said, embracing her friend.

"You know you always look like a million dollars," LeeAnn said.

"That's a flat out lie, and you know it, but I'll take it," she said lifting her chin.

LeeAnn, as always, was dressed impeccably in a crisp white blouse tucked into a mid-length navy blue pencil skirt with sensible heels. Her dark brown hair was set in a style that never changed, a bouffant piled high on top of her head that gave her the extra height she didn't have naturally. Her classic beauty blending effortlessly with the elegance of her surroundings.

"I can't wait until your garden comes in. Spring's right around the corner, you know," LeeAnn said cheerfully.

"Yes, believe it or not, I've already noticed things sprouting in my garden. You know me, a little hint of spring, and I'm getting my hands dirty." She held up her hand and pointed to the dirt under her nails.

"You are a marvel. But you really should think about wearing gloves," LeeAnn said, shaking her head.

"It's good therapy. You should try it sometime," Addie said with a teasing smirk.

"And, you should try being a secretary. On second thought, I think we are both very well suited for the jobs we have. I never liked to dig in the dirt, and you would be like a worm in hot ashes if you had to sit behind a desk all day," LeeAnn said, laughing.

"We know each other too well," Addie chuckled.

"I know you didn't come here to shoot the breeze with me—he's in his office," LeeAnn said, nodding toward Lester's closed door.

"Well, as much as I've enjoyed our visit, I do have some pressing business to discuss with him. I promise not to take up too much of his time," Addie said.

"You know as well as I, there's nobody on this earth he'd rather see than you. Go on in."

"Thanks, honey. I'll see you shortly," Addie said, as she walked toward Lester's door.

Addie knocked softly on the closed door but didn't wait for Lester's response. She turned the knob and walked right in. He was seated at his desk; his head bent over a document of several pages. She took note of the furrowed lines on his forehead; obviously troubled by the document spread before him.

Lester's six-foot-four frame commands attention, but in sharp contrast, his demeanor is that of a big ole teddy bear. Southern to the core, Lester embodies the very essence of a bona fide gentleman. His irresistible gentle nature and the way he embodies all that is good about humanity draws people to him like bees to honey.

Today, as always, Lester was wearing an ivory linen suit, of which he had many and wore year-round. This, despite the fact that every good Southerner knows—linen is worn only in summer. Even though Lester had flung this golden rule to the wayside, Addie couldn't imagine him in anything else. Quite simply, it was his signature look, and he pulled it off with charm and grace. Completing his attire was a white bowtie tied at the neck of his crisp white shirt, and always white socks, and tan loafers. His thick, wavy brown hair (which he secretly hoped would someday turn snow white) gave him an adoringly boyish appearance.

Upon hearing the door open, Lester looked up from his work. The furrowed lines on his forehead vanished instantly when he saw Addie standing in the doorway. He slapped his large palms on the desk, pushed back his chair and hurried to greet her. As always, he pulled her into a tight embrace. "My girl! You're a sight for sore eyes!" he said, lifting her off her feet and twirling her around.

Holding back tears, she said, "Oh, Lester, I can't tell you how good it is to see you!" She squeezed him tightly. A stray tear emerged and fell down her cheek. Staring into his questioning eyes, she added, "I'd like to say that it's just my usual checking in, but unfortunately, today isn't the case. I've got trouble—trouble like nobody's business. If you're smart, you'll run me out of here before it's too late."

"Awh now, hon. You know there's nothing in this world I wouldn't do for you. Come on over here and have a seat and tell ole Lester what's troubling you."

Lester opened his door and called out to LeeAnn. "Hey darlin', would you mind calling the Morgans and rescheduling their eleven o'clock for later this afternoon? And hold my calls. I'll be tied up for a while—I've got an important client here."

LeeAnn nodded. While he was still talking, she had the receiver in her hand dialing the Morgans' number.

He threw her a thumbs up and softly closed the door. Guiding Addie by the elbow he led her to the leather sofa and positioned a pillow behind her back. He sat on the opposite end and turned his body so he could look directly at her as she spoke.

"I hardly know where to begin. It's a pretty wild tale," she said, as her hands busily smoothed out imaginary wrinkles on her dress.

"Just take your time and begin at the beginning. I've got all the time in the world when it comes to you," Lester said. He placed his arms over his middle and clasped his hands together, a gesture Addie had seen him do many times.

Tears welled up in Addie's eyes, and the reality of what she had come to ask of her dear, devoted friend suddenly hit her like a brick. She fidgeted in her seat, beads of sweat forming at her hairline. She hadn't given it an ounce of thought until now. *How could she ask Lester to put his good reputation and his lucrative career on the line for her? He could lose everything. If she were a true friend, she wouldn't have come here today.* A guilty feeling came over her, and she suddenly wanted to flee from his office before it was too late.

"Oh, Lester," Addie said, shaking her head. "I don't know what I was thinking. I can't involve you in this mess. Before this moment, I couldn't wait to come here, knowing you would do whatever I asked, and help in any way I needed. But I hadn't given the first thought to how it could affect you and your reputation, not to mention your very lucrative business, and...."

Lester interrupted her. He leaned in and patted her hand. "That's enough of that kind of talk. Come on, let's hear it. I'm a big boy—I can handle it."

Addie inhaled deeply. She took Lester's hand and squeezed it tightly. "I want this clear from the start; you are under no obligation whatsoever to involve yourself in this. It's morbid and entirely unethical.

"You can't stop there, I'm hooked," Lester said.

✱✱✱✱✱✱✱✱✱✱✱✱✱✱

Lester rubbed his chin thoughtfully, letting her predicament sink into his brain. "So, Jessie is how old?"

"Oh, Lester, that's the saddest part. She's only seven. According to the little bit of information I've been able to get from Lizzie, she's had a miserable childhood and now this. I lied to the child and told her Jim Bob wasn't dead. So now I must dispose of him, for good. I don't want Lizzie or Jessie to know anything about it."

"And you have somewhere in mind?"

She knew that if she was going to involve Lester in this mess, she had no choice but to tell him the whole sorted tale. "You already know some of this story—Lord knows, the whole town does—but only I know the rest of the story, and it's a dilly; best you sit back for a wild ride," Addie said.

Lester put his feet up on the coffee table in front of him and leaned back into the soft leather cushions. He swept his arm in her direction, giving her the floor.

Addie closed her eyes, breathed deeply, and began to unravel the long, woebegone tale.

Chapter 6

She closed her eyes and let her mind drift back to that Wednesday in late October. Reggie's face came into clear view as if he were standing there in the room. She barely heard the words that were spilling from her mouth. The secret she had kept for so long was now being exposed....

"It was barely past noon, and Reggie was seated atop his usual stool at The Hangin-in Saloon, a whiskey glass raised to his lips. With his elbow propped on the counter to steady his hand, he sipped the strong drink. He never knew when to quit, and he stopped counting altogether after two. He swayed this way and that, his words slurred as he raised his glass and called out to Buck for another round. Somewhere, he had gotten the idea that his card playing skills improved when he was *all liquored up*, as he liked to say.

"Reggie was drunker than Cooter Brown when the local cronies gathered around the poker table in the back of the room. He left his seat at the bar and joined them. His gambling, like his drinking, was out of control. He had no money to cover his bets, but the locals allowed him to place his bets with the few valuables we had left to our names. Because of this, he was a welcome player at the table. It was a win-win situation for them; their wives were happy with the things they brought home and they, in turn, weren't harassed for being out gambling. Also to their advantage was Reggie's foolish idea regarding drinking and gambling. Even if he had a winning hand, he was easily tricked into losing, due to his extreme level of intoxication. Not only did the locals take advantage of him, but word had gotten around, and outsiders began to show up on a regular basis.

"Several hands had been played, and more pieces of our silver had been sacrificed when a stranger entered the bar. At that time Reggie was taking a break and had returned to his stool at the bar. The stranger stood just inside the door, surveying the room before making his move. He'd heard about Reggie; he'd made a living by swindling men like him out of their money and valuables. But he hadn't come for money or even valuable trinkets—his eyes were set on a far more lucrative asset.

"The stranger was dressed from head to toe in black. Strands of greasy black hair fell into his beady black eyes. He sat down on the stool next to Reggie and immediately began to set his hook. He introduced himself as Slick Parks from Chicago, said he came to town looking for a good time. He bought Reggie round after round of drinks. Slick was a pro. He knew just how to make a fool feel like he's suddenly got a new best friend.

"It wasn't long until Slick had persuaded Reggie and some of his cronies to join him in a game of poker. He had no interest in the other players, only Reggie. As the hands were played, Slick encouraged Reggie to double and triple his bets. To nobody's amazement, Reggie lost hand after hand, but Slick, playing him for the fool he was, let the games go on until Reggie's losses were exorbitant. This is when Slick abruptly called an end to the fun and games and demanded his money.

"As he always did when it was time to pay up, Reggie stood, put his hands in both pant pockets, and pulled out the empty linings. This usually brought hysterical laughter from his drinking buddies, but Slick wasn't laughing.

"Slick carried out the rest of his game the same way he'd done with the other misguided fools he'd hustled. He made sure there were witnesses so there would be no doubt Reggie had lost fair and square. Reggie insisted he had no way to pay him monetarily, but could pay him with valuable items—if he would accept that in exchange. That was when backstabbing, double-dealing Slick pulled out a gun and pointed it at Reggie's head. He told him that the deed to his property would cover his debt just fine. He gave him an hour to go and get it then he was to meet him down by the old, abandoned mill—a place he'd noticed when driving into town.

"Reggie was scared stiff—terrified is more like it. I heard him when he came through the door. He didn't call out to me like he usually did but instead staggered straight to his office; next thing I knew, he was headed for the door, a folder under his arm.

"I stopped him and demanded to know just what he was up to and what was in the folder. He told me some made-up cock and bull story that I didn't believe for one minute. I insisted that he tell me the truth. His voice was shaky, and his hands were trembling when he came out with the whole sordid tale. He was desperate to leave, saying that Slick would track him down if he didn't show up.

"I had no intention of letting some greasy weasel like Slick take away the only thing we had in the world. With little time to think, I hurriedly came up with a plan and convinced Reggie that it was our only hope. We jumped into the car, and as Reggie drove, I went over the details.

"The plan went like this: we'd meet Slick just as he'd instructed. Reggie would approach him from the front, and I'd make my way quietly through the woods and position myself close behind Slick and wait. When the time was right, I'd make a noise behind him. He'd turn around, and that's when Reggie would jump him and knock the gun away. That was how I planned it—how I hoped it would play out.

"When we got to the mill, Reggie parked the car several yards away. I quietly opened the door and slipped off into the woods. With the deed in hand, Reggie walked toward Slick, who was already waiting at the designated spot, his gun at his side. Clearly, he had an itchy trigger finger and was prepared to use it.

"I was in position behind Slick and stepped on a dry branch. Slick turned around just as we had hoped he would, but here is where our scheme went to hell in a handbasket. When Reggie jumped at him, Slick didn't drop the gun, but he held onto it. The two of them ended up on the ground wrestling for control of the gun. From my point of view, it looked like Slick was winning the match, and then a shot rang out. I could only hear the sound of my heart pounding in my ears. The two men lay on the ground, neither of them moving. I stood frozen—terrified. Then Reggie moved his right arm. I realized I was holding my breath. I breathed deeply and released a huge sigh of relief. I went to Reggie and knelt at his side. He was stunned and shaken but not injured. I studied the man on the ground beside him. Slick lay still as a board—obviously dead.

"I knew it was an accident, but who else would believe it? There were witnesses who knew Reggie had lost fair and square. How would it look if they knew Reggie had shot him? For sure, he'd go to jail. That's when I knew we had no choice, none at all. We had to hide the body—and fast."

****

Addie opened her eyes and looked around the room, suddenly realizing where she was. She noticed Lester had moved from his comfortable position to the edge of the sofa, his eyes wide. Her lower lip trembled, knowing she had just revealed a deep secret, a secret that could land her in prison for the rest of her life. She'd gone this far—she trusted Lester with her life. Carrying on, she went to the part of the story that mattered most.

"To say the least, we had a giant dilemma on our hands. What on earth to do with a dead body? Thankfully, out of the clear blue sky, it came to me where to put it—it was perfect—the place where nobody would ever think to look for him.

"You know Lester, those vines growing on my house, the ones I've nurtured for years and fed with The Formula? They're so thick and tangled, you could hide a car in there and nobody would find it. Reggie was skeptical, but I knew it would work—it had to."

Lester looked at her quizzically. Addie shifted in her seat.

"Well, it took some doing, actually a lot of doing; it was the most exhausting thing I'd ever done in my life. But what had seemed absolutely ridiculous and totally impossible had actually worked."

"So, ole Slick is buried in your ivy? Only you could think of that," he said, shaking his head. But there's more, right?" His lawyerly mind knew the story didn't end there.

"Oh, yeah, there's more," Addie said.

"Now I had to consider our next move. Someone like Slick, who was a known swindler, must be a wanted criminal. It occurred to me that the reason he had spent so little time in Beau Ridge was because he was on the run. I figured this could play to our advantage.

"It made sense that Slick was on the run. He must have been tipped off that the law was closing in. The Feds would want to question the townsfolk, find out what they know, and had they seen him? They would get the story from Reggie's cronies and come here looking for him. This is where we had to play it cool.

"The Feds showed up just as I predicted, fully informed about the gambling debt and Slick's threat on Reggie's life. They had been to the mill, where it all went down. We had taken great pains to cover our tracks, picking up the shell casing, and covering the blood with leaves and debris. We left his car untouched, thinking the Feds would determine that Slick had either fled on foot, or one of his cohorts had aided in his getaway.

"We sat on our porch, where we casually sipped lemonade and answered their questions, and they filled us in on Slick's many criminal acts. They had been on his trail for over a year, calling him a con artist who had been accused of swindling everyone from poor little old ladies to rich landowners—like us. I guess they hadn't done their homework—rich hardly described us.

"I was surprised how quickly they believed our story. We didn't even have to lie. They came up with scenarios that took Reggie totally out of the picture, some of the same ones I had predicted. They drew the conclusion that he left his car so he couldn't be tracked and had some of his low-down buddies pick him up. They deduced that he was lying low for a while, that he was headed for another state. We just sat in silence, nodding occasionally as they spun their predictions.

"Reggie's eyes grew wide when they said Slick had been known to leave only to return and harass or murder his victims. But, they said this shouldn't worry us because they had a team of agents in neighboring towns tracking him, and they were sure he'd be caught soon. I worried that Reggie's guilty looks would give us away, but these guys seemed only interested in their quest for Slick.

"They thanked us for our assistance, handed us their cards to call if Slick should show back up, and they left. Of course, we didn't call, and they never came around again.

"Following the fiasco, Reggie was never the same, especially after having killed a man. He stopped going to town to his usual establishments, and his cronies had abandoned him. He lost interest in everything except the one thing he had left—the land. From morning until it became too dark to see, he sat in his chair on the front porch staring out across the cotton fields.

"Then one day, as was my daily routine, I was bringing him his lunch when I saw him slumped over in his chair. Beside him was an empty glass. I picked up the glass and saw tiny granules in the bottom; I recognized them immediately. They were—to my sorrow—The Formula. Reggie had taken his own life, a life that he could no longer bear."

Lester reached over and patted Addie's hand. "I've got to say that's some story. In fact, it's just about the most incredible, enthralling, and saddest tale I've ever heard. It must have been hard to keep a secret like that for so long."

"I swore I'd take it to my grave," Addie said.

"Correct me if I'm wrong, but I think you've come to ask my help in burying low-down Jim Bob in there with scumbag Slick, am I right?"

"You're a quick study," Addie said, nodding affirmatively.

"This is a risky proposition. Like you said, it could result in an end to my very lucrative career," he said, thoughtfully rubbing his chin. He shook his head from side to side. Then he clapped his hands so loudly it made Addie jump. "Count me in. I need some excitement in my dull existence!"

"You're one crazy guy," Addie said, wrapping her arms around Lester's large frame and kissing him squarely on the lips. "I won't blame you one little bit if later you have second thoughts, but for now—I can't thank you enough. How on earth will I ever repay you?"

"You could marry me," Lester said with a grin.

"I could never do that to you—I love you too much," Addie said, her eyes tearing.

"You know I'll never stop trying," he said, gazing at her with large puppy dog eyes.

"I can promise you this: I'll remain your true and faithful friend for all the days of my life," she said.

"You're impossible," he said, shaking his head.

"You're my hero," Addie said, placing a kiss on his cheek.

"Oh, get out of here," Lester said, a wide grin lighting up his face. "I'll see you at three o'clock—ready, willing and able."

Chapter 7

After her parting conversation with LeeAnn, Addie left Lester's office with one thing on her mind—finding a crib and highchair for Lillie. She strolled across the street to Frugal Freda's and paused to admire her prettily decorated window.

A wooden swing, its slats missing and paint peeling, hung from the ceiling, draped in lavender wisteria and filled with colorful throw pillows. Terracotta pots overflowing with silk flowers sat atop a faded floral rug. On the door, a grapevine wreath dripping with wisteria offered customers a warm welcome.

The bell over the door jingled as Addie strode into the shop. A moment later Freda stepped in from the back room, her curly red hair shining, touched by the morning sun.

"Addie!" Freda exclaimed cheerfully. Hastily she made her way to Addie and drew her into a tight embrace. "I've missed you terribly."

"It has been a while, hasn't it? These days I seem to lose track of time." She placed a friendly kiss on Freda's cheek. Changing the subject, she said, "How do you do it? Every season you seem to outdo yourself—the window dressing is absolutely gorgeous."

"Thanks, I'm glad you like it. I got the idea from a picture in a magazine. Call it serendipity, but just yesterday I found that old swing out by the curb, peeling paint and all, just like the one in the magazine. I could hardly believe it. I loaded it up in my van and voila!"

"That's incredible, what luck!" Addie said, recalling other stories Freda told of just the same kind of good fortune. *Maybe it was her Irish heritage that brought her luck—and maybe, just maybe, a little of it would rub off on her.*

"What special thing are you looking for today?" Freda said.

Addie cast a sideways glance at her friend. *Is she psychic as well as lucky?* "What I need is very special indeed. I've got my fingers crossed that you might have a crib and a highchair," Addie said, holding up her crossed fingers.

Freda wiggled a finger in her ear, pretending to clean it out. "I don't think I heard you correctly. I surely didn't hear you say a crib and a highchair."

"Don't worry, there's nothing wrong with your hearing—you heard right," Addie said, playfully keeping her friend in suspense.

"What on earth for? And don't try to tell me you're pregnant because I won't believe a word of it," Freda said, her tone showing her growing curiosity.

Addie was just about to explain when she heard a familiar sound. Plunk, shuffle, plunk, shuffle, plunk. She knew the sound all too well—it made skin crawl. She had assumed they were alone but knew instantly that wasn't the case. She turned to see Birdie Banks, the town's most notorious gossip, coming toward them, her cane making a plunking sound as she shuffled across the wood floor.

Freda's face turned the color of her dark red hair. In her excitement over seeing Addie, she'd forgotten to enlighten her of Birdie's presence in the back room.

Addie hated to criticize another person, but Birdie had a way of getting under her skin, and she wasn't alone. Birdie's malicious gossip had touched almost every resident in Beau Ridge—no one was off limits.

Just seeing Birdie brought her most vicious rumor to mind: Charlie Jacobs was helping his best friend Roddy Reid replace shingles on his roof when Roddy lost his footing and fell to his death. It was a tragic accident. The whole town mourned his passing. Of course, Charlie, being the good friend that he was, did what he could to comfort Roddy's wife, Tess, in her time of loss. It seemed that Birdie couldn't resist a chance to cause harm. In her mean and spiteful way, she started the rumor that Charlie had pushed Roddy to his death so that he could have Tess for himself. Some people in town had believed this horrible lie. Tess was a timid soul who couldn't bear the nasty whispers, and the way she was shunned by those she thought were her friends. A month after Roddy's funeral, Tess sold the home she had shared with her beloved husband and left Beau Ridge for good.

Addie shook the memory from her mind and stared into Birdie's thick glasses that magnified her eyes, making them look too large for her face.

In her needling tone, and her gaze locked on Addie's stomach, Birdie said, "Did I hear you say you're in need of a crib?

Nothing good ever came from Birdie knowing anything. Addie knew she had to set her straight before she had the whole town talking. With a quick roll of her eyes in Freda's direction, Addie then turned her gaze back to Birdie.

"As I was just about to tell my good friend, Freda, my sister and her children are visiting for a while. The youngest is an infant, and yes, she needs a crib." Addie said, in a tone she hoped would show her irritation, all the while knowing that nothing ever fazed Birdie. She was like silicone—things just rolled right off.

"Oh, your sister. I don't remember her name, but I recall she was wild as a Betsy bug, ran off with that Thornhill boy, and broke your mother's and father's hearts. Sent them to an early grave, she did. I bet you'll be glad when they go back where they came from, won't you?" Birdie said, her beady eyes staring into Addie's.

Addie's eyes narrowed. "Birdie, they're my family, and I'll thank you not to speak ill of them. I'm so very sorry that my private conversation with my friend has taken you from whatever you were doing in the back room. I won't be in the least offended if you go back to doing whatever it was."

Freda cleared her throat, not sure where Addie's next words were going. "Yes, Birdie, we hadn't meant to disturb your good work. Collecting clothing with holes and stains for the downtrodden is such a worthy cause."

Addie clutched her hand over her mouth to hide her amused grin.

"Well, I had been making good progress until I was interrupted," Birdie said. She shuffled toward the back room, then stopped and turned to face Addie.

"Is your sister's husband staying with you as well?" she probed.

Addie choked back laughter, realizing that, yes, he actually was staying with her, so to speak. She quickly recovered and cast her eyes downward, shaking her head sorrowfully.

"You've obviously touched on a delicate subject, Birdie. I think we've interrogated Addie enough," Freda said, looking to Addie for affirmation.

"Well, it's just that I have so much to do today, and I feel guilty for engaging in idle conversation when I have company waiting at home. I'm sure you understand, Birdie," Addie said, hoping she'd gotten the message loud and clear.

Birdie opened her mouth to say something. Freda reacted by placing a hand on her back and giving her a tiny push in the direction of the storeroom. They could hear her mumbling something under her breath as she shuffled and plunked along, obviously perturbed that she was unable to pry out more of the juicy details.

With Birdie out of sight, Addie and Freda ran for the door. Out on the sidewalk, the two doubled over with hysterical laughter.

Through her giggles, Freda said, "Oh, Addie, I'm so sorry to put you through that. Although I have to say, that's the first time I've ever seen Birdie Baxter shut down—it was a glorious thing to behold."

Addie pulled Freda into a tight embrace. "You don't know how much I needed a good laugh. "So—do you have a crib?"

"This, my dear, is your lucky day. It just so happens that Cindy Sue Bush just brought in the most adorable one I've ever laid my eyes on—you know what a clean fanatic she is. It looks like it's never been used and there's a highchair, too." Freda said, obviously pleased that she could supply Addie's needs. She took Addie by the hand and led her back inside the store.

"You were right—this is my lucky day!" Addie said, running her hand over the slick wood finish on the crib. "I couldn't have bought a brand new one that would be as nice, and the highchair's perfect too."

"So glad to be of service." Freda flexed her muscles and said, "Let's get them loaded."

****

The Piggly Wiggly on East Main was deserted except for Loretta, the cashier—who had worked there for as long as Addie could remember, and the stock boy—whose name she didn't know—she'd given up trying to remember their names, it seemed to her that they were here today and gone tomorrow.

Addie knew the shelves and the inventory like the back of her hand, enabling her to hurry through the aisles collecting the items on her list. When she came to the produce aisle, she sighed as she always did. Nobody had vegetables like hers, but until her garden came in, she begrudgingly chose the best of them and put them in her cart.

Steering the loaded cart up to the checkout area, she greeted Loretta while placing one item at a time onto the conveyor belt. "Hey, Loretta, nice day, isn't it?"

Loretta skipped over the niceties, "You must have company coming," Loretta said, eyeing the number of items and her unusual selections.

Addie knew Loretta was just making small talk, but today, it seemed intrusive. Her loaded-up cart would naturally spark Loretta's attention, especially since she never used a cart but always carried her usual few items in her arms.

"Yes, for a few days," Addie said. Then she remembered Jessie, grateful for a reason to change the subject. "I need a gift for a young girl. Is there something you could recommend?"

Loretta pointed to the rotating display filled with all sorts of things intended to entice children while their parents shopped. She picked a package from the display and held it up for Addie to see. "I bought my niece this rhinestone ring and necklace for her birthday, she wears it all the time."

"That's very nice, any little girl would love it." Addie said. Still, wanting to check out all the options, she turned the display until something caught her eye: a cellophane package containing a watercolor set with twelve paint colors, a brush, and a tablet. Addie picked it off the rack and held it to her chest. "This is perfect! Thank you for pointing that out. Of all the times I've been in this store, I'd never even noticed it."

"If you had kids you'd have noticed," said Loretta, shaking her head. Kids drive their poor parents crazy, begging for the things they can't live without. Most of the time their parents buy it, too—just so they'll hush. Kids are spoiled rotten these days. I think a good sound spanking would do them all good, but nobody's asking me. I just do my job and keep my mouth shut. Like you, I never had kids—we're the smart ones."

"Maybe so," Addie said, but lately she wasn't so sure.

* * * * * * * * * * * * * *

Addie unloaded the groceries from the truck and put them away, then went to check on Lizzie and the children. She found them in the parlor, plied together in the overstuffed rocking chair, sound asleep. Not wanting to disturb them, she backed quietly out of the room but turned around when she heard a voice whisper softly.

"Aren't we the laziest bunch you've ever seen?" Lizzie said.

"Yes, you are, but you have every right to be—don't get used to it—I have very little tolerance for slackers," she said, winking. "Since you're awake, I can't wait for you to see what I bought for the baby, and I've got a surprise for Jessie, too," Addie said, forgetting to lower her voice.

Hearing her name, Jessie's eyes popped open. Quick as a wink she scrambled out of her mother's arms and rushed to her aunt. Taking her by the hand Addie led her to the kitchen, where she promptly presented her with a brown paper bag.

Jessie hugged the bag tightly before opening it. Tears spilled onto the clear wrapping, and she quickly wiped them away. "Oh, Aunt Addie! I love It! Thank you!" she said, hugging her tightly.

"I needed some pretty pictures to hang on our walls, and I thought you'd be just the person for the job," Addie said. "I was thinking, too, that an artist should have a studio, a place of their very own. Maybe later we can search for that perfect place for yours? How does that sound?"

Jeanne Vaughn

Through the flood of tears streaming down her face, her words came out broken and trembling, "I would love that more than anything."

"Then it's a deal," Addie said, sealing it with a handshake.

****

Lester arrived promptly at three o'clock, which was no surprise to Addie. He'd never been late a day in his life—a habit drilled into him by his regimented father.

"Are you up to doing a little moving?" Addie said.

Lester bent his right arm to show off his triceps. "Ready and able. What are we moving besides dead bodies?"

"Funny," Addie said. "We've got a baby who needs a bed, and sooner than later, she'll need a highchair, too, and it just so happens that I have both in my truck."

"Well, let's get to it," Lester said, giving her a playful push toward the door.

Outside, Lester took the reins and gave Addie instructions as they unloaded the crib from the truck and carried it into the house. Maneuvering it through doorways proved to be a challenge, but little known to her, Lester had experience in this area.

"I worked in a furniture store when I was in college. They always put us college boys on the moving crew," he said.

"What can't you do?" Addie said, shaking her head.

He leaned over and whispered in her ear. "Bury bodies," he teased.

Addie rolled her eyes in response.

Lester insisted the bed be placed on the inside wall away from drafty windows, which made perfect sense, but Addie wasn't sure she would have thought of it by herself. Standing in the doorway, she nodded approvingly at the room; the crib looked right at home.

With the crib in place, Addie went to find Lizzie, and instructed her to close her eyes. Taking her by the hand she led her down the hall and stopped at the doorway of her room. "Ok, open your eyes," Addie said.

Lizzie peered into the room; her eyes glistened with tears. She walked over and ran her hand across the bed's smooth finish. She went to Addie and hugged her tightly as her gaze fell on Lester, standing in the background.

"Lizzie, you remember Lester, don't you," Addie said.

"Why, of course I do. It's been a long time," Lizzie said softly. She put out her hand to shake Lester's but instead found herself caught up in one of his trademark bear hugs. "I'm so glad you're here to help Addie. I'm sorry to say I've been no help whatsoever."

"Well, of course you haven't. I understand you've been through quite an ordeal," Lester said.

"You could say that," Lizzie said. "But rest assured, I plan to pull my weight around here just as soon as I'm able."

"I have no doubt you will. You're a Richardson and Richardson women are tough—Addie's proof of that," Lester said, with a wink in Addie's direction.

"We are that," Lizzie said. "Plus a few other things, like headstrong, sassy, and...,"

"Say no more. I'm a pushover for headstrong, sassy women, as you can see." Lester said, slightly nudging Addie and enjoying the banter.

"Well, Lester, as much as I hate to be a party pooper, we have a pressing job awaiting us," Addie said.

"What are ya'll up to now?" Lizzie said.

"Oh, just a little job Lester promised to help me with outside. We'll be out there for a bit. You get your rest. We'll be done before you know it," Addie said. She had high hopes that the job would go smoothly, knowing that Lester, on his worst day, would be a thousand times more helpful than Reggie had been. "We'll have a relaxing dinner after we're done," she called back as they headed out the door.

****

Dressed in coveralls and wearing leather work gloves, Addie and Lester stood before the wall of English ivy that covered the entire side of the house. Lester appeared mesmerized by the thick, tangled mass of woody vines.

Addie noticed the astonished look on his face and probed his thoughts. "Pretty awesome, isn't it?"

"I'll say, very impressive," Lester said, his eyes studying it as if seeing for the first time.

He pulled a measuring tape from his pocket and pushed it deep into the mass until it met the siding. From there to the outermost vines measured three feet.

"Wow!" he said. "For once in my life, I'm at a loss for words."

"So, you can see what a great hiding place it is; look closely. Do you see anything besides vines and leaves?"

Lester stepped closer and peered intently, scrutinizing every section along the wall. He chuckled and gave Addie a playful slap on the back. "Ok, you got me. I must admit you really had me going. Fun and games are over, Sis. Now, what's the real plan?"

"I swear it on my life: Slick's all snuggled in like a bug in a rug. I used to worry that a bone would work its way out, but thankfully, that's never happened. Don't you think it's the absolute perfect place?" Addie said, a look of pride on her face.

"To tell you the truth, I thought this was a hair-brained idea, but hey, I know better than to doubt you," Lester said. "Now, fill me in on how this is going to work. Time's a-wastin'." He danced around like a boxer preparing for a match, his playful nature on full display.

"I just love an enthusiastic worker. So, here's the plan: we start from the ground and work our way up. We'll need a ladder. I can show you better than I can tell you," she said.

Tugging her gloves further up her arm, she approached the wall and carefully pulled away a section of vine. She turned to look at Lester, making sure she had his full attention. Convinced he was watching intently, she continued.

"In a way, the process is similar to a ground burial. Only instead of a shovel digging into dirt, we'll be digging into the ivy with our hands. Like the dirt dug from the ground, the ivy will be used later to cover the body. It's important to leave the vine attached to the main root."

She held up a long leafy vine and let it drop from her hand. With its aerial roots detached, it dangled freely from the main root.

Lester gave an understanding nod.

"As we get deeper into the vine, that's where the old, ropy vines are—they'll be more of a challenge. She got a good grip on one the size of a broom handle and pulled. Its strong roots held it firm. Taking a step back, she readjusted her grip and pulled again. This time the vine released and sent her toppling to the ground.

Lester let out a deep, hearty laugh. "I'm not sure I got that. Could you show me again?" he said, reaching out a hand to help her up.

Addie pulled his arm with both of hers and brought him down beside her. They laughed until tears were streaming down their faces. In no hurry to get back to work, they sat side by side staring at the imposing ivy.

"Look!" Addie said, pointing to the wall where a sizable, gaping hole was exposed. Recharged, she jumped up and resumed her work, while giving Lester play by play instructions.

''This is great! We're already making progress. We just keep on until we've cleared a section large enough for the body. Then we put old Jim Bob in the bed of the truck, back him up to the wall, fit him into the cavity, and weave the vines back over him," Addie said, dusting her hands. "Easy, peasy, huh?"

Lester looked adoringly at her dirt-smeared face and the twigs sticking out of her head like tiny antennas. Shaking his head, he pulled out a twig and held it up for her to see.

Laughing, she took the twig from his hand and stuck it behind his ear.

"Uh, I was just thinking. Since you've got experience under your belt and doing such a bang-up job, you could just carry on. I'll be happy to take the job of supervisor. Besides, the view from back here is much more to my liking." He gave her a boyish grin and patted her backside.

"Sir, if you don't mind, I'd prefer that the help keep his hands to himself and his mind on his work," Addie said, her chin raised as if offended.

"Yes, ma'am," he said, raising his hand to his forehead in a salute.

"As for me doing all the work and you watching the scenery—I could do that, if you don't mind being called a wimp," she said, playfully nudging him toward the wall.

Lester stumbled forward. "By the way, where is ole Slick anyway? Are you sure we won't be disturbing his peaceful slumber?"

"Sure, and certain," she said, tilting her head in the direction of the chimney. "He's down there."

"I'm still not totally convinced that a traditional grave wouldn't be a better way," Lester said, rubbing his chin thoughtfully.

"Think of it this way: who's going to look for a body in a bunch of twisted vines?" Addie said.

"You've got a point there," Lester said. He gave her a thumbs up.

Taking turns, they pulled out sections of the vine, Lester insisting that Addie leave the larger ones for him. After a long session, Lester suggested a break. Addie, being accustomed to working long hours in her garden, hadn't given it a thought. She looked at Lester, who was dripping with sweat, and realized a break was in order. She went to the house and came back with a full pitcher of water and poured them each a large glass. Sitting shoulder to shoulder, they relaxed on the grass.

"Just so you know, I plan to repay you for this," Addie said.

Lester cocked his head and gazed quizzically at her.

Addie caught the baffled look on his face. "Something wrong?"

"The thought just occurred to me that you know exactly how to get me going. Like putting a carrot in front of a mule to make him work faster," Lester said, his face set in a teasing pout.

Addie grinned. "I wish I could say I'm that clever, but if it worked, Sir…"

"Darn right it did, Ma'am," he said. He got to his feet and went straight to work, reaching in and pulling at the vines with renewed vigor.

Addie laughed as she watched him attack the vines like tomorrow might never show up. For over two hours they worked tirelessly.

Lester, who was on the ladder, paused and turned to look at Addie. "Maybe digging a hole wouldn't have been such a bad idea after all," he said, wiping away the rivers of sweat that streamed down his face.

She disregarded his comment, taking in their progress instead. "Lester!" she said, clapping her hands excitedly. "I think we're done. Come down and see for yourself."

Lester climbed down from the ladder, stood next to her, and gazed wide-eyed at the wall. "By George, I think you're right." He took out his measuring tape. "Hallelujah!" he said. He lifted her off the ground, twirling her around and around.

"I hate to put a damper on your enthusiasm, but that's just step one," she said, with a nudge of her elbow into his side. "Step two is getting ole Jim Bob settled in."

Lester followed Addie to the shed where he helped her into the bed of the truck. He hoisted Jim Bob onto the tailgate, and Addie kept the body stable as Lester drove the truck to the house and backed it up to the wall. It took both of them to stand him up and place him in the crevice. The ladder worked like a charm to hold the body against the wall.

Addie worked from the ladder as Lester held it steady. Starting with the inner vines and working her way to the outer ones she weaved layer upon layer in a meticulous fashion over the body until it was completely concealed. Standing back from the wall, she and Lester surveyed their work. Their eyes scrutinized every section, detecting nothing but leaves and vines. Their handling of the leaves caused them to be limp, but since it was technically still winter, this would appear natural.

"A good dose of The Formula will perk those leaves right up," Addie said.

"I'm speechless," Lester said, wiping sweat from his brow.

Addie rubbed her lower back. "I have a feeling, dear friend, that tomorrow we'll be moving slow—my back is killing me already. You head on inside and clean up while I park the truck in the shed. I'll be there in a jiffy to fix us a bite of supper."

****

Walking into the kitchen, Addie stopped and smiled at the scene before her. At the table sat Lester with Lillie in his arms, Jessie was happily painting a picture of a house with green grass and blue flowers, but there was no sign of Lizzie. Addie looked quizzically at Lester.

"When I came inside, I took one look at her and insisted she lie down; I promised I'd take good care of the children. I think you should go check on her," he said.

Addie washed her hands at the kitchen sink and slipped out of the room. At Lizzie's bedside, she gasped at her sister's ghastly skin tone. "Oh, honey. You've been up way too much. I feel just awful. My nurturing skills are definitely lacking. You hardly have enough strength to breathe, much less take care of yourself and the children. I'm so sorry. I promise I'll take better care of you, now that I've gotten these little jobs out of the way."

Lizzie looked into Addie's tired eyes. In a shaky voice she said, "You have nothing at all to be sorry for, you've selflessly attended to our every need. And don't try to pretend that you're not tired—I can see you're exhausted."

Yawning, she said, "You always could see right through me. Thankfully, this day has almost drawn to a close. After dinner it's off to bed for everybody."

****

Although hardly able to put one foot in front of the other, Addie somehow managed to throw together a simple but satisfying meal of chipped beef and gravy on toast. Talk around the table was almost nonexistent and each set of droopy eyes, including hers, told her that it was time to call it a day.

"I'm exhausted," she announced. This brought on a unison chorus of shared sentiment laced with tired laughter.

Moving slowly, Lester gathered up the dirty dishes and took them to the sink to wash, while Addie, holding Lillie, followed Lizzie and Jessie to their room.

Lillie's little head nodded in Addie's arms. She laid her in her new crib, changed her diaper, and dressed her in a clean cotton nightgown. Pulling the covers over her, she lightly kissed her forehead. "Sleep tight, precious angel," she whispered.

Lillie found her thumb, and soon her soft sucking sounds gave way to a hushed sleep. She hesitated for a moment longer over the sleeping child and marveled at what a good baby she is and how she never cries. *How could anyone not love this child? Only the monster we buried today. Darn you Jim Bob!* The contempt she had for the man caused her blood to boil.

Turning away from the crib she was surprised to see Jessie standing quietly behind her. She reached for her hand and said, "Now, it's your turn, sweetie, let's get you into your pajamas."

Addie helped Jessie undress then tugged a crisp white nightgown over her head. Gently, she laid her in the bed beside her mother. "Snug as a bug in a rug," she whispered. Tucking the blanket under Jessie's chin she placed a kiss on her cheek. "Sleep tight, precious one. I'll see you when the morning comes."

At the doorway, Addie glanced back at her new little family—safe and sound. A wave of emotion swept over her knowing that this could be the first time they'd felt safe. She took a deep breath and slowly exhaled it—*darn you Jim Bob*—the thought resounding in her head.

Returning to the kitchen she found Lester with his head resting on his crossed arms at the table. She sat beside him and tenderly laid her hand on his arm. At her light touch he raised his head.

"I guess today told us that we're not so young anymore," he said, rubbing his shoulders.

Addie scooted her chair closer to his. Skillfully, she massaged his neck and shoulders. He groaned as her hands worked deeper, releasing the tension in his knotted-up muscles. She leaned in close to his ear and whispered, "What on earth would I ever do without you?" Tenderly she placed a kiss on his cheek. "Thank you for today. What you did was over and above anything a friend should ever be asked to do. As always, you came through—just as I knew you would."

"All in a day's work," Lester said, with a shrug. He put his arm around her and kissed her forehead.

"Well, Mr. All in a Day's Work, you need to go home and get some well-deserved rest. I'm going to try to do the same."

At the door, Lester pulled Addie into his arms and whispered in her ear. "Don't think for a minute that I've forgotten about my payment for all my hard work."

"Oh, don't you worry, you'll be paid with interest," she said, and gave him a look that had him almost dancing out the door.

The moon cast its light on Lester as he strode to his car. With his hand on the car door, he turned and called back. "I'll be on pins and needles until then," he said.

Addie watched as his car grew smaller and smaller until it disappeared. She walked back inside and leaned against the closed door. A fluttering feeling, like the brush of butterfly wings, spread through her body, and she smiled.

Chapter 8

Before retiring to her room, Addie stopped to look in on the children. The room was dark except for the sliver of light from the crescent moon. She listened. All was quiet—all was still. She turned to leave the room and heard a small voice call to her.

"Aunt Addie," Jessie said.

Addie stepped back into the room.

"Yes, sweetheart, do you need something?"

"Could you stay while I say my prayers?" she said.

"I'd like nothing better," Addie said.

They knelt beside the bed, their hands clasped, fingers pointed toward the ceiling.

Jessie bowed her head and prayed: "Dear God, please be with my mama and make her better, and thank you for not letting my daddy take baby Lillie. And thank you, God, for Aunt Addie—for her bringing us here to live with her in her nice house. Amen." She lifted her head and gazed into Addie's eyes. In her sweet, young voice, she said, "I love you."

Addie blinked back tears and pulled Jessie into her arms. "I love you, too, sweetheart." She helped her back into bed and pulled the covers up under her chin. "Now, if you need anything at all during the night, you just come and get me, okay?"

Jessie nodded and closed her eyes.

Outside the room, tears streamed down her face as thoughts of her sister consumed her. *I have to hand it to you Lizzie. You've certainly done a remarkable job raising your children despite the horrible things you experienced at the hands of a wretched husband and father. At least that nightmare is over—for good.* A warm feeling ran through her, knowing they were safe now.

Before getting into bed, Addie knelt and did what she had neglected for far too many years: she put her hands together and prayed: "Dear God, it's me Addie. I know it's been a long time since I've asked for Your help. I've always thought I could go it alone, and time after time, I have. But this time, I'm in over my head—little children are involved. I want to do what's right for them and for Lizzie, but I need Your help. Show me how to care for their needs, and give me the strength to endure the trials that lay ahead. And please, God, hold Lizzie and her children close and fill their broken hearts with hope in the way that only you can do. Amen."

When she finished, the front of her nightgown was damp from her tears. The instant she crawled under the covers an unexpected calm spread through her body, drawing her into a deep sleep.

****

Roused by the morning sun, Addie sat up in bed and stretched, feeling alive and more energized than she had in years. She looked out the window and gave a nod toward the heavens with new assurance that she could handle whatever came her way.

Sliding her feet into her slippers, she took her robe from the bedpost and wrapped it snuggly around her. Pattering softly on the bare floor, she made her way to the kitchen, being careful not to wake Lizzie and the children.

The room gave off a soft amber glow sending a warm sensation from her head to her toes. She walked over to the windows and pushed the curtains open to let the sunlight fill the room. Starting the coffee brewing, she hummed softly. She fixed Lillie's bottle and set it in a small pot of hot water. While the coffee perked and the bottle was warming, she went into Lizzie's room to see if the children were awake.

Lillie had kicked off her blanket and was happily playing with her toes. As quietly as she could, Addie pulled down the side rail, made a quick diaper change, and lifted her out, speaking softly into her ear. Noting that Jessie was still asleep, she quietly left the room, closing the door behind her.

In the kitchen, with Lillie on her hip, she took the bottle from the water, turned it upside down, and shook a few drops onto her wrist to test the temperature. Positioning Lillie in her lap, her tiny hands went eagerly around the bottle, sucking greedily as her little legs kicked sporadically.

This experience was new to Addie. Holding a baby in her arms was a feeling like none she had ever known, and to her surprise, she was growing increasingly fond of it. Blissfully, she closed her eyes and gently rocked as Lillie drank contentedly from her bottle. Feeling a slight touch on her arm, she opened her eyes to see Jessie standing beside her, wide-eyed and shaking.

"Good morning, honey bear," Addie said, missing the tormented look on Jessie's face.

"I woke up, and Lillie wasn't in her crib," Jessie said.

Addie exhaled an exasperated breath and shook her head. *How could I have been so insensitive?* She hadn't given any thought to how seeing Lillie's empty bed would affect Jessie. Quickly she said a silent prayer for God to help her shield Jessie from her demons.

"Oh, honey, I wanted to let you and your mama sleep a while longer, and Lillie was awake. I'm so sorry—I didn't mean to worry you."

"Lillie likes it here, just like me," Jessie said, changing the subject, obviously sensing her aunt's distress.

"Sweetie, I'm so glad. Nothing pleases me more than having you here, all of you." She wrapped her free arm around Jessie, bringing her in close.

"Now, what would you like for breakfast? How about chocolate chip pancakes, but only if you help me make them."

A big, wide smile and an affirmative nod were the only answer Addie needed. "Lillie's almost finished with her bottle. I'll make her a pallet on the floor where we can watch her while we cook. How does that sound?"

"That sounds great!" Jessie said, brimming with enthusiasm.

The two cooks were busy adding the finishing touches to the pancakes when Lizzie walked in the room. "What are my best girls up to?"

"We made chocolate chip pancakes, Mama," Jessie said, smiling broadly and revealing chocolate covered teeth.

"I hope you saved one for me," her mother said.

Jessie held up the plate piled high with pancakes.

"Oh, sweetie, those look super yummy. My mouth waters just looking at them," Lizzie said.

Jessie walked over to the china cabinet, and selected a plate covered in pretty yellow flowers. On it she placed two pancakes decorated with chocolate chip smiley faces and topped with melted butter and warm maple syrup. Proudly, she set the plate before her mother.

Lizzie made a production of placing her napkin in her lap, picking up her fork, and cutting into one as it smiled up at her. She took a bite, raised her fork in the air, and turned to face Jessie. "My compliments to the chef! You've simply outdone yourself, Madame. These are the most delicious pancakes I ever tasted."

Jessie's whole face beamed like sunshine. "Really, Mama? The best you ever tasted?"

"The absolute best! Yum, yum, yum, yum, yum," Lizzie mumbled, her mouth full of pancake.

Seeing Lizzie in her role as a mother deeply touched Addie's heart. She saw no signs of the former Lizzie, whose main focus was herself. Her sister had been transformed into a loving and devoted parent, whose first and foremost concern was the well-being of her children. *Miracles do happen.*

Following breakfast, Lizzie and Lillie were back in their beds, leaving Addie and Jessie alone to get better acquainted. Addie started clearing the kitchen table to make room for Jessie's art materials, but remembered her promise to find Jessie a special place to do her art.

"How about we go find that special place of yours?" Addie said.

"Oh, can we?" Jessie said, clapping her hands excitedly.

"Artists need light, you know. A room with windows where natural light comes through would be a good choice. We'll walk through the house and check out every room. Since you're the artist, you get to choose any room you like."

Jessie took the task seriously, scrutinizing every room. After surveying all the downstairs rooms, Jessie started up the stairs. Addie almost protested but stopped herself. For several reasons she kept those rooms closed off, but she had told Jessie that she could choose any room she liked, which perhaps was a mistake, but she had no intention of going back on her word.

All of the rooms on the second floor intrigued Jessie, and she spent time in each one running her hands over the walls, appraising the view from the windows and the amount of light each provided. One room in particular piqued her interest. The floor to ceiling window filled the room with radiant light, the wallpaper—though peeling in places—was like a being in a field of tiny pink roses, and the view overlooked the immense front lawn.

"Aunt Addie, this is it!" Jessie said, her eyes wide with excitement.

Addie had to admit, it was perfect. What could she say? This child needed assurances, not broken promises. "You have a great eye—the eye of a true artist. I think it's perfect! But I think we should clear it with your mother first. If she says yes, then it's settled."

"I think she'll say it's okay, but I think we should ask her."

Addie had no confidence in her own ability to decide what was best for a child of seven, and she had no desire to start off on the wrong foot with Lizzie. She was glad for Jessie's gracious agreement to involve her mother in the decision. "We can start looking around for things you'll need. Once we've gotten the all-clear from your mom, we'll get right to work."

They set out on a mission to find items that could be used from Addie's sparse furnishings. In the kitchen was a small table that they determined would make the perfect desk. And in the garden, they spied a little wooden chair that would be just right for the desk. Addie suggested that the two could be painted in Jessie's favorite colors, and that they could make a pretty cushion for the chair. Their creative minds churned out idea after idea. Jessie clapped her hands and hugged her aunt at every new find.

A pleased smile spread across Addie's face. *This is joy at its purest.*

Every few minutes Jessie would go to the door and peek into their room. After making at least ten trips, her mother finally stirred. She made a beeline to her side. "Mama, would it be okay if Aunt Addie and I make a special room for me to do my art? Aunt Addie let me pick the one I wanted, and I found the perfect one," Jessie said, her words rushing out, breathless and full of hope.

Lizzie sat up and patted a place for Jessie to sit beside her on the bed. "So, tell me what you and your aunt have been cooking up," she said, cocking her head.

Jessie's excitement caused the pitch of her voice to rise, and she spoke in a hurried tone. "It's up there," she pointed upward. "It's the best room ever with lots of light—like real artists need, and a big window that looks out over the front lawn. We found furniture to put in it, and we're going to paint it and make a cushion, too. Oh, Mama, it's so perfect! Please say it's okay."

Addie was standing in the doorway, listening to their conversation. Lizzie looked at Addie who shrugged sheepishly.

"Let me talk to your aunt about it, sweetie. I want to make sure those rooms are safe; can I have just a few minutes alone with her? I promise I'll have an answer for you right away."

Jessie kissed her mother on the cheek and limped from the room, leaving the two alone.

Addie walked over and sat on the bed beside her sister. "I may have jumped the gun," she said guardedly. "I didn't mean to step on your toes, but I just have this strong urge to make Jessie happy. I can't seem to say no to her."

"You and me both," Lizzie said, nodding her head. "So, do you feel that the rooms upstairs are safe? I know you've had them closed off."

"Well, structurally, yes; it was just too costly to heat the rooms I wasn't using. I feel confident that it's safe, although there's nothing at all up there, and it can be cold in the winter. I suppose if we leave just that door open, the heat from below would warm the one room adequately," Addie said.

"That's all I needed to hear. If Jessie says it's the perfect room, then how can I object?" Lizzie said. She placed her hand on Addie's arm. "I'm so pleased that you've been so kind to Jessie and have shown her so much love. I don't know if you've noticed—she's so much like you.

Addie's face lit up. "You think so?"

"I know so," Lizzie said with a grin.

Still beaming, Addie said, "Well, she does have my features, but I've never been that sweet or that good. And it would be downright impossible for anyone not to love that child."

"I know one person who didn't, but goodness knows, he didn't even like himself," Lizzie said.

"I know things were bad with you and Jim Bob. I have a feeling it was pure misery, when you're better we can talk about it. Right now, your little daughter is anxious to hear your decision."

Lizzie called out to Jessie, who despite her injured leg, came running like she had wings on her feet.

Taking Jessie's hands in hers, Lizzie said. "It's decided. You now have a room you can call your very own. I'm expecting great works of art from you, young lady."

"Mama, you and Aunt Addie are the best! Thank you! I love you so much," Jessie said, wrapping her small arms around them both.

Addie was as overjoyed as Jessie; she couldn't wait to start painting and sewing.

* * * * * * * * * * * * *

At bedtime that evening, as Addie was helping with Jessie's bath, she noticed that the wound on her leg was terribly swollen and had turned blackish. She had kept it clean, applied ointments, and wrapped it in bandages, but apparently, that wasn't good enough. Now, she feared infection had set in. She made up her mind that they would see the doctor first thing in the morning.

"Honey, does your leg hurt?" Addie said.

"Sometimes," Jessie said, then added, "but, not too bad."

Addie doubted that to be true. From the looks of it, she knew it had to hurt like crazy.

"I think we'll have to go to town tomorrow and let the doctor look at it. Would you be alright with that?"

Jessie looked down at her leg as if seeing the injury for the first time. "It looks pretty bad, doesn't it? He won't hurt me, will he?"

"No, sweetie, he wouldn't hurt you for all the tea in China. He'll know just what to do. It just so happens that he's my doctor, too, and I trust him completely."

"I've never been to a doctor before. Will you stay with me and not leave me?"

"Of course I will. I won't leave you for a single second, I promise. If we don't go, your leg could get worse."

"Well, I do want it to get better," Jessie said.

"Okay, then it's settled. We'll go in the morning. Let's get you in your pajamas and off to bed so that you'll be well rested for tomorrow."

Addie knelt with Jessie as she said her prayers then pulled the covers over her and kissed her goodnight. She softly shook Lizzie awake and motioned for her to follow her into the hallway where she filled her in about the condition of Jessie's leg and the need for her to see a doctor.

"I was hoping that it would heal on its own. She's never been to a doctor, and a wound like that is sure to raise suspicion. I've heard tales of children being taken away from their parents for things such as this," Lizzie said, her voice suddenly shaky.

"I'll be right there with her; I won't let her out of my sight. I fear if she doesn't receive the proper care, something bad could happen, and I couldn't bear that, and neither could you," Addie said.

"There I go, back to my old self-centered ways. Of course I want her leg to heal. I hope you know that. I just know how it will look, but yes, she must go, and the sooner, the better."

"Well, it's a good thing you're not taking her in your condition—it would sure raise concerns," Addie said, grinning.

"We would be a pair for sure, I can hear the talk now," Lizzie said, and they chuckled at the thought.

"In the morning before we leave, I'll get Lillie's bottle warmed and put her in bed with you; she'll probably go right back to sleep. I'm hoping we won't be long," Addie said.

"That's not necessary, I can do that; you are babying me too much."

"My motives are purely selfish. My goal is for you to get better as quickly as possible. You'll just have setbacks if you're up doing things too soon, as we've already witnessed. You're just going to have to indulge me on this, Sis," Addie said, her hands on her hips—her authoritative attitude on display.

"As always, dear sister—you know best," Lizzie said, showing signs of her old sassiness.

Addie smiled; it was good to see her sister's spunk returning.

In her bed, Addie closed her tired eyes and within minutes she drifted off. Suddenly her eyes popped open—she saw a strange man wearing a red baseball cap. He was watching the house, watching them. Her vision was foggy, she couldn't see his face, but one thing was perfectly clear—trouble was brewing.

Chapter 9

Long before the sun had a chance to peek through her window, Addie was awake. Her vision of the stranger had disrupted the good night's rest she desperately needed. Since her bed offered no solace, she climbed out, hurriedly dressed, and twisted her hair into a messy bun. Quietly, so as not to wake the others, she made her way to the kitchen.

After her dreadful night, what she needed most was coffee and lots of it. While it perked, she washed some fruit and made oatmeal for their breakfast. She prepared two bottles for Lillie, just in case she and Jessie didn't return before lunchtime.

At the table with her coffee cupped in her hands, her thoughts went to her vision of the man. She was troubled that it was so vague; it left her with a lot of questions—questions she had wasted far too much time agonizing over.

Forcing her mind away from the subject, she remembered the chair cushion she'd promised to make. Taking her pattern box from the shelf in the storeroom, she rifled through her neatly organized patterns and found the one she was looking for. She had just begun to pin the pattern to the fabric when Jessie shuffled sleepy-eyed into the room.

Looking up from her work, Addie said, "Sweetie, did I wake you with all my clamoring around in here?"

"No, I've been awake a while. I'm a little bit scared about today, Aunt Addie," she said.

She detected a slight quiver in her niece's voice. "Oh, honey, I feel the same way when I have to see the doctor—it's perfectly normal. Remember, I'll be with you the whole time. You're going to like Doctor Loggings. Best of all, when it's time to leave, every good patient gets to pick a toy from his treasure chest. Believe me, there's some really good stuff in there."

"A treasure chest!" Jessie said, her face lighting up. "I think I'm not scared anymore."

"Good girl!" Addie said. "Now, what do you think of this fabric for the chair cushion?"

"It's perfect, I love it!"

"Before we get started on it, I think we should have some breakfast and get you ready to go. We'll get back to it and our other projects when we get home. Does that sound okay?"

"I think it sounds great—I can't wait!" Jessie said, twirling around in circles.

* * * * * * * * * * * * * *

Addie helped Jessie up into the truck. The uneasiness she felt earlier about the man in her vision had returned. She scanned the house and lawn as she slowly drove away.

As she drove down the lane, Addie pointed out things of interest to Jessie: the biggest magnolia tree on the property, the buttercups just beginning to peek their green leaves out of the ground, the oak tree where the hoot owl lives, and the large fields where cotton was grown.

"Cotton, like my dress?" Jessie said, her fingers rubbing over the soft fabric.

"Yes. I suppose you didn't know that cotton grows from a plant. That seems funny, doesn't it? Cotton has been grown on Kent land for four generations, starting in the 1840s by my husband's great-grandparents. A lot has changed since those days," Addie said.

Jessie's eyes grew wide as she took in the vast amount of land. She pointed in all directions. "Is all this land yours?"

Addie nodded. "Everything you see around us, a thousand acres in all. Sounds like a lot, doesn't it?"

"I don't know what an acre is, but I know that a thousand is a whole lot."

"You're right about that, but the arrangement I have with Farmer Jones has made my life simpler. He takes care of everything related to the land, and I get to do the things I enjoy: my garden and sewing—which are much more fun," Addie said, smiling.

"I want to be just like you, Aunt Addie. I love it here. Being here is the best feeling I've ever known."

Addie reached over and took Jessie's hand and squeezed it. She opened her mouth to express the joy she felt, but the words stuck in her throat.

"Could you tell me stories about you and Mama, things you did when you were growing up? I'd like to write them in my diary—they're much better than mine.

"Sure, I will, honey, but I have a feeling your stories are way better than you think, so keep writing them," Addie said.

Like a tour guide, Addie pointed out interesting facts about the place she had lived her entire life. Jessie listened intently. Like a sponge, she soaked up all the details that would later go into her diary.

With only a few miles to go, Addie couldn't delay the dreaded subject any longer. She needed to have a heart-to-heart talk with Jessie about her injury and what they would tell the doctor. "Sweetie, you know the doctor is going to ask how you hurt your leg, and it will be best if you let me tell him. I might need to tweak the truth just a wee bit. It's always best to tell the truth, but just this time, a little fib might be necessary. Are you okay with that?"

Jessie simply replied, "Yes."

Addie nodded, astounded that she was so young to understand so much.

When they arrived at Dr. Loggings's office, Addie opened Jessie's door and helped her out. Hand in hand, they walked inside.

Margie, the receptionist, greeted Addie warmly. "Good morning, Addie. So good to see you. And, who's this you have with you?"

Addie smiled. "It's good to see you, Margie. This is my niece, Jessie, my sister's oldest daughter."

"Well, I'm very pleased to meet you, Jessie," Margie said.

"Thank you. I'm pleased to meet you, too," Jessie said, parroting Margie's greeting.

Addie's eyes went to the appointment book on the counter, seeing no empty time slots, she sighed before turning her gaze back to Margie. "We don't have an appointment, but we have a situation that I feel needs immediate attention. Would it be possible for the doctor to see Jessie today?"

"Certainly, we can arrange that. He has a full schedule today, but an emergency always takes precedence over routine appointments. What exactly is the problem?" Margie said.

"It's Jessie's leg. I'm afraid I've waited too long to bring her in. Her wound seems to be terribly infected," Addie said.

Margie had a soft spot for children and could sense their apprehension a mile away. She took Jessie's hand in hers and felt her nervous tremble. "Sweetie, don't you worry one little bit. Dr. Loggings will make everything better, I promise."

Margie turned her attention to Addie. "I'll let the doctor know you're here. If you'll just have a seat over there, he should be right with you," she said, pointing to the chairs lined along the wall.

With Jessie's hand still holding tightly to Addie's, they seated themselves in the uncomfortable plastic chairs. Addie watched as Jessie's eyes darted around the room. On the walls were framed photographs of forests and mountain streams. She felt Jessie's grip loosen, and her rigid posture relaxed slightly. *Maybe, it's not the scary place she had imagined after all*.

A couple of minutes later, Margie reappeared. "If you'll come this way the doctor will see you," she said. She led them down a hallway and into a small room where she instructed them to take a seat, then closed the door, leaving them alone.

Along one wall were two plastic chairs, like the ones in the waiting room, where they sat awaiting the doctor. Addie watched Jessie scan the room, taking in every detail—details that would no doubt go in her diary.

In the middle of the room was a tall metal table with a long sheet of white paper on top. At one side of the table was a round metal stool on wheels. The walls weren't painted but were wallpapered with images from nursery rhymes.

Jessie pointed to the large shoe with children hanging out the windows and whispered to Addie. "The Old Woman Who Lived in a Shoe."

Addie smiled and nodded.

They had only been seated a few minutes when Dr. Loggings entered the room. His long strides made his way straight to Jessie.

The doctor reached for Jessie's hand and shook it vigorously. "Well, well, so you're Addie's niece. I'm Dr. Loggings," he said, kindly. "It just so happens that my favorite aunt's name is Jessie. Do you know what the name Jessie means?" He was just about to impress her with the answer when Jessie spoke up.

"It means God's gift," Jessie said, her angelic voice giving credence to her name.

"It certainly does," he said. He gave her hand a tender pat. "A very special name, to be sure, and I can see you are a very special little girl."

"Thank you. My whole name is Jessica Hope," she said, warming up to the doctor.

"I can't think of a more fitting name for such a sweet young lady," he said.

Addie smiled, impressed at the doctor's warmhearted way with children. He had certainly put Jessie at ease in mere moments.

"Addie, it's good to see you," Dr. Loggings said, turning his attention momentarily away from Jessie. Then, getting down to business, he said, "So, I understand this young lady has a wound that seems to be infected."

"Oh, I blame myself, and I feel just terrible," Addie lied. "You know, I've never had children around my place, and until now, I was never aware of all the dangers lying around— everywhere."

"So, what happened?" he asked.

"Well, there was this piece of pipe sticking up from the ground in my garden. I knew it was there and always walked around it. My goodness, I don't know where my mind was— I forgot all about it. I was showing Jessie around, and she tripped right over it. The rough metal cut right into her leg. I feel just awful—now it's all infected."

"What kind of pipe was it?" he asked, still trying to get all the details.

"I think it was an old water pipe. My goodness," Addie went on, "I just hate that she got hurt—it was terrible."

"I'm sure it was," replied the doctor. "What did you do?"

"I cleaned it promptly and applied a liniment. It didn't appear to be deep, so I just bandaged it up good. Since then, I've been applying the ointment and putting on a fresh bandage every day. That was two days ago, but last night, I noticed how black her whole leg had become. Why, it scared the life out of me. I hope I haven't waited too long to bring her in."

"Best we have a look at it," he said, rolling the stool close to Jessie. Holding her leg in his hands, he put on his glasses and examined it carefully.

"How bad is it, Doctor?" Addie said, wringing her hands.

"The blackened area is a bad bruise that will eventually go away, and the wound should heal just fine, but it's the hematoma that most concerns me." He pointed to an area that was taut and puffy.

"I'll need to perform a small procedure. I know that sounds scary, but it will be over before you know it, and all that bad pain will go away just like that," he said, with a snap of his fingers.

"What will you do?" Jessie said, always wanting all the details. Still, her voice had a detectable quiver.

In a soothing tone, he began to explain the procedure in terms she could understand. "First, I'll make a tiny opening in the skin," he pointed to the puffy area, "to allow the blood that has collected there to come out; it will feel like a gush of warm water, and that quick, it'll be over, and your pain will be gone. We'll put a clean bandage on it, I'll give your aunt some medicine to kill the bacteria, and in a few days you'll be as good as new. How does that sound?"

Jessie sat up straight in the chair, put on her brave face, and nodded affirmatively.

"Then we're all set." Carefully he helped her onto the tall metal table. "Now, lie down and relax, close your eyes if you like. Your aunt will be right here beside you the whole time. I promise you will hardly feel a thing."

Just as the doctor had said, it was over before they knew it. Still, Addie noticed the faint quiver in Jessie's body. She perceived this to be perfectly natural, especially given her understandable apprehension.

"That wasn't so bad, was it?" the doctor said, giving her a tender pat on the hand.

"Not so bad," she answered, truthfully.

Dr. Loggins turned to face her aunt. "Addie, you should childproof your yard. Not that you can prevent every accident, but a rusty pipe sticking out of the ground is undoubtedly a recipe for disaster," he scolded.

"I plan to do just that," Addie said, realizing that she did indeed need to childproof her yard now that children were around. "I want to thank you for seeing us on such short notice. I was terribly worried that her leg was in a bad way. I never dreamed it could be fixed so easily."

"I'm glad it wasn't worse. I hope there isn't a next time, but if there is, you should come in right away. We can usually prevent things from getting to a critical stage—if we're able to tend to an accident immediately."

"I've learned my lesson," Addie said. With her finger she made an imaginary cross on her heart.

Dr. Loggings handed a small pill bottle to Addie. "She gets one pill twice a day with milk, and also, clean the wound and change the dressing twice a day until it's healed."

He turned to Jessie. "You were the perfect patient today and for that you can choose any toy you want from The Pirate Treasure Chest," he said, pointing to the camelback trunk in the corner of the room.

With eyes as big as saucers, Jessie made her way over to the chest and knelt in front of it.

Addie watched her lift the lid and peer inside. She noticed how she took her time, contemplating over each and every toy. Realizing how even the smallest things meant so much to her little niece filled her heart with a warm fondness.

While Jessie was busy choosing a toy, the doctor pulled Addie aside for a private conversation. She hoped he hadn't sensed her lie about Jessie's injury and was going to interrogate her to get at the truth. If he had done a thorough examination, he would have seen that her little body was covered with bruises—then she would really have some explaining to do. To her great relief, he only wanted to inquire about her own health.

"Seeing you today reminded me that you haven't been in for your annual check-up. I had Margie pull your chart and discovered it's been two years since your last visit. Our well-being should come before everything else, dear lady," he said in a lecturing tone.

Addie breathed a sigh of relief. Although grateful that his attention had shifted away from Jessie, her feathers were ruffled for being called on the rug for what he saw as her lack of attention to her "well-being". "I'd have been here with bells on if something was wrong, but I'm happy to report that I'm fit as a fiddle," she replied, hiding her annoyance.

"Well, I just don't like to see people neglect their health issues—it's so important. I just can't stress that enough to my patients. You really should make an appointment before you leave here today. You know it's vital for us to keep a close check on things as we age."

What health issues, and is he really implying that I'm getting old? I'm twenty-eight, for goodness sakes, and as I see it, healthy as a horse—hardly ready for the rocking chair. And what gives him the right to lecture me, especially when my visit today had nothing to do with me—and to involve his receptionist—that's going way too far!

For some reason it had all just rubbed her the wrong way. She was tired, and her stress level was showing. She chided herself for being so sensitive. It was so unlike her to let such a small thing get under her skin. He is her doctor, after all, and she supposed that did give him some justification to inquire. And besides, he had been so very kind to Jessie; she decided put on her best Southern manners and try to be gracious.

"You couldn't be more right," she said sweetly, but with a dash of underlying vinegar. She had no intention of making an appointment. These days she had no money for needless doctor visits. *My herbs will cure anything that ails me—thank you very much.* She thanked the doctor politely and walked back across the room where Jessie was seated on the floor by the toy chest. In her arms she cradled a velvety white rabbit with pink ears.

Smiling brightly, Jessie held out the rabbit for Addie to hold. "Isn't Fluffy soft? Can we make her some clothes?" she said, her face full of hope.

"I think that we must," Addie said.

After paying the bill, Addie took Jessie by the hand and they made a hasty exit, hoping to avoid further discussion of an appointment for herself. She had never been so relieved to get out of a place in her life.

****

Following Jessie's anxiety-ridden doctor visit, Addie wanted to make the rest of the day special for her. Side by side and hand in hand, they strolled down the sidewalk until they came upon Kune's Five and Dime. Before entering the store, they stood and admired the window filled with an assortment of items intended to lure young children inside. There was a stuffed brown bear, a yellow tricycle, a red wagon filled with multi-colored blocks, a green motorized tractor, a life-sized baby doll, a baseball bat and glove, all of which sat atop a spiky green rug that gave the appearance of a grassy lawn.

Addie looked at Jessie's reflection in the glass. Her eyes wide and transfixed on the enticing display.

"Oh, Aunt Addie! I've only seen things like that in my storybooks," Jessie said.

Addie squeezed her hand and led her inside. Her days of lavish spending were long gone. Nowadays, she had to be careful with her money, especially now that she had four mouths to feed. Today was special. Before leaving the house, she had dipped into her cookie jar where she hid the little bit of money she'd been able to save. She slipped a five-dollar bill into Jessie's hand. "This is for you to spend anyway you want."

Jessie held the bill tightly as if she feared it might suddenly vanish. Her eyes glazed with tears, and she wrapped her arms tightly around her aunt.

Addie wiped tears from her eyes and said, "I could make a suggestion. You might want to choose a fabric for Fluffy's clothes."

Jessie's eyes widened, "Oh, yes! I do want to do that!"

Jessie studied all the fabrics carefully and after much consideration, chose one with pink and white polka dots, and at Addie's suggestion, some white rick rack for trim. With money left over she bought scarfs for her mother and Addie in pretty spring colors and a pink bunny rattle toy for Lillie. Jessie's generous nature touched Addie's heart—especially since the child had so little herself.

****

In the few short days that she had been with her, Addie had learned a lot about her niece. She was curious, smart, generous, and selfless. Now she had learned another of her traits—she didn't forget anything. On the drive back home, Jessie reminded her of her promise to tell her stories about when she and her mother were growing up. Addie thought for a moment, then said, "Has your mother ever told you our given names? I mean our full names, not Lizzie and Addie."

Jessie shook her head.

"Well, our parents—bless their hearts—didn't much care how a name sounded. They just pulled ours straight out of the family hat. My given name is Adeline Beatrice. I was named after a dear aunt of our mother's, and our father's beloved sister. Your mother was named Elizabeth Rosalie, names taken from our mother's mother and our father's mother. Even though our two names didn't quite roll off the tongue the way Southern names are supposed to, our parents insisted on using them both. Heaven forbid they play favorites and pick one name over the other."

Addie chuckled at the memory. Jessie grinned with delight.

Addie continued, "I always thought Adeline Beatrice sounded like fingernails on a chalkboard, and although Elizabeth Rosalie had a slightly better ring to it, it wasn't exactly harmonious either. Well, thank goodness for small favors. When your mother began to talk, naturally, she couldn't say my big ole name, so she called me Addie. Then thankfully, everybody else began to call me Addie, too. It was the same with me when I began to talk. I called your mother Lizzie. That's how it was with the two of us. We always seemed to have each other's backs."

"I love that story, Aunt Addie. My mama told me how I got my name. She said before I was her little girl, she was really sad, but when I was born, she said I was her gift from God. My second name is Hope. She said that I gave her hope that things would be better—now that she had me to love."

"You are God's gift, precious," Addie said, "and that is a beautiful story."

"Will you tell me another one?" Jessie said.

"Oh, sweetie, I could go on and on forever, but we're almost home; we'll have plenty of time for more stories. I'll make sure of it."

As Addie pulled the truck around to the back of the house, her gaze was instantly drawn to the wall of ivy that appeared in a state of disarray. Something had been digging at the base, and some of the vines had been pulled away. Alarmed, she hurriedly parked and helped Jessie inside. Thoughts were swirling around in her mind. *What in heaven's name could be digging in the ivy? Surely, it's some critter—she'd check into it later.*

For Jessie's sake she had to hide her concern. Although she hadn't shown signs of having the sight, she had something else. She was instinctive and insightful, not one to be easily fooled. No, she'd have to stay calm until she could go out alone, inspect the damage, and figure out exactly what had caused it.

Chapter 10

Seeing that Jessie's leg was swollen to almost twice its normal size, Addie insisted she lie down. She blamed herself for dragging her all over town when she should have brought her straight home after seeing the doctor. Where the child was concerned she had the best of intentions, but she still had so much to learn.

Helping Jessie into bed beside her sleeping mother, she propped her leg up with pillows, and placed a kiss on her forehead. Silently, she tiptoed out of the room. She couldn't wait a minute longer. She was itching to get to the bottom of what had been digging in the ivy.

Silently she made her way to the back door, slipped into her warm coat and tugged on her tall boots, then stepped outside. She paused mid-step as a sickening stench crept into her nostrils. She gagged and pulled the collar of her coat over her nose then moved in closer. Her eyes were instantly alerted to the pasty white hand that dangled from the vines. She shrieked, and quickly placed her hand over her mouth.

With an instinct she didn't know she possessed, she studied the ground for tracks, or feathers, or anything that might shed some light on the mysterious culprit. Whatever it was had to be some nasty critter or even a buzzard, something that feeds on dead carcasses. And she knew that most likely it wouldn't stop as long as the odor was there to attract it. Whatever it was, it had to be stopped—immediately. Addie quickly devised a plan. *If the culprit returns, which I'm certain it will, I'll be waiting for it.*

****

She went about gathering the things she would need for her stakeout: a blanket, her slingshot, and rocks she had collected earlier. Before going back outside, she peeked in on the girls. All were sleeping except for Lizzie, who had been waiting for Addie to make her usual rounds. Seeing her in the doorway, Lizzie quietly slipped out of bed and led her sister into the hallway.

Lizzie kept her voice low so as not to wake the children. "Something happened today while you and Jessie were in town—we had a visitor. Lillie was sleeping, and I was in the kitchen when I heard a loud commotion outside. I walked to the back door and peered out to see a large dog attacking the ivy, grabbing large pieces with his mouth and growling ferociously. I clapped my hands and yelled at him. I guess I put the fear in him—he took off like a bullet. The dog must have been after whatever died in there—there's a horrendous stench."

Addie put her hand to her chest. "What a relief!"

Lizzie looked puzzled.

"When we got home, I noticed that something had been up to no good. I was prepared to sit up all night, waiting for whatever it was to return. I'm glad to know it's not some wild man-eater." Addie bit her bottom lip to keep from showing her amusement at her choice of words.

"My guess is he'll be back alright. Now that you know what you're dealing with, you shouldn't have to wait up to catch him. You'll hear him loud and clear." Worry lines deepened on Lizzie's brow. "Now to the most important subject—what did the doctor say about Jessie?"

"Oh my, I should have come to you right away with the report. Dr. Loggings took extremely good care of her today. I was so impressed with the kindness he showed her and how he instantly put her at ease. One look at her leg and he quickly diagnosed the problem as a hematoma. Of course, Jessie wanted all the details, and in simple terms he explained every step of the procedure. Seconds later, it was over. He prescribed an antibiotic for infection, said to keep it bandaged, and that soon she'll be good as new."

"Did the doctor give her a full examination? They usually do that with new patients," Lizzie said, twisting a strand of hair.

"Luckily, due to his full schedule, he only had time to address the wound on her leg."

"He surely asked how it happened," Lizzie said.

Addie scrunched up her face. "Well yes, he did, and I told a straight-faced lie. In case anybody asks, we need to have the same story—she tripped over a metal pipe in my garden."

"Shame on you, Adeline Beatrice," she said, jabbing her with her elbow.

"I know. I'm probably going straight to hell for all the lies I've spun lately," Addie said.

"I'm glad you can think so quickly when the situation calls for it. Your lies just might keep us out of jail," Lizzie said.

"Or get us locked up for life," Addie said.

They laughed, but worry showed on their faces.

"Seriously though, you should be so proud of that child. She was perfect today in every way. I swear, Lizzie, I don't know how you managed to raise such an angel."

Lizzie shook her head. "If you're wondering how someone as wild as me ended up with a child as good as Jessie, join the club—I ask myself that same thing every day."

"Well, I wasn't going to put it quite like that, but you were known to do some pretty crazy stuff—Elizabeth Rosalie," Addie said, gently returning the elbow jab.

As children, the two had a word they used when it was time to end their sisterly bickering.

With a smug grin, Lizzie held up two crossed fingers and declared: "Truce."

Addie did the same and responded, "Truce."

A warm feeling ran through Addie, and she smiled. This is what she had missed, the closeness they had once shared. Thankfully, fate had given them another chance.

****

The full moon cast its light into Addie's room, making it feel more like morning than the middle of the night. But that wasn't what had kept her awake; it was the dog that seemed hell-bent on uncovering her secrets. She lay listening, knowing animals were likely to be on the move when the moon was full.

Hours passed, and she'd begun to nod off when she heard a faint bark, then a deeper one, and then pawing and scratching. She jumped out of bed and slipped on her robe that was weighed down with the slingshot and rocks she had placed in the pockets. Hurriedly, she made her way to the back door.

Making as little noise as possible, she opened the door and peered out—thankful for the bright light the moon cast over the lawn. In her bare feet she stepped gingerly down the back stoop, slipping quietly to the side of the house.

Her heartbeat quickened—she'd caught him in the act. The big dog had a long, ropy vine tight between his teeth, pulling backwards with all his might. The vine gave a little, but it was stronger than he was. Still, he persisted in his quest. While the dog was busy tugging at the vine, she moved in closer to get a good shot. Taking a rock from her pocket, she inserted it into the band of the slingshot, drew back, and let go. The rock flew out, resulting in a most pitiful yelp from the large beast. He rolled about on the ground, howling as if he'd been hit by a cannonball. She watched cautiously at a distance as he continued rolling and whimpering pitifully.

This dog is an actor. Why, I couldn't have hurt him that badly. That rock wasn't any bigger than an acorn—big baby. But, she had a soft heart, and this pitiful display was more than she could stand. Cautiously, she walked over to the dog, who was still whimpering like he was dying. With big, sad eyes he gazed up at her. Her heart melted on the spot. Kneeling beside him, she rubbed his side as he licked her hand with his slobbery tongue.

"Okay, you're a good boy, but you need to go home, wherever that is. And I insist that you quit messing around with our dead body. Now, get going! Go!" she demanded in a gruff tone.

Still, he just lay there nudging her with his nose. Again and again, she tried to coax him up, but he wouldn't budge an inch. *Now, what? I certainly can't bear hitting him with another rock, and he's not staying here to create more havoc.* She made a hasty decision. "You're going into the shed—just for tonight, then tomorrow—you're out of here."

She went inside and returned with a large ham bone and a bowl of water. Lured by the enticing bone, the dog followed her into the shed. The second she laid the bowl of water on the ground, he drank as if he hadn't had a drop in days. Then he lay on the bare ground and began gnawing contentedly on the bone.

"We've got a deal, right? Tomorrow—you go home." She closed the door to the shed and walked back to the house, thankful that she didn't have to contend with a ferocious canine. But she still had a problem—a big one. He wasn't going anywhere, not after getting food and water. He could leave on his own accord, though she found that highly unlikely.

****

In her bed, the big, silly dog occupied her thoughts again, but this time in a different way. He didn't seem afraid, and he'd made himself right at home when most dogs would have gone berserk when being locked up in some strange place. She pondered this until sleep overtook her.

With tranquility restored, she slept peacefully until awakened the next morning by a small voice beside her bed. Jessie was saying Lillie was awake and beginning to fret— and so—her day began.

Chapter 11

Soaking. That was the word Addie's father had used when she and Lizzie were nestled snuggly in his arms in the early mornings. Seated at the kitchen table with Jessie's and Lillie's warm bodies against hers, Addie felt her father's presence. She closed her eyes and let her gentle rocking take her back to that time of childhood bliss. She began to hum softly—the familiar tune her father had hummed to them. In a small voice, Jessie hummed along, and Lillie cooed softly while twisting strands of Addie's hair around her tiny fingers.

Their blissful mood came to a sudden end when they were jarred awake by a loud noise that, to Addie's dismay, sounded like a barking dog.

Jessie scrambled from Addie's lap, went to the window and peered out, "Aunt Addie, what was that?"

"Oh, honey, it's just an old stray dog that came around last night; he wouldn't leave, so I put him in the shed. After Lillie goes down for her nap, I'll let him out."

"If you hadn't put him in the shed, wouldn't he just have gone back home?" Jessie said.

Addie smiled, seeing this as more proof of Jessie's sensible thinking. "Well, he seemed intent on tearing up the lawn; I put him up so that he couldn't do that," she said, hoping that was enough information to put her questions to rest.

The barking continued, getting louder by the second. Obviously, it awakened Lizzie, who appeared in the doorway, rubbing sleep from her eyes.

Addie, knowing what she would have to deal with if she let him out, wasn't in a hurry to do so. But his continued barking left her with no choice. "Well, I guess it's time to let him out. It's plain to see that we won't have peace until I do." She placed Lillie in Lizzie's lap and went to the door. Putting on her coat and boots, she headed outside to the shed, mumbling to herself all the way. "You just had to break up our quiet time, didn't you—you old mutt."

Standing outside the shed, Addie was still apprehensive about the dog's temperament. Cautiously, she opened the door. Out he bounded, wagging his tail happily. In the light of day, she could see that this dog definitely wasn't a mutt; she sensed there was something special about him. His shiny, copper-colored coat and the way his tail wagged constantly said he had been well cared for—even loved.

Instead of running for the hills, he sat beside her and nudged her hand with his head. "Oh no..." Addie said. "We've got a deal, remember? You're going home. Shoo! Go! Go on now—go home!" In response, he licked her hand affectionately. Addie let out a deep sigh and rolled her eyes.

Jessie had been at the window watching her aunt interact with the dog. Addie heard the screen door slam and turned to see Jessie making her way toward the dog with her arms held wide. Bending to his level, she wrapped him in a tight embrace.

Addie shook her head—*this is not good.* She could see herself fast losing ground with this hound.

"Oh, Aunt Addie, he's so beautiful and so sweet," Jessie said, rubbing her face into his coat. "Can we keep him?"

Stuck between a rock and a hard place, she inhaled deeply. The last thing she needed was a dog, especially one intent on uncovering her secrets. But—as she had learned—it was impossible to say no to this child. "A dog can be a whole lot of trouble, and they bark a lot, and they make big messes," Addie said, hoping Jessie would submit to reason.

At the sight of Jessie's downcast eyes, Addie's resolve softened. "He is kind of cute, although smelly," Addie said, holding her nose.

Jessie put her nose closer to the dog's coat. "He kind of smells like whatever that is over there," she said, pointing to the side of the house.

Addie's face turned scarlet. "Oh, that. I think there's something dead in the ivy that he was after. And the bad boy was destroying the vine. That's why I had to lock him up." So far, her answers were truthful.

"If we give him a bath, can he stay?" Jessie said, her green eyes widened with hope.

Her hopeful look tugged at Addie's heart, and she'd run out of excuses. This time it was her decision to make—she didn't need Lizzie's approval.

"I'll tell you what, why don't we give him a try — see if we like him, and he likes us? There's also a big possibility that he belongs to somebody, and then we'd have to give him back. Also, he'll have to stay in the shed. So, for now, he can stay on a trial basis—after he's had a bath. Deal?" Addie said.

"Deal!" Jessie got to her feet and wrapped her arms around Addie. "Thank you!"

"Remember, he's on a trial basis, and don't forget, there's a big possibility that he belongs to somebody. It won't be easy to give him up," Addie said, covering her bases.

"I remember, and I won't forget." She returned her attention to the dog, showering him with hugs and kisses.

Oh brother—what have I done? Addie buried her face in her hands, questioning her sanity. *This is the big bad dog that could land us all in jail, and now I'm giving him a home. Well, it's not the first lunatic decision I've ever made, and I'm sure it won't be the last.*

****

The day had warmed to the mid-fifties, not ideal for bathing a dog, but it was going to happen just the same. She pulled a large, galvanized tub under the faucet and filled it with water.

Hands on her hips, she locked eyes with the dog. As if he knew what was about to happen, he stiffened and planted his feet firmly on the ground. Grabbing hold of the rope around his neck, Addie pulled him toward the tub—he didn't budge. She tried pushing him. Still, he remained anchored to the spot. "You're getting a bath, like it or not," Addie said. Once again, she pushed his body toward the tub—he resisted. Determined not to let this beast win the battle, she took in a deep breath and gave a mighty shove. The dog lurched forward and landed feet up in the tub as a wave of water splashed out over her.

Jessie couldn't contain her amusement. She dropped to her knees, laughing and clapping her hands.

Hearing her laugh brought a smile to Addie's face, and before she knew it, she was laughing too. Then, getting back to business, she said, "Sweetie, would you go to the house and grab a towel? You can help dry him when this is over."

In the meantime, to prevent his escape, Addie held the dog by his makeshift collar with one hand while washing him with the other. It only took a minute to see that he loved to be rubbed, and soon he quit fighting her and stood still as a statue. When the job was done, and the rubbing was over, he bounded from the tub. Sidling up to her, he shook off gallons of water—covering her from head to toe. She sighed heavily. "You just insist on trying my patience, don't you?"

He looked at her with his big, pitiful eyes and rubbed his wet body against her.

When Jessie returned with the towel, she took her time drying him, all the while telling him what a good boy he was. When he was thoroughly dry, she brushed his coat to a glossy sheen.

"I thought his coat was pretty before, but you have him shining like a brand-new copper penny," Addie said.

Jessie's eyes lit up. "Copper! Wouldn't that be a good name for him, Aunt Addie?"

"I think Copper fits him to a T—Copper it is!" Addie said, giving Jessie a thumbs up.

****

Copper proved to be more of a problem than Addie had anticipated. Jessie had talked her into allowing him to run free in the front yard. His good behavior was short-lived, and in no time at all he was back to his old tricks—tearing away at the ivy. Addie would have to stop what she was doing and tie him to the back porch railing, where he whimpered like he was being mistreated. When her patience had worn thin, she would retreat into the house, leaving him tied and whining.

On this particular day she was seated at the kitchen table wondering how on earth they could coexist with this troublesome dog when something behind her made her jump. She turned around to see Copper, happily wagging his tail. In her absentmindedness she'd left the door ajar. Somehow, he'd freed himself from the railing and the open door was an invitation for him to come inside. He ambled over to the rug by the door, circled it twice then lay down. The annoying whimpering had stopped. He seemed content—now that he was inside.

Sighing heavily, she said, "What am I going to do with you?"

Copper gave her a sad, quizzical look.

"You just lie right there while I think this through," she said, wagging her finger at him.

****

At lunchtime, Jessie made a beeline to the back door to check on Copper. She shrieked with excitement upon seeing him lying on the kitchen rug. Kneeling beside him, she rubbed his sleek coat and spoke softly in his ear. When she heard her mother calling for her, she left the room with Copper following on her heels.

It dawned on Addie that Copper was the first friend Jessie had ever had. The bond between the two was instant.

Now, on top of everything else, she was left to worry that an owner might show up to claim him.

****

With his gentle way and his big sad eyes, Copper made his way into all their hearts. His temperament did a complete turnaround once he was allowed inside the house—displaying none of the obnoxious behavior he had shown when left outside. Never would she have thought that a seventy-pound dog would be happy as a house dog, but clearly, he was happy as a clam.

Copper was as taken with Jessie as she was with him, and he wouldn't leave her side. He slept beside her bed, and in her studio, he lay at her feet while she wrote in her diary and painted her pictures. He was her best friend and constant companion. Addie's heart swelled as she witnessed the bond they shared.

Copper's good behavior, they were soon to realize, was limited only to the indoors; as soon as he was outside, he was on his usual path of destruction. Addie pondered the dilemma and saw only one solution: Copper must not be allowed outside unsupervised at any time.

****

As if she didn't have enough to worry about, Addie learned that the trip she and Jessie made to town had opened up a can of worms. Once the word got around that a seven-year-old girl was living with her, it set off a chain reaction. The sheriff was the first to hear of it. He alerted the truant officer, who went straight to the school board with the news. The school board appointed a representative to investigate the situation. It seemed to Addie that the small town didn't have enough to talk about, so they jumped on any gossip, no matter how trivial, and spread it around like butter on a biscuit.

They were all napping when Addie heard the sound of tires on the gravel drive. Not expecting company, she rose and went hurriedly to the door and peered through the glass. A paunchy man with a slick bald head got out of his car and was making his way up the porch steps. She stayed out of view until he had knocked three times.

She opened the door and eyed him suspiciously. "Can I help you?" Addie asked, her tone lacking its usual warmth.

"Yes. Uh, hello, are you Mrs. Kent?" the man said.

Addie only nodded. He extended his hand.

"My name is Alfred Bass. I'm from the Clayton County School Board. I'd be obliged if you could spare me just a minute of your time, Mrs. Kent."

"I'm terribly busy at the moment," Addie lied. "What is this concerning?"

"A matter has come to the board's attention regarding a school-age child living here with you. I assume that information is correct," the man pressed.

Addie saw this as more of a statement than a question. When she didn't respond, he continued.

"If you don't mind, I'd like to come in to discuss the matter with you. I promise I'll be brief."

"Of course," Addie said, seeing no other option. "Please, come this way." She led him down the hall to the parlor and motioned to the most uncomfortable chair in the room. "Please, have a seat. Can I offer you some sweet tea or lemonade?" she asked, making an effort to be hospitable.

"That's very kind of you, but I'm fine, thank you. I don't want to take much of your time, I know you're busy. Arriving unannounced as I have, I'll get straight to the point. The state of South Carolina has very explicit rules regarding the education of all children from age six to eighteen. The county school board is responsible for seeing that these rules are strictly adhered to. If I am correct, the child residing in your home is seven years of age," he said, raising his eyebrows.

Again, it was more of a statement than a question, and again, Addie didn't respond. As a rule, she preferred straight talk as opposed to beating around the bush, but she instantly disliked the man—she had a strong desire to withhold information.

"Is she your child?" Mr. Bass said.

Addie bit her tongue in an attempt to hold back the insulting words that were forming as a reply. She was a fixture in the county, known to young and old. He certainly hadn't done his homework, or he would have known she had no children of her own. "The child, to whom I believe you are referring, is my niece, my sister's daughter."

"Well then, I suppose I should be speaking with your sister as well. Is she here?"

"My sister is recovering from a horrible stomach virus," Addie lied. "I'll be glad to relay your message to her when she's feeling up to it."

"I suppose that will have to do. Actually, I've been instructed to take the child with me today, but this document has to be signed first." He reached into his briefcase and produced a document. "This order basically states that the guardian of a school-age child has been notified that said child must be enrolled in our school system and attending classes immediately or within five days of receipt of this order."

"That's short notice, don't you think, Mr. Bass?" Addie said.

"I don't make the rules, Mrs. Kent. I'm only here to inform you of them. As your sister is the legal guardian of the child, I must obtain her signature on this document." He pointed to a dotted line at the bottom of the page.

"Well, Mr. Bass, I can assure you my sister is presently in no condition to sign her name. Why, she can barely raise her head. Every time she does...well, let's just say she's very ill."

Mr. Bass was a pushy man, obviously used to having his way by implementing intimidation. Addie noticed his frustration mounting as he rubbed his greasy bald head.

"This order, Mrs. Kent, is to be signed and witnessed by me. It is not negotiable," he said, his agitation made clear.

"I realize your plight, Mr. Bass—believe me, I do." Addie adjusted her posture to stand taller. "Today is quite simply not the day. I'll inform my sister of your visit and relay your message. Now, if you'll follow me, I'll show you out." She held the document by one corner as if it was contaminated with the ghastliest of germs and led him to the door.

"I'll be back to get that signature and the girl in five days, Mrs. Kent. There are serious consequences if your sister doesn't comply."

"I'm sure there are, Mr. Bass. Enjoy your day," she said, closing the door soundly behind him.

After he had left, Addie made her way out the back door. She hadn't heard Copper behind her. He bounded out the open door and, in the process, turned over a metal bucket that clanged and banged noisily. Startled by the sudden chaos, she quickly gathered her senses, grabbed him by the collar and herded him back inside.

Unaware that Mr. Bass hadn't left, Addie was startled to see him appear around the corner of the house.

"I heard a loud noise and thought I should investigate, make sure everything's alright," he said, immediately holding his nose. "What on earth is that horrible smell? It seems to be coming from that vine," he said, pointing to the ivy.

Oh, Lord, have mercy—what's he doing back? Quickly, she came up with another lie. "We think some animal, maybe a squirrel, got in there and died. At any rate, it is a disgusting odor to be sure." She felt she was becoming quite a liar. "I appreciate your concern, but there's nothing to worry about. Have a good day, Mr. Bass," she said, praying he would take this as his cue to leave.

"I could send someone out to get rid of whatever it is for you—that odor is enough to kill a dead person."

Addie bit the inside of her cheeks to conceal her amusement. He didn't know how close he was to the truth.

"That's very thoughtful of you, but I've already talked to our neighbor about doing just that. He's coming by later this afternoon," Addie lied—again. "Good day, Mr. Bass."

"Good day, Mrs. Kent," he said, pinching his nose and looking backward over his shoulder as he walked away.

Addie made her way back inside and found Copper sitting by the door. She bent down, looked him square in the eyes, and scolded him in a gruff tone. "You were a very bad boy! No more going out without permission, understood?"

He dropped his head, and his big, sad eyes gazed up at her apologetically.

She gave him a pat on the head. "Sorry doesn't quite get it, buddy. You need to learn to stay out of trouble, or you'll be looking for a new home."

Copper loped off to find Jessie. Addie joined Lizzie at the kitchen table.

"What was going on out there? I heard a loud clanging noise and voices," Lizzie said.

Addie sighed wearily, "We have a situation on our hands. Beau Ridge is a great place to live, but it's a small town, and word travels fast. People like to have something new to talk about, and it seems they've found it. Apparently, our visit to the doctor opened up a can of worms. We had a visitor, a representative of the school board. He was sent here to inform us that we have five days to enroll Jessie in the local elementary school, or, as he put it, there will be serious consequences."

"For heaven's sake," Lizzie said. She lowered her voice. "We need to talk privately; I have no doubt that little ears are listening."

Addie motioned toward the door, and the two of them retreated to the garden where they sat side by side on the stone bench.

"Addie, it's entirely out of the question, I can't allow it. Jessie isn't like other children. She's timid, and so very vulnerable. Add that to what she has been through, and it spells disaster. No, I put my foot down! Let them do what they will to me. They can take me to jail, but she will not be enrolling in their old school—period."

Seeing Lizzie's passion return brought a smile to Addie's face. "I thought you'd feel that way. I have a plan if you're willing to take a chance, and it won't involve anybody going to jail. Are you game?"

"You bet I am—spill it!" Lizzie said.

Chapter 12

The air was chilly, so Addie went inside and came back with a blanket. She and Lizzie sat like two peas in a pod, wrapped up in its warmth. Lifting her gaze into the bright sky, Addie prayed that she was leading them down the right path. "I only have this one plan. If it doesn't work, I suppose we'll have no choice but to abide by the board's rules," Addie said.

"I'm sure already that I'll like your plan—anything will be better than their stupid old rules." Lizzie said, with a smirk.

"I can think of no other way than to prevail upon Lester—again. With his brilliant legal strategy, he can plead our case before the school board. I've written down some pointers to give him for starters." Addie paused then added, "Mind you, these are just pointers. Lester will do an amazing job preparing a proper request for Jessie to be home schooled.

Lizzie propped her hand under her chin and listened intently.

Addie cleared her throat and began "Reasons Jessie should be allowed to be homeschooled:

1. She's been the victim of abuse. 2. She lacks confidence. 3. She's timid. 4. She's naive. 5. She's fragile.

6. Her brilliance would be drastically jeopardized if forced into an unfamiliar environment. 7. Her well-being demands that she be surrounded by people who understand and embrace her vulnerable nature."

When finished she placed the paper in her lap and turned her questioning eyes to Lizzie.

Lizzie remained silent for several minutes, then looked tenderly at her twin. "Addie, I suppose I can attribute your all-knowing account of Jessie's fragile life to the sight. How else would you know these things?"

"The sight definitely played a part, but mostly, I have this weird connection to Jessie; it's like I can see into her soul. I'm aware I don't know the whole story, but...."

"But you're on the right track," Lizzie said, laying her hand on Addie's.

Addie smiled. "Lester can work miracles, and he carries a lot of clout in this town. If anyone can persuade them— he can. I assume it will require some work on our part— letters, and whatnot. Lester will inform us of anything he needs us to do. We must act fast, though. I'll have to meet with him today. How do you feel about it?"

"I rather hate the idea of the whole town knowing of my sweet child's tormented childhood, and we both know she has so much to overcome without the gossip. But, to put her in the hands of uncaring strangers would be the worst thing in the world for her. I certainly don't have a backup plan, and I'm not fond of the idea of going to jail, so I say— let's see what Lester can do," Lizzie said.

With that settled, they returned to the house, where Addie dressed hurriedly and left for town. She made a mental note to buy Copper a proper collar and a substantial leash. If she was going to have to keep pulling him out of one predicament after another, she needed something stronger than a piece of twine.

****

With her notes in hand, she waltzed into Lester's office. As always, LeeAnn was seated behind her desk in the front room. Upon hearing the door open, she looked up from her work and gave Addie a questioning gaze before greeting her.

"Twice in one week—that's a record," she said, her curiosity showing on her face.

"Life is full of surprises. My life seems to get crazier with each passing day. Seeing you brightens it, though," Addie said warmly. "Is Lester in?"

"He's been working on a divorce case that's driving him to the brink. He'll welcome a pleasant distraction," LeeAnn said.

"I don't know how pleasant this visit is going to be. Chances are I'm only adding to his troubles," Addie said.

"Believe me, nothing could be worse than dealing with those two people and their endless bickering. We both want to run and hide when we see them coming. Seeing you will take his mind off them for a while," LeeAnn said.

"I hope you're right," Addie said. She knew Lester would be glad to see her, still she worried that one day her wild requests would push him away.

When she reached Lester's closed door, she stopped and turned back to face LeeAnn. "There's something different about you today."

"It's my hair," LeeAnn said, covering her head with her hands and looking as though she was about to cry. "Pixie, at Sweet Pixie's Beauty Parlor said this was the latest style, right out of Paris. It's horrible—just go ahead and say it."

Turning her full attention to LeeAnn's hair, she had to admit it was terribly unbecoming. "Well, it's not horrible, but I do think your old style suits you much better," Addie said diplomatically.

"Well, you can bet money that come tomorrow, my bouffant will be back. I haven't felt like myself since I walked out of Pixie's Parlor. We Southerners could teach those Paris women a thing or two about style," LeeAnn said, nodding her head assuredly.

"LeeAnn, you're one of the most stylish ladies I know. Those Paris women could learn a lot from you," Addie said.

"Thank you, Addie. You're a good friend. I can always count on you to lift me up."

Addie blew her a kiss and turned to knock lightly on Lester's door. At his invitation, she stepped inside. His face lit up upon seeing her.

"Addie! What brings you in again so soon?" he said, coming around his desk and greeting her with his customary bear hug.

"I know every time I walk in here, you're thinking—here comes trouble," Addie said.

"Actually, you are the only kind of trouble I would welcome—any day of the week," he said.

"Well, I'm giving you the right to throw me out of here if I've gone too far this time. On second thought, that would have been the last time I was in here." The remark brought rich laughter from them both.

"Ok, so what's going on this time? Not another dead body, I hope."

"Funny," Addie said, giving him a gentle punch in the side. "No, you can rest easy. This is more along the lines of corruption."

"A little diversity. I like it—keeps things interesting," Lester said.

"Lately, things have been a little too interesting," Addie said.

Taking her seat on the couch beside Lester, she took a deep breath and began to unravel the latest crisis. "It all started when I had to bring Jessie in to see Dr. Loggins about her leg. Apparently, it got people talking about the school-age child who is living with me. Then, word reached the school board and, of course, they made it their business to check into it. So, this morning, a representative from the board, a Mr. Alfred Bass, paid us an unannounced visit."

Addie paused to catch her breath. Lester's hand was cupped under his chin, listening intently.

"He had come to confirm Jessie's age. When that was confirmed, he promptly presented me with this letter." Addie said, handing him the letter.

Lester quickly scanned it and returned his attention to Addie.

"He said we must enroll 'said child' in the elementary school within five days, or there would be 'consequences'. Lester, this would be a disastrous thing for Jessie. She's an intelligent, wonderful child, but through no fault of her own, she has issues. I know this is a lot to ask, certainly over and above what a friend should ask of a friend, but it would mean the world to me if you could help us. I don't mean to pressure you...but you're our only hope."

"I don't suppose you tried to reason with Mr. Bass, plead your case?" Lester said.

"Plead with that incorrigible little man with his greasy bald head? I would have tried, but he didn't seem like the type to give an inch, he seemed to thrive on authority. Besides that, he rubbed me the wrong way. He came intending to leave with Jessie today. That just wasn't going to happen—plain and simple. Thankfully, I managed to buy us some time…"

"By weaving a little white lie?" Lester said, with a wink, knowing her tactics well.

"When all else fails," Addie said, giving a shrug.

"I assume you have a plan," Lester said.

"Always," Addie said with a confident air. "We'd like for you to be our spokesperson and plead Jessie's case before the school board. We're asking that she be allowed to be home-schooled. As a starting place, I've written out some points for the petition," she said, handing him the paper with her handwritten notes.

"You sure don't make things easy," Lester said, rubbing his chin. "This could cost you a dinner and a good bottle of wine."

"You're not afraid of the price it could cost you? Going against the school authorities could create big problems for you," Addie said.

"I'll look forward to it. There's nothing like a good brawl. Give me a day or so to get the petition together. I'll come out as soon as I know the outcome. And not that I don't enjoy coming to your house, but when are you going to get a phone?"

"You are an absolute dear," Addie said, squeezing his hand and giving him a kiss on the cheek. When you come you can be sure I'll have a nice dinner and that bottle of wine ready, but I owe you so much more than that. About the phone, I hold firm on my position—I absolutely have no use for one—total waste of money."

She left his office feeling like a hundred-pound weight had been lifted off her shoulders.

Chapter 13

In her studio, with Copper at her feet, Jessie sits at the window, her chair positioned so that she has a clear view of the expansive lawn below. She keeps a vigilant watch like a mother bird guards her nest. Her view, high above the ground, allows her to peer into the robin's nest and to even count the number of tiny blue eggs nestled inside. She sits for hours, just watching the birds that fly from branch to branch, the bugs that crawl along the window sill, and the squirrels that scurry about the lawn and then climb with ease up the tree trunks and scamper from limb to limb.

She pays no heed to the mouse that darts under her chair and across the room; the way she sees it, every living thing needs a home. That's how Copper came to live with them. He needed a home. Truth be known, she needed him just as much.

She loves being at her aunt's house, where everything is so peaceful. At last she feels like she has a real home and family. So different than the way it was at Little Hope.

In Little Hope, most of the time, it was just she and her mama; her daddy was gone a lot. He'd never been a real daddy, that's why she'd never called him that—he was Jim Bob—the man who sometimes lived in their house and made her mama sad.

Today, for some reason, he was on her mind. She didn't know where he went after that terrible night. She only knew that he didn't follow them to her aunt's house, and for that she was glad.

"I hope he never comes back to try to take Lillie or to hurt Mama. You'll protect us, won't you Copper?" she said, giving his head a gentle rub.

He moaned softly.

She moved to the floor and rubbed her hands through his soft coat. Tears filled her eyes. "Jim Bob was mean. I guess he never got the love he needed when he was a little boy. Maybe that's the reason he couldn't love me."

Copper laid his head in her lap and moaned.

"Mama couldn't change the way he felt, so she said she loved me enough for the both of them." Thinking of her mama made her think of the good times they had—when Jim Bob was gone. "We listened to the radio, and Mama would twirl me around the kitchen floor. We played lots of games. I helped her cook and do house chores. We sang silly songs that we made up. She taught me how to read and write. I had my lessons every day, just like the school children. Mama said I was a quick learner."

Copper stopped moaning. He sat up, listening.

"Mama spent very little time on subjects like arithmetic and geography. She said they weren't her favorites when she was in school, and she didn't see the point in learning what you'd never use. That was fine with me, I didn't like them either. We mostly worked on reading and writing—writing is my favorite. I like to write stories, some are true and some are made up. I write about the stories Mama and Aunt Addie tell me, too—theirs are the best.

Copper begins a low growl; his ears stand up.

"What is it, buddy?"

She looks around the room to see what's upset him. "Is it that old mouse?"

He's on his feet now, looking out the window. "What is it, boy?"

She looks where Copper's eyes are fixed. At first, she sees nothing unusual. Then, she sees him. A man, in the lane leaning against a tree like a statue, but he's no statue. She moves to the side of the window where she watches him.

She whispers to Copper. "Shush, it's okay, boy. He sits quietly at her feet.

The man is too far away—she can't see his face. She notices the faded red hat he's wearing, like the kind baseball players wear. There's a single letter on the hat, but she can't quite make it out. She squints and looks again. The letter A becomes clear. She doesn't move. The man is staring straight at the house—he's not moving either.

In a low voice she says to Copper, "Wonder what he's up to. Maybe he's just passing by and thought this was a nice place to rest for a bit before moving on. But why is he staring straight at the house?" She keeps her eyes locked on him.

For a long time, she stays back—watching. She hears her mama calling her to come to lunch—she wants stay and keep an eye on him. Her mama calls again. She leaves the window and goes to the kitchen and sits at the table between her mother and her aunt.

Looking from one to the other, she says, "Why do you think a man would be in the lane staring at the house?"

The two look at each other, then at her.

"What man, sweetie? This house?" they asked in unison.

She answers, "Yes, he's out there now, leaning against a tree in the lane, just staring up at the house."

They didn't say a word but took off running up the stairs, and she followed them. Standing to the side of the window, they all look out, but the man's not there.

"He was there, I promise," she says, her gaze going all around, but it's true—he's not there.

"We believe you, honey," Mama said. "Did you get a good look at him? What did he look like?"

"I couldn't see his face, he was too far away. He was wearing a faded red hat with the letter A on the front," she said.

Mama looked at Aunt Addie. "Red and the letter A—A for Alabama. What else could it be?" Mama said.

"Before we jump to conclusions, it could stand for Arizona, or Alaska, or apple or any number of words starting with the letter A," Aunt Addie said.

Mama frowned. "Yes, but I'm putting my money on Alabama. Who could he be? Why is he here? What does he want?" Mama said.

"I thought he might be just passing by and needed to rest a little while, but he gave me the heebie-jeebies being so still and staring straight at the house like that. He was there for a long time before I came down for lunch," she said.

"You're probably right, Sweetie, just somebody needing to rest a bit. He probably won't be back, but just in case he returns, promise that you'll let us know right away, okay?"

She nodded, "I promise."

Chapter 14

At the first hint of daylight, Addie sat up in bed and stretched her arms over her head. The mysterious man and his reason for being there was something she decided to push from her mind, and instead turned her thoughts to a more pleasant subject—her garden. She tugged on her jeans, and pulled a T-shirt over her head. Without a single glance into the mirror, she pulled her hair into a messy ponytail. *Who cares if I look a fright?*

Hurrying through her morning routine, thoughts of spring and the tasks that lay ahead ran through her mind: tidy up the beds, prune, deadhead, make compost piles, prepare The Formula, start seeds, plant seeds, and apply The Formula. *At least my mind's still intact,* she thought—recalling how Dr. Loggings had made her feel like she had a foot in the grave.

****

She was up to her elbows in dirt when she looked up to see Lester walking toward her. With the back of her hand, she pushed her hair out of her eyes. "Hey there, do you prefer a rake or a shovel?" she said playfully.

"Not my cup of tea, Ma'am," he said in his slow Southern drawl.

"What brings you out here so early? Want some coffee?"

"Love some," he said.

While the others were still sleeping, they sat alone at the kitchen table and sipped their coffee in silence. Addie sensed Lester's hesitation. The morning sun that filled the room accentuated the worried lines on his forehead.

The suspense was more than she could take—she broke the silence. "Is this about the school board? Surely, they didn't turn down our petition," Addie said, her chin rising in defiance.

Lester shook his head. Addie studied the troubled expression on his face and sensed his reluctance to add to her troubles. Whatever was on his mind had caused him to bring the news in person—not that he had a choice.

"No, it's something else entirely," he said. He leaned forward in his chair and laid his crossed arms on the table, a gesture Addie had seen him do many times when the situation was serious.

"I came to warn you about a disturbing development that's come to my attention. A stranger has been asking questions around town about plantation homes in the area. He says he's writing a book about the history of the South and that he's been traveling around in search of homes that are still in existence. I know for a fact that some of the townsfolk have told him about Magnolia Place. If you ask me, his story doesn't pass the smell test. My advice to you and Lizzie is to keep your guard up at all times; you never know; the guy could be a convict," Lester said.

"Well, that explains everything," Addie said, releasing a heavy sigh.

"Explains what?" Lester said, tilting his head, his eyes questioning.

"The man in the lane. Jessie saw him yesterday, leaning against a tree and staring toward the house. She said he was wearing a red ball cap with the letter A on it, and Lizzie is convinced that the A stands for Alabama. I'm with you, Lester—I smell a rat. He's not a writer seeking information about plantations—I'd bet the farm on it."

Lester rubbed his chin. Addie could see the wheels turning in his analytical mind.

"This guy might be from Alabama, huh? And Jessie's right on about the ball cap, the guy was said to have been wearing one fitting her description. That sheds a whole new light on the subject. In my opinion this spells trouble with a capital T. He could be on the up and up, but I wouldn't put my money on it. You girls need to be very careful," he said.

"Heaven only knows what this guy's got up his sleeve. We'll be on our guard all right—you can be sure of it," Addie said.

"I'll keep my ear to the ground and keep you posted with any new developments," Lester said.

Addie took Lester's hands in hers and looked deeply into his eyes. "I know I say this all the time, but it's true. What would I ever do without you?"

She wrapped her arms around him. He drew her closer. Neither one was eager to pull away. It was Addie who finally did. She took Lester's hand and walked him to the door. Standing in the doorway, she watched as he made his way to his car.

With his hand on the door handle, he turned and called back to her. "Do us all a favor—get a phone."

She blew him a kiss. He shook his head. Behind the wheel he drove slowly away while keeping his eyes peeled for the stranger who could be out there now, lurking around her property.

****

Addie knew the time had come for that heart to heart with Lizzie that she'd been putting off. Considering the recent revelations, delving into the fine details of her life could lead to discovering the mystery man's identity. The opportunity presented itself after lunch. Lillie was down for a nap, and Jessie was painting in her studio.

"I've got some news that you need to hear," Addie said.

"Good news, I hope," Lizzie said, biting her bottom lip.

"Well, I wouldn't exactly call it good, enlightening is more like it. I had a visit from Lester this morning; he shared some news that's being spread around the Beau Ridge rumor mill. It seems that a stranger has been in town asking questions. Says he's interested in plantation houses in the South—writing a book, so he says. Some people have helped him out by giving him directions to my house, which explains the man Jessie saw in the lane."

Lizzie's eyes narrowed. "Writing a book? I don't buy a word of it. I smell an Alabama rat."

Addie grinned at her sister's spirited response. "I don't buy it either, but for our safety, we have to be extremely cautious. He's obviously snooping around here for something. If you're right about him being from Alabama, then my bet is—it's got something to do with you, in one way or another."

"I'm drawing that same conclusion. Since we don't know what he's up to, do you think Jessie's safe up there by herself? I'll be honest, I'm feeling threatened by this guy," Lizzie said.

"Right now, I think, yes. We don't have time to sit and watch out the window, but Jessie loves doing just that. If he returns, she'll know, and she knows to alert us immediately." She eyed her sister suspiciously. "You seemed convinced that the guy is from Alabama. I'm curious, what makes you so sure?"

"It's just a feeling. I have nothing to base it on, but we were living in Alabama when Jim Bob came up missing. It makes sense to me that somebody would want to know where he is. He had no friends, none that I know of anyway, but he could have owed somebody money, or he could have taken something from somebody, and they want it back. I think whoever this guy is, he's looking for me, thinking that I can lead him to Jim Bob," Lizzie said.

"I think you're headed down the right track—it makes perfect sense. If that is the case, I have no doubt that we haven't seen the last of him."

"No doubt about it," Lizzie agreed, "he'll be back."

Addie sank into her chair and focused her gaze on Lizzie. "I think it's time we had that talk about your life in Alabama. It could just hold the key to our stalker's identity."

"Just be forewarned—it's not for the faint of heart," Lizzie said. She sighed deeply and lowered her head. Speaking softly she began to reveal the tragic tale that had been her life.

"I guess the best place to start is at the beginning. I'd like to blame it all on stupidity. I was so in love with Jim Bob—he was all I cared about.

Blinded by love as I was, there were things I just didn't see at the time: his extreme possessiveness, his anger issues, the hate he had in his heart. I didn't see it as a problem that he wanted me to depend only on him and nobody else, especially not Mother and Father. In some weird way, I thought this was a sign of true love. That he wanted to be the one to take care of me, like no one else would; I thought he loved me that much—the same way I loved him."

Tears blurred her vision, and she paused to wipe them away. "From the day I ran off with Jim Bob, my life has been cursed." Her tears were flowing now, and she couldn't look Addie in the face. "I caused it all," she said through her tears. "I thought that you, Mother, and Father spoke lies about Jim Bob, and I told him so. I told him every bad thing that had been said about him, and he hated all of you for it.

"Jim Bob held a tight grip on grudges and a tighter grip on hate. I was angry. He was angry. We jumped into marriage without a care for anybody but ourselves. We left Beau Ridge in a cloud of dust and took off for Alabama. In time, I realized this was his way of separating me from my family. We were alone in the world. Knowing I was to blame for him taking me away was the hardest thing to live with. Regret burned inside of me—it still does."

Addie felt it in her soul—the extreme guilt her sister carried. Softly, she laid her hand over her twin's, their pulse beating as one. They sat in silence, feeling their shared emotions as their eyes met through a vale of tears.

Lizzie took her hand away and sighed deeply. In a shaky voice she continued. "When I got word that Mother and Father had died in a car accident, I cried until I thought my heart was going to break. I knew then there would never be a time of reconciliation—it tore me apart."

"Sweetie, we all have regrets of some kind or other. Unfortunately, it seems we can't go through life without them. I have plenty myself. The best advice I can give is for you to find a way to forgive yourself. Otherwise, it will consume you. Believe me, I've been where you are with my own regrets," Addie said.

Lizzie sat up a little taller, and her voice seemed a little stronger. "Being here with you has already started a healing process. I thought you would never accept me back into your life. I know I don't deserve it, but you've welcomed me into your home and showered me with love."

"We're family, that's what we do. We stick together through life's storms, and we come through them stronger and hopefully smarter," Addie said, tears glistening in her eyes.

Lizzie raised her chin, and Addie detected the trace of a smile returning.

"I'm curious. Why did Jim Bob decide on Alabama? Did he know anyone there?" Addie said.

"His stepbrother, Eddie, lived there before he went to prison. He talked about it like it was heaven on earth. That got in Jim Bob's head, and he was determined that Alabama would some day be his home. Little to my knowledge, one day he drove down there looking for a place for us and settled on Little Hope. He took a job as an auto mechanic— that happened to be his dream job—and paid a month's rent on a house on the outskirts of town."

Lizzie lost Addie at the word prison. While she talked on, Addie's mind was piecing the puzzle together—*Eddie and prison—this couldn't be a coincidence, could it?* She forced her attention back to Lizzie's story.

"I was so excited about starting our new life together and was convinced it was going to be all that I envisioned it would be. I couldn't wait to see the house; Jim Bob said it needed a little work, but by his description, I just knew I was going to love it. I found it hard to sit still in the worn seat of his old beat-up car. With every charming town we came to, I sat up taller to get a good look through the window, and I hoped we'd be calling one of them our home." Her face fell. "I don't know how many times I asked him, 'Is this it?' He'd answer with a firm 'no'. As we drove farther south, we encountered one run-down, pathetic town after another. Then, at last, Jim Bob had me close my eyes. My heart was pounding like a drum, anticipation coursing through my body like electricity. Then he announced, 'Open your eyes! Welcome to Little Hope—our new home'."

Lizzie shook her head as she relived the memory.

"I opened my eyes to see the dirtiest, most run-down place of them all. My heart literally stopped beating for several seconds. I wanted to cry. Through my blurry eyes, I saw abandoned buildings with broken windows; shards of glass and trash littered the sidewalks. Graffiti was spray painted on the block exteriors, most likely the favorite pastime of the local hoodlums. Addie, I tell you the truth, it felt like we had just entered through the gates of hell. Jim Bob's face lit up as he pointed out the dingy mechanic shop where he was now employed. I heard a thump and thought it had to be my heart hitting the floorboard."

"I can't imagine your disappointment. I suppose you were thinking of what you'd left behind, our beautiful town of Beau Ridge," Addie said.

"There are no words to describe how I felt," Lizzie sighed. "Well, from there, we drove on for another mile or so before Jim Bob instructed me to close my eyes again. He stopped the car and helped me out. With his arm around my shoulder, he guided me as I stumbled over trash and beer cans. He walked me to the front of the house, where he stood and pridefully announced, 'Behold your palace'. If he hadn't been holding me up, I swear I would have collapsed right there on the spot.

"Dreadful doesn't even begin to describe it. It was nothing more than a dilapidated shack, with paint peeling off the siding like dead petals from a flower. Inside was even worse and filthy to boot. The odor in the house would knock you down. I clenched my nose tightly. The smell made me nauseous."

Lizzie shivered and put both hands over her nose. "Just the thought of it takes me back there. I don't think that stench will ever leave me."

Addie could see that the memory held a tight grip on her sister. Lizzie sat as if frozen with her eyes closed for several minutes. Addie watched the return of an old habit Lizzie had when she was distressed; she began twirling a strand of hair around and around her finger. When she spoke again Addie heard the hurt in her voice.

"Well, Jim Bob played it down. He said the Landlord had explained that sometimes the sewer overruns—nothing for us to worry about—it only happens a couple of times a year. I asked him why we didn't have the landlord fix some of these things. His answer was that we got the place dirt cheap, and if he went complaining to the guy, the rent would go up for sure."

"Lizzie, I just can't believe this story. How awful for you."

"Well, Jim Bob finally agreed that the place did need a little work. Ha! The place would have been better burned to the ground."

Addie suddenly choked and beat on her chest. "A little matter that's been taken care of," she said smugly.

The corners of Lizzie's mouth turned up, and she said, "At least there's one good thing about this sad story. Well anyway, he said we could have fun doing the repairs together; you can guess that never happened. I did my best to fix what I could. Whenever I did ask for Jim Bob's help, his response was always, 'Let's see about it tomorrow. I'm too tired today.' I learned to quit asking when his answer came across loud and clear with his fist. My busted lip and the deep cut on my cheek was all the lesson I needed. I knew he could be mean, but that was the first time he had raised his voice or his hand to me. At that moment, he had declared himself king of his castle, and I was his slave.

"In order to make the place livable, I cleaned until my fingers bled while he sat in his duct-taped recliner and drank beer after beer, and tossing the empty cans on the floor."

Lizzie stopped talking and listened. Lillie had awakened and was beginning to fret. She started to rise from her chair, but Addie gently put her hand on her shoulder.

"Let me, you could use a breather," Addie said, leaving Lizzie alone with her thoughts.

When Addie returned with Lillie, she placed her in Lizzie's arms. "I'll warm her bottle while you two soak."

"Good morning, precious," Lizzie said, placing kisses on her cheek.

Lizzie wrapped the thin blanket snuggly around Lillie and gently rocked her. Lillie cooed softly and twisted a strand of her mother's hair in her fingers. Addie's heart swelled at the sight of mother and child sharing the tender moment.

When the bottle had warmed, Addie scooped Lillie from Lizzie's arms and cuddled her as she suckled contentedly.

With her hands free, Lizzie went back to twisting her hair and, with sad eyes, continued her story. Her body visibly trembled as she relived her horrific past.

"Over time, I learned to overlook Jim Bob's outbursts. As long as I didn't ask him for anything, or ask him to do anything, I managed to keep things fairly peaceful. That changed the day he came home mad as a hornet, cursing and throwing punches at the wall. He had gotten fired from his job for hitting his boss and breaking his nose in the process. That event changed everything for Jim Bob; he lost his pride, his reputation, and what was good in him vanished like a puff of smoke."

She paused to take a sip of water, and her hand shook so violently that most of it spilled before reaching her mouth. She sighed heavily and continued. "After that fiasco, Jim Bob began to drink day and night, and he wouldn't stop until he was out of his mind drunk. Then he would become combative, lashing out about anything and nothing. He would go away for days, saying he was looking for a job that he never seemed to find. The worst part was that he would come home so drunk he could hardly walk, but upon entering the door, he was hellbent on picking a fight with me.

"In the beginning, I stood my ground. I would hit back and scream at him. You know me, Addie, I wasn't going to let anybody get the better of me—until he did. His size and the force of his fists, I'm sad to admit, made me cower to his fits of rage."

Addie closed her eyes in sorrow, finding it hard to bear the horrible tale she was hearing. "Lizzie, I can hardly believe that you, of all people, submitted to this abuse. Why in the world did you stay? You had no children by him. You could have left."

Lizzie dropped her head, ashamed to admit the cowardly reason she didn't leave. "Well, I did try to leave once. I packed a bag and started for the door. Jim Bob slammed me against it, saying the only way I was leaving him was in a body bag. I believed him—he'd become that evil. Then, there's the other reason. You know as well as I, how stubborn I can be. I had too much pride to go home and confess that I had made such a disastrous mistake. I felt it was my due punishment; I resolved to stay, come what may."

Addie gave a small laugh to lighten the heaviness that had sucked the air from the room. "You were definitely stubborn—no one can argue with that."

"Stubborn and stupid," Lizzie said. She sighed deeply; the hurt in her heart was too great to share in the amusement.

"You're being way too hard on yourself, kiddo. You were seventeen and clueless, like every other girl our age," Addie said.

Lizzie shrugged. Her eyes were beet red, and her voice told of her immense regret. She continued to weave her story as her hands shook more noticeably now than before, and her right eye had begun to twitch.

"Three years into our marriage, the one thing I hoped would never happen, happened—I was pregnant. I was pretty ticked off with God. I had prayed constantly that he wouldn't allow an innocent child to be brought into my hopeless life."

"I can certainly understand your distress and your fears," Addie said. "How did Jim Bob feel about having a child?"

"I was sure he would be furious, but he wasn't, not at first anyway. He treated me with kindness and gentleness throughout my pregnancy. I found this odd, but it gave me hope that things were going to be better. Jim Bob insisted on a midwife to assist with the birth, saying we couldn't afford a hospital—which was true. Luckily, all went well, and I gave birth to my beautiful baby girl. Jim Bob had paced anxiously outside the room, waiting to hear the news. When he was told the baby was a girl, he exploded in a fit of rage. He was out of control—a madman. Nothing was going his way, and the fact that I didn't give him a son was the last straw. He rammed his fist through the wall and called me a tramp, saying I was pathetic and useless."

"Oh, Lizzie, my heart breaks for you. What kind of father would deny his child because of the gender?"

"The self-centered, loathsome, wretched kind," Lizzie said, wiping away the flood of tears that cascaded down her cheeks. "But that wasn't all. He left us that day saying he was done with the crap he had to put up with, and he hoped we starved to death because he was through providing for us. He stormed out of the house. I didn't know if he was truly gone for good, but at that moment, it was an answer to a prayer."

"But he did return didn't he?" Addie said.

"Sadly, yes. He would show up when I least expected it, and there was never any rhyme or reason to his timing. He could be gone for days or weeks at a time. I came to realize that I was never going to be completely free of him. After Jessie was born, I feared for the baby he so despised. I kept her out of his sight. His drinking became even more of a problem. The times he did come home he'd be out of his mind drunk. The least little thing would set him off, and sometimes he would beat me until I couldn't stand. At those times I found it was best to lie motionless on the floor until he settled into his recliner and fell asleep—only then would I tidy up his mess and tend to my wounds."

"Oh, Lizzie, I don't understand any of this. How could you stay there with this monster and then with a baby?"

"It's hard to explain to someone who hasn't been a victim of abuse. It's not that I didn't want to leave or that it never crossed my mind—it did. Every time he came home with his violent rages, I swore to myself I was going to leave. Now that I had Jessie, and he knew how much I loved her, I feared that he would track us down and kill us both, or maybe just her to hurt me in the worst possible way. I could take the abuse of his hands, but the thought of him hurting or possibly taking the life of my baby kept me from leaving."

Addie saw the pain on Lizzie's face—it was tearing her heart out. "You're so right. I haven't lived it, but you've explained it so well, now I understand. Still, it makes me furious at that monster. Why if he weren't already dead and buried...." Her face flushed scarlet. Covering her mouth with her hand, she gazed sheepishly at Lizzie and murmured—"oops."

Lizzie gave her twin a sideways look. "I've played along—knowing there'd be a time when you'd spill the beans. I know Jim Bob's dead, and I also know where you put him. You felt you needed to protect me, and I love you for that. If I thought he was still alive, I couldn't sleep at night for fear he'd find us. I'm glad he's dead, but I'm sorry that you had to be the one to dispose of him—it should have been me."

A sly smile returned to Addie's face. "I should have known I couldn't fool you, though I'm relieved that the cat's out of the bag. You'd probably like to know how he died. I can assure you it was an accident—pure and simple. He's dead, and I plan to make sure his body will never be found. You can all breathe easier—he can never hurt you again. It's in our best interest if we let sleeping dogs lie and never speak of it ever again."

Lizzie nodded. "I'm glad to have you in my corner, Sis."

Lillie began to squirm in Addie's arms. She moved her onto her lap and murmured soothing words in her ear. "Isn't that just like grownups to ignore the sweetest girl in the room? You're such a good baby." She rocked her gently in her arms while continuing to whisper softly in her ear until her eyes grew heavy, and her tiny body went limp.

"I'm impressed," Lizzie said, her brows lifted in surprise. "I had no idea you had such a way with babies; I was under the impression that they weren't your cup of tea."

"Oh, I love babies. I just never wanted one of my own. I was too busy being the queen of society to have time for a child—talk about regrets—that's one of my biggest," Addie said, her eyes never leaving Lillie's sweet face.

"Well, you can claim both of mine as part yours, and you didn't even have to go through the hard stuff to get them," Lizzie said with a slight laugh.

"Thank goodness for that," Addie said. "I've always been a wimp when it comes to pain. Now, getting back to your story, how did you manage to survive if Jim Bob wasn't paying the rent or providing money for food and things for the baby?"

"That's the part that made no sense at all. Like I said, after being gone for days he'd return, and when he did he gave me money for the rent, but little extra. I don't know where it came from, but I knew better than to ask. His stays were brief, usually only a day or so, depending on his mood. Then he'd leave again, always looking for that job he never seemed to find. At that stage of our lives, Jim Bob had few redeeming qualities, but I have to give him credit for that little bit of money he provided, it kept a roof over our heads."

"Well, at least he did that," Addie said, rolling her eyes.

"There was so little money—I scrimped on everything I possibly could. We ate dried beans and cornbread until I thought starvation would be better. When Jim Bob showed up, he berated me for the meals I prepared, the way I looked, the way I kept house. Nothing suited him, and everything led to a fight."

Lizzie paused and cast her gaze upon Addie. "I know all of this sounds dismal, and it was, but for all the bad times, there were some good times," Lizzie said, her tone lifting a little.

"I should hope so," Addie said, giving Lizzie a half grin.

"The good times came when Jim Bob was away. Heaven only knows where he went or what he did while he was gone—I quite simply didn't care. But I made the best of those times for Jessie's sake. As she got a little older, she became my best friend. She was super inquisitive at an early age. She asked questions and I found myself telling her things she should have never heard, especially at such a tender age. Of course, I left out the worst of it, but still it was wrong of me to tell her such things," Lizzie said, shaking her head sorrowfully.

"I can't see that you were wrong. Jessie possesses a selfless love, it's a rare gift. It seems to me that she saw your broken heart and wanted to help, and by confiding in her you made her feel needed. She adores you. I see it every time she looks at you," Addie said.

"Thank you, Addie. I really never looked at it that way. And, I'm amazed that you've come to know so much about Jessie in such a short time. That's exactly how she is. I made amends with God after she was born, thankfully he knew best. What would I ever have done without my precious little girl? She's my rock," Lizzie said, her eyes glistening.

Addie took Lizzie's hand and held it in hers, and they sat in silence as the sun filled the room with radiant light. There was still so much Addie wanted to know, but she could see what a toil it was taking on her.

"Are you okay with going on? We can talk another time if you'd rather."

Lizzie sighed, "No time like the present."

"So, was there a time when you thought Jim Bob was gone for good?" Addie said.

"Pretty much every time he left, especially when he began to stay away months at a time. That was when there was no money at all, but I found I could make money on my own, despite Jim Bob's claims that I had no skills. Our landlord was a kindhearted man who sympathized with my plight. We worked out a deal. I did his laundry, ironing, and mending for a very generous reduction in the rent. Kind man that he was, he put out the word in town that my services were available, and others began to bring their laundry. The money I made was enough to make ends meet. All was good, and Jessie and I were happy—until the night Jim Bob returned. He was drunk as usual, but this time with sex on his mind. He hadn't touched me in that way in years. He forced himself on me. I was repulsed, but for Jessie's sake, and my own, I didn't resist. The next morning, he was gone.

Lizzie closed her eyes and took a deep breath. "He didn't come around again until the night I gave birth to Lillie. I was lying in bed with Lillie in my arms, and I heard the front door open and heavy footsteps in the hallway, and then his frame appear in the doorway. He walked to my bedside, looked down at the baby wrapped warmly in a pink blanket, and said in disgust, 'Another girl! All you're good for is filling this world with losers like you!' He stormed off, and that was the last time I saw him until the night he came for Lillie."

"That's the most puzzling part of all," Addie said, scratching her head. "If he had such an aversion for his little girls, why would he want to take Lillie?"

Pondering the question, deep wrinkles formed across Addie's forehead and thoughts of their stalker returned to her. "You said Jim Bob's brother had lived in Alabama before he went to prison, so there's the connection with the ball cap and the letter A. And funny thing, Lester had implied that the guy could be a convict. I suppose it's possible that Eddie could have been released, and if so, he'd instantly become our prime suspect. It's probably a far-fetched idea, but it wouldn't hurt to check into it. Do you know his full name? I could ask the police to do a search into his prison record. That would be a start. I'd feel better if we knew who we're dealing with here."

"I only know Jim Bob called him Eddie. I never met him, but when Eddie's mother married Jim Bob's dad, it's possible that he took his name. Could be that he goes by Thornhill."

"I'll get right to work on it. Even if we find out that he's been released from prison, it's not proof that he's our mystery man, but my instincts are going in that direction," Addie said. She rose from the table just as Jessie burst into the room.

"He's back! The man is back! This time he's closer to the house than before. He saw me watching him from the window and winked at me."

That was all it took. Addie hurriedly took Lillie to her room, laid her in her crib, and then rushed up the stairs with Lizzie following close behind. At the window, Addie peered out, keeping Lizzie hidden behind her. Just as Jessie had said, he was there, only a few yards from the house and making no attempt to hide. She got a good look at his face. He tipped his hat to her, then turned and casually retreated down the lane.

"The nerve of him!" Lizzie said, her hands planted firmly on her hips. "What gives him the right to stalk us? He's sending us a message—a threatening one. You got a good look at him, didn't you?"

"I certainly did—it'll help when I get to the police station. I'll get to the bottom of this—one way or another," Addie said.

Chapter 15

An urgency coursed through Addie's body as her old pickup sped toward town. Leaving Lizzie and the children alone and vulnerable had her nerves on edge. She wanted to get to the police station, obtain the information about Eddie, and return home as quickly as possible.

The stranger and his threatening behavior had her mind ticking off a series of what-ifs. *What if he hadn't left but was close by watching the house? What if he saw her leave? What if he made an even bolder move and broke into the house?*

A cold chill ran through her at the thought of her family being ambushed. Before she left, a bad feeling had settled over her. She'd given Lizzie and Jessie strict instructions: "stay inside, keep the doors locked, and don't open the door to anyone." The lines across her forehead deepened. She had no idea what this guy was up to, but his latest appearance on her property had crossed the line—she wanted him gone. *He can be thrown in jail or thrown out of town—either way will suit me fine.*

As she drove, her eyes scanned the roadside for any sightings of him, knowing he could easily hide his vehicle out of view or conceal his body behind a tree. That she hadn't encountered him, didn't calm her nerves.

The tight grip she had on the steering wheel loosened a bit when she reached the city limits. She took several deep breaths to calm herself. It helped that the police station was close by—soon she'd have the answers they desperately needed.

Reaching the station, she parked the truck and strode purposefully to the entrance, pausing at the door to take another long breath before going inside. It was the place she came once a year to obtain a permit for her stand, and she always had the same impression—*how could anyone work in such a depressing environment?* Everything from floor to ceiling was the drabbest shade of gray.

She made her way over to the gray metal desk where Deputy Dan Raskin was seated holding the telephone receiver to his ear. He looked up and gave Addie a friendly nod and pointed to a chair situated at the front of his desk. Addie smiled, returned his nod, and perched on the edge of the gray metal chair. She drew her shaking hands into her lap, clasping them tightly together and waited impatiently for the deputy to end his call.

Addie studied the man behind the desk. She had grown up with Dan and had gone through all twelve years of school with him. In his high school years, he had been a powerful linebacker for the football team. His massive, muscular build made his opponents tremble in their cleats. He had been hailed as the best player to ever grace the Tiger team. With his large belly and his double chin, he no longer bore any resemblance to that boy of years ago, but no one cared. His outstanding record had never been broken, and at almost thirty years old, he remained the hometown hero.

Addie sat taller in her seat upon hearing Dan's conversation drawing to a close.

"We'll be on the lookout and alert you if we hear of anything," Dan said. He hung up the phone and slowly lifted his oversized body out of the chair. "Addie," he said, extending his hand across the desk. "What brings you in today? Oh, before we get to that, I should tell you. That call was from the police station over in Tremont. Said their cadaver dog has been stolen. Seems someone called them and reported seeing a man with a dog fitting its description a couple of days ago out near your place. The officer didn't have a description of the man, but he said the dog's coat is the color of copper. Said they paid a fortune to have him trained. They sure seemed anxious to get him back—even got a reward out for him. If you happen to see him, let me know. Now that we've got that behind us, what can I do for you?"

Upon hearing this enlightening news, Addie's face turned blood red. Her whole reason for being there changed in that instant. She couldn't ask about Eddie, given this revelation. She had to come up with an alternate reason for being there—fast, then get out quick.

Her hands trembled. She could hear her pounding heartbeat in her ears. Putting on her sweetest smile, she attempted to hide her anxiety. "I was doing some errands in town, and it occurred to me that I should check on the location for my stand, you know, make sure it'll still be available this year. Things have a way of changing, and with spring coming on it won't be long until my garden will be producing. I'm just thinking ahead," she said, hoping her trembling voice and rambling words weren't causing suspicion.

"I don't know why it wouldn't be, but you're smart to ask. You never know what the city council will do from one year to the next," Dan said.

While making her way to the door she said, "You'll be sure to let me know if you find out anything to the contrary, won't you?" she said sweetly.

"You bet ya. Brenda Sue would be the first to complain if you weren't able to have your stand in your usual place. She counts on doing some shopping downtown and getting some of your good produce all at the same time—very convenient for everyone," Dan said.

Addie tapped her foot impatiently. "That's certainly nice to hear. Well, you have a lovely day. Tell Brenda Sue I said hello," she said, her words flowing fast and high-pitched.

Being careful not to draw attention to her nervous energy, Addie walked to her truck at a normal pace and drove slowly through town as sweat beaded on her forehead. When she got out of the city limits, she put her foot to the floorboard. "Holy cow! Can it get any worse?"

Breathing deeply, she counted to ten as she willed herself to calm down, knowing she did her best thinking with a cool head. This was a much more problematic situation than it appeared on the surface.

She started recounting the events that had taken place over the last couple of days concerning the man and the dog. The man stalking them, obviously, is the one who stole the dog, who she now strongly suspects to be Jim Bob's stepbrother, Eddie.

He was proving to be someone to be reckoned with on a grand scale. He was obviously clever and intuitive, most likely skills he mastered during his many years in prison. Of course, until confirmed, Eddie's involvement was pure speculation on her part, but all of the moving parts led her to believe she was on the right track. Still, she needed proof that Eddie was no longer incarcerated, then her suspicions would be validated.

If it was Eddie who stole the dog, he had to have strong suspicions regarding Jim Bob's whereabouts. He must have reason to believe that Jim Bob is dead. Addie couldn't shake off the troubling questions rolling around in her mind. *He's either on a fishing expedition, or he knows something.* She scratched her head. The latter was the most troubling.

Hadn't she taken extreme care to cover their tracks? Nobody had seen her set the house on fire or load Jim Bob's body in the bed of the truck—or had they?

Warning sounds were going off in her head, alerting her of impending danger. The urgent feeling she had when leaving the police station had grown to an intense level. She had to get home, home to Lizzie—to inform her of this new revelation and of her fearful suspicions. Being pushed to its limit, the old truck rattled as if it might shake apart at any moment. Regardless, Addie didn't let up on the gas pedal until she braked to a screeching halt at her back door.

Exiting the truck, she rushed up the steps. Breathlessly, she entered the kitchen where she found Lizzie sitting peacefully at the table, Lillie in her lap drinking from her bottle, and Jessie beside her, spooning cereal into her mouth.

One look at her sister and Lizzie's eyes widened with concern. She turned to Jessie and said, "Sweetheart, are you about finished? I thought you could get back to that painting, I know how anxious you are to finish it, and I can't wait to see it," Lizzie said, her tone downplaying her unease.

She needed no further encouragement, She quickly spooned in the last few bites, placed her bowl in the sink and turned to her mother, "May I please be excused?" she said politely.

"Of course, Sweetie, go and make it the prettiest painting of all," her mother said.

Jessie happily exited the room with Copper, as usual, following in her wake.

Addie sat beside Lizzie and Lillie at the table. "How are you feeling today?" she asked, struggling to keep her voice casual.

"If you're wanting to know if I'm up to hearing the bad news, the answer is no," Lizzie said, only half kidding.

"Is it that apparent?" Addie said,

"Oh, yeah. I knew from the moment you walked in the door that something big was brewing," Lizzie said.

"Big is an understatement," Addie said, shaking her head. "You're not going to believe what I found out. I went straight to the police station, fully intent on gaining information about Eddie. Well, when I arrived, Deputy Dan was at his desk talking on the phone. The call was from a neighboring police district concerning a stolen dog that had been trained to sniff out, get this—cadavers. And the dog just happens to be copper in color. Are you seeing where this is going?"

"I'm seeing that you're thinking the stolen dog is our Copper," Lizzie said.

"It's a pretty definite thing. There were reports that a man with a dog fitting Copper's description had been seen in our area. Then Copper shows up here—and then the man."

"Oh, my great day!" Lizzie said. "So, the man stole the dog and then he shows up here. How on earth would the man know to come here?"

"Putting two and two together, I'm convinced that the man is Jim Bob's brother, Eddie, and that he has strong suspicions that Jim Bob is buried here—he stole the dog to help find him. The dog apparently got away from him and he's looking for him, I'm sure he suspects we have him. What he plans to do from here on out is anybody's guess— it's up to us to figure it out. We sure don't need to be sitting ducks when he makes his next move."

"Did you ask about Eddie's release from prison?" Lizzie said.

"Thank goodness I was clear headed enough not to go there. That could have opened the biggest can of worms that ever was. If Eddie is our stalker, and if's he is indeed out of prison, the police would begin to look for him. Eddie would surely tell them his suspicions that we have the dog. We could even be seen as the ones who stole him. Then, Eddie could also tell them about his missing brother, and how he thinks we're responsible for his disappearance, or worse, his death. That would bring a passel of law enforcement agents digging around here. No, I was just glad to get out of there without being implicated in the situation."

"How on earth will we ever get out of this mess? My head is spinning. We could both end up in prison," Lizzie said, shaking nervously.

"I'm not going to jail, and neither are you. We have to be smart, make a plan, and stick to it. I've determined that Eddie is cunning. For our survival, we have to be, too," Addie said.

"We're criminals, too, in a way," Lizzie said. "Maybe we should use that to our advantage—think like Eddie."

"That's brilliant!" Addie said. "We'll think like Eddie. But that will take getting to know him, don't you think? We start right now, at this very minute. We put our helpless, fearful notions aside, and we no longer hide behind the curtains. We go into full-blown damage control. Next time he shows up, I'll go out and talk to him. I think you should stay out of sight for the first meeting while I go on a fishing expedition."

"We know one thing—he wants Copper back. That means we must keep him inside and under our control at all times," Lizzie said.

Addie was glad to see Lizzie taking charge. If they were to avoid jail time, it would take them both—planning and scheming. And her sister was the best schemer she'd ever known. "I like the way you think. Got any other suggestions?" Addie could see the wheels turning in her sister's brain.

"This guy may think because we're women, he can overtake us, so we have to be armed. We have a watchdog, and we need to be watchful ourselves and never, ever let our guard down as long as he remains a threat." Lizzie's face took on a devilish look, her old spunk on full display. "We can play his game. When he plays a card, we'll play a better one. The key to our success is to anticipate his moves before he makes them."

Addie grinned, pleased that the old Lizzie had come to play. "You said we'd be armed. You're aware I don't own a gun. Just what do you have in mind?" Addie said.

"Booby traps," Lizzie said, her face lighting up. "I used to set them all the time to keep the pesky boys from following me. I fixed their little red wagons good and sent them home crying to their mamas. Oh, how that brings back memories. You'll probably find my methods a bit shocking, but I can assure you they work. I have to admit I had some pretty awesome traps. The best one worked like a charm. I'd tie back a tree limb and cut it loose just when the boy got close. That trick always resulted in a lot of hollering and cursing along with some cuts and bruises," Lizzie said, her face aglow.

Addie's eyes widened. "Ouch! That's a little extreme, don't you think?"

Lizzie shook her head. "Believe me, they got what they deserved. I had other methods just as shrewd. There's the one I called mud-in-the-face. I dug a hole, filled it with water, and covered it with leaves. When the boy came to it, he'd stumble and fall down—face first. When he got up he'd be covered from head to toe with mud and muck. Oh, how I miss those days!" She grinned broadly, obviously enjoying the memory of her brave past exploits—that had long since vanished.

"Lizzie, where did you learn such devious tricks? You were heartless!" Addie said, a broad grin spreading across her face. "No doubt about it, your expertise will be very valuable in dealing with our situation. When you have a concrete plan of action, we'll set it in motion. I'll leave you alone to think." She retreated to her garden—the one place where she could take refuge from her escalating problems.

Chapter 16

The varying shades of spring green in her garden refreshed Addie's soul. She took a moment to gaze across the landscape and breathe in the aromas of Mother Earth. With so much going on the past couple of days, she had neglected the chores that were so crucial at this stage. Now was the time to start her seeds in the lean-to greenhouse positioned on the east side of the shed. There, the seeds received the benefits of the warm morning sun. The seedlings required a certain amount of time to germinate and could only be planted in the ground once the sun had warmed the soil and frost was no longer a threat.

Starting the seeds at just the right time was imperative, but like everything else, Addie never left this to chance. She had a proven record of when the task was to be performed. The records, which she painstakingly kept, were her guide each season and the reason her garden was so successful year after year.

Behind the garden shed her worktable sat empty, awaiting the job that lay ahead of her. She arranged empty pots on the table and systematically, in each pot, added her soil mixture and the seeds, then watered and labeled each one. From under the table, she retrieved a wooden crate and was just about to fill it with the pots when she caught a glimpse of Lizzie at the back door, wildly waving her arms. Alarmed, Addie let the crate slip from her hands and made a mad dash toward her.

"He's here!" Lizzie whispered, pointing to the front of the house. "He's sitting on the porch swing whistling like he doesn't have a care in the world—he's so bold. Who does he think he is just moseying up here and making himself at home? I want to go out there and give him a piece of my mind."

Addie took Lizzie by the hand and pulled her inside. "Let's not do anything rash—not yet. The smartest thing we can do now is stay with our plan. I'll go talk to him. You can listen through the door, but until we know his intentions, I think it's best for me to deal with him," Addie said.

"I guess you're right. But if we don't like what he has to say—then I'll deal with him—I feel up to a good fight!"

Addie patted Lizzie on the shoulder. "Hopefully, a fight won't be necessary, but be ready—just in case."

With a pinched expression on her face, Addie stomped down the hallway. She opened the door, keeping her hand on it—prepared to slam it shut and throw the bolt if necessary.

At first, he paid her no mind, continuing to whistle while casually swaying to and fro in the swing. This obvious dismissal of her presence had Addie seeing red. Hands on her hips, she glared at him. Slowly he turned his gaze to her while still whistling the annoying tune. Addie stood firm, her eyes fixed on his. Refusing to be intimated, she said, "Sir, you do know this is private property." It wasn't a question.

Addie studied his face that was riddled with deep lines which she assumed to be the result of his years of hard living. His brown hair curled around the sides and back of his cap, and long unruly sideburns framed a face that, surprisingly, she found to be somewhat handsome. His cool gray eyes revealed nothing at all—he spoke not a word.

"Since you've boldly made yourself comfortable on my porch, you could at least speak. I demand to know why you've been stalking me, and it's not that you're seeking information on plantations, so don't try that one," Addie said, her tone calm, her eyes locked on his. She noticed the corners of his mouth turn the slightest bit upward but just as quickly returned to a poker face.

Addie preferred to handle matters in the tactful Southern way—kill 'em with kindness—however, when provoked, she could take a totally different approach and be frank and blunt. This was just such an occasion. "I assume you can speak. You'd better start talking, or I'm calling the police."

He looked at her and laughed. "Why don't you just go ahead and do that? I'll be right here waiting."

He's shrewd. By his reply, she knew he had noticed that there were no telephone lines running to her house. Still, she played it cool. "For now, let's just get back to why you've been snooping around my house. Stalking is a very serious offense that could send you straight to prison, mister." It was an empty threat, but it had caused his face muscles to twitch.

He leaned forward in the swing and placed his elbows on his knees. "I've got reason to believe you have my dog. We were walking out this way the other day, and he wandered up your lane to do his business. Next thing I knew, he was headed toward your house—haven't seen him since."

"Why in heaven's name didn't you come here and ask about him that day? He's had plenty of time to wander off— no telling where," Addie said, thinking her quick response was quite clever.

"You got a dog?" he said, ignoring her question.

"Yes, I have a dog. I've had him for years." Addie touched her nose, thinking she actually felt it grow. "I fail to see what my having a dog or not having one is any of your concern."

"Well, I want to see this dog of yours," he said.

"You can't just come on my property and make demands. Your dog isn't here," she said emphatically. "I insist that you leave the premises immediately."

"I'm not going anywhere until I find my dog. He's here, and I know it. I'll be reporting to the cops how you stole him."

"Mister, you go right ahead and call the police. I'll be right here waiting for them."

Addie raised her chin, her eyes narrowed. "Where did you come from anyway?"

"Long way from here, and I won't be leaving without my dog. The sooner you turn him over, the sooner you'll be rid of me," he said.

Addie saw that their banter was getting her nowhere, so she decided to take a different approach—pour on the Southern charm.

"I can see you're very attached to your dog, but I can assure you I haven't seen him. I know how hard it would be if I lost my sweet Tessie—why, it would just kill me. Why don't you give me a number where you can be reached? I promise if I see him, I'll let you know right away," Addie said.

He stood and shifted his weight from one foot to the other before answering. "My name's Eddie. I'm staying in town at The Shady Inn. You can leave a message at the desk if you have any information. Like I said, I'll be around until I find my dog."

On the outside Addie showed no reaction, but on the inside, her heart was doing summersaults. She had just gotten the one bit of information that confirmed her suspicions, and it was easier than she thought—she kept fishing. "What does your dog look like? What's his name? Does he have a collar?"

"He's the color of a copper penny, his name's Stud, and he don't have a collar," Eddie said.

Addie covered her mouth and coughed to hide her amusement. *Stud. Where did he come up with that one?*

"I'll be sure to get word to you if I see Stud around here. Now, if you'll excuse me, I have supper on the stove, and I'm sure you have things to do, like looking for your dog somewhere other than here," she said.

Before leaving, there was one last bit of information she wanted to pry out of him. "Oh, what do you drive? You surely didn't walk all the way out here from town."

The look on Eddie's face showed his annoyance at her obvious probing questions. "I appreciate your concern, but yeah, I walked all the way," he said.

Realizing he wasn't going to divulge any more information, Addie promptly dismissed him. "Have yourself a nice afternoon, Eddie. I'll be sure to let you know if Stud shows up here."

Eddie gave her a salute and sauntered slowly down the lane.

She watched until he was out of sight. "He'll be back, no doubt about it," she said, stepping inside then firmly shutting and bolting the door.

.

Chapter 17

Prison—the thought of it sent shivers down Eddie's spine. He rubbed his neck and shoulders to ease the tension that stemmed from the mere mention of the word. The sister's empty threats didn't scare him in the least, but they did provoke memories that he was trying hard to forget.

Following his ordeal with the sister, he was back in his room at the Shady Inn. Alone with just his thoughts, his mind trailed off to the years before he'd been incarcerated, the time he referred to as BP—Before Prison.

His mother had been a disaster when it came to choosing a husband. Whenever the marriage turned sour, they'd board a Greyhound bus—bound for some other small town. By the time Dickie Ramsey—husband number five—came along, he'd made it clear that it wasn't a package deal—he wanted no part of raising a kid. She had no choice, his mother had said as she walked, suitcase in hand, to Dickie's waiting car. At the time he'd been greatly relieved to be left behind—he hated Dickie's guts.

If he'd had a say in it, he would've liked to have gone back to South Carolina to live with stepfather number three, Toby Thornhill. Although he held no real fondness for the man, he had become close to his son, Jim Bob, during that short marriage.

But it wasn't meant to be. When his mother married Dickie, he'd been left instead with stepfather number four—Roddy Parks.

Roddy was rougher than a corn cob and although he didn't mistreat Eddie, he wouldn't win "father of the year" either. At the age of thirteen, Eddie had been forced to fend for himself whenever Roddy wasn't around, which was more often than not—he couldn't seem to stay out of jail.

Roddy had quit school at the age of ten and always thought that he was better off for it. He said he had a better plan than to learn stuff he'd never use in the real world. At that young age he'd begun working alongside his father, learning the ins and outs of The Trade—as they called it— the long-time family tradition of car thievery.

When Eddie and his mother came to live with Roddy, he was on a roll, though his rolls were always short lived. Just as he was riding high, he'd get careless and end up in the local jail for brief periods of time. His profession didn't seem to bother Eddie's mother, but she couldn't tolerate him being a jailbird. She wasted no time in finding a replacement, who shortly thereafter, became husband number five.

After her departure, Roddy's carelessness increased to the point of being locked up for months at a time. Eddie often wondered if his stepfather had stopped caring about being caught—he kept doing the same dumb things over and over that ultimately resulted in his arrest.

The times Roddy was locked up, which was most of the time, Eddie learned to take care of himself. That was when, he too, took up the family tradition as a means of survival. From the young age of fourteen, he could hot-wire a car and be gone in sixty seconds.

He considered himself lucky to have been taken under the wing of an established a businessman—a man he trusted, even though he questioned his morals. His name was Harry Heckle and he dealt in used cars—no questions asked. As dubious as it was, the connection enabled Eddie to leave Roddy's house and go out on his own. After that, he lost all contact with his stepfather—where he was now—was of no concern to him.

Eddie had learned well. For over ten years he eluded the police until one summer day when his life took a fateful turn. He'd thrown caution to the wind when he got behind the wheel of the fire-engine-red convertible Corvette. He hadn't planned to steal it. He was casually strolling down the sidewalk when he saw it parked at the curb with the keys dangling in the ignition. It was an open invitation—far too tempting and way too easy.

Taking that particular car went against the basic rule of car thievery—never take the flashy ones. When the owner of the Corvette reported it missing, it had stood out like a sore thumb and the cops had no trouble spotting it. Eddie had made it even easier for them by leisurely cruising about in plain sight. He was twenty-four when he was hauled off to jail. The courts charged him with Grand Theft Auto, which landed him in Rockville Prison confined to a six-by-eight cell for a term of ten years. He'd thrown away his freedom on that day, in that swanky car with the top rolled down, a gentle breeze brushing his skin, and feeling invincible. If he only had the chance to relive that day—he'd admire the car and keep walking.

He sighed heavily, recalling those long years behind bars, how he was challenged from the very first day he walked through the prison gates. Just like in the movies, the tough guys came around to intimidate him—letting him know, in no uncertain terms, who was boss.

Being bullied wasn't new to him, and neither was fighting. In his rough upbringing, fighting was a way of life. He ran his fingers over the scar on his neck where Mean Marty Monroe had cut him with a switchblade knife for not giving him a quarter. He had retaliated by giving Mean Marty a bloody nose. That was the way it was: a guy hurts you—you hurt him back.

He was reminded of when he was twelve, and a new boy, Truck Bates, moved into town. As his name implied, he was huge—three times the size of any of the local boys—meaner than a rattlesnake. His mouth was always set in a deep frown, and his squinty eyes spoke volumes of his meanness. Everybody cleared the way when they saw Truck coming.

One day, in the school hallway, Timmy Brown was tying his shoelace and failed to see Truck approaching. Truck picked him up and slammed him into the row of metal lockers. Timmy was rushed to the hospital with three broken ribs. After that, he wore only penny loafers.

Truck had terrorized the entire town. Polly Sue Wigs was only ten, just a little girl walking home from school. For no particular reason, Truck started following her—day after day. He would yank on her ponytail and step on the heels of her shoes, often causing her to fall and skin her knees on the rough surface. His refusal to leave her alone caused her father to get involved. The meek school principal, Mr. Mosley, sympathized but offered no solution. Come to find out, he too had received threats from Truck, who had said to him, "Give me any trouble, and you'll be sorry." Eddie recalled how nervous Mr. Mosley always appeared, and how he constantly looked over his shoulder.

Nobody was off limits. Whenever Truck was spotted in town, the merchants all rushed to their doors, put out the closed signs, turned the locks, and pulled down the shades.

The tough boys, Eddie being one of them, held a meeting to decide what to do about Truck. They all looked at Eddie. Eddie knew he didn't stand a chance in a fight with Truck—he'd be smashed like a bug. He knew a better way to settle a mild conflict without the situation coming to blows.

He had been in fifth grade when Moose Townsend, who was on the verge of failing, walked by his desk and snatched up his homework. When he reached to grab it from his clutch, Moose pulled back his fist. Eddie had looked him square in the eye and said, "Think about it, Moose, you'll just be getting yourself into more trouble—teacher knows my handwriting." Moose looked at him through narrowed eyes; he had closed his, bracing for the hit. To his surprise, Moose unclenched his fist, put the papers back on his desk, and shuffled dejectedly back to his seat.

It had worked once, and he wondered if the same tactic would work on Truck. The situation presented itself when he and some of his buddies were eating lunch in the school cafeteria. He was just about to bite into his hamburger, when Truck appeared. With one massive paw he swiped it from his hands. This was the only good meal Eddie would get all day, and he darn sure wasn't going to let Truck get away with taking it. He stood and faced Truck with rage in his eyes. Truck dangled the sandwich in front of him and said, "Whatcha gonna do about it, wimp?" Holding his knotted fist at his side, he had pondered the question, then he said, "I'll tell you what I'm going to do about it." He reached into his pocket and pulled out a dollar bill. Quick as a wink, he grabbed his sandwich from Truck's hand, and stuffed the bill in its place. The room grew silent; all eyes were fixed on Truck—waiting for the inevitable ball to drop. For several seconds Truck appeared stunned. Then he shook his head, shoved the bill into his pocket, and sauntered off. Following that event, there was a noticeable change in Truck's behavior, but not a single tear was shed when, a year later, his family packed up and moved away.

Eddie had been stunned at how easy it had been to calm the situation. The simple strategy had come to him out of the clear blue. From then on, he applied the tactic whenever he found himself in a challenging predicament. Even while in prison, when coming face to face with the most ruthless characters, his words of reason and non-confrontational tactics managed to still the waters. The guards liked that he kept a cool head. His way of avoiding conflicts had earned him special privileges as well as an early release.

A contented smile crossed his face. As long as he lived, he'd never forget the elation he felt the day he walked through the imposing prison gates—a free man. He'd been offered a job and a place to live, arranged for him by the Department of Corrections. It was a privilege given to only a select few. Why him, he didn't know—but he accepted it with gratitude.

He rubbed his fingers over the thick calluses on his palms. For the last six months, he'd been working on a construction crew in Tennessee. The pay was good, and he liked the work. He took great pride in knowing that his small contribution played a part in turning a stack of raw lumber into a sturdy and fine structure. For the first time in his life, he was learning a legitimate trade—honest work for honest pay. At last he could hold his head high.

With little need for money, he saved most of what he earned. In a couple of months, he'd saved enough to buy a car. Granted, it was the cheapest one on the lot, but he'd beamed like the summer sun when he laid the cash on the salesman's desk. He strode with pride to his new ride, keys clinched in his hand—his hot-wiring days behind him.

A noise out on the street brought him back to the present and to the reason he was in Beau Ridge in the first place. It all started two days ago when his boss, Mr. Roberts, surprised him with a week's paid vacation. Eddie had been overwhelmed by his generosity, especially since he'd only been on the job six months. Roberts had told him that he believed in rewarding employees who showed dedication, worked hard and did their jobs well—a quality he said he'd seen in him. His chest had swelled with pride when Mr. Roberts told him he'd make a fine project manager someday.

After work that day he'd gone home to his small apartment and pondered how he'd spend a solid week on his own. He got along well with his fellow workers, but they all had wives and children; he didn't fit into their lifestyles.

As was his way to unwind after a hard day's work, he'd settled into the cushy sofa, taken off his shoes and propped his socked feet atop the coffee table. Here he had a clear view out the window of his parked car—always the wary ex-thief.

Subconsciously, he had taken the keys from his pocket and jingled them in his hand. That was when the idea of looking up his family came to mind. There was only one member that he had any interest in seeing again—his stepbrother, Jim Bob. While in prison, his stepbrother had been the only one who had cared enough to reach out with an occasional letter or phone call.

He'd been so wrapped up in navigating his new life on the outside that he hadn't let Jim Bob know of his release. He looked at the keys, still in his hand, then out the window at his car. In that instant, he knew how he'd spend his time off—drive down to Alabama and surprise his brother.

****

A comforting feeling came over him as he recalled being in his car and studying the map that Jim Bob had given him. Seven hours—out on the open road—like a bird out of a cage. He chuckled, realizing how true it was. *Must've been a jailbird who came up with that line.* The outside air had been chilly, but instead of turning on the heat, he had rolled down all four windows and let the fresh air fill his senses.

Everything was fresh and new. He took mental snapshots to preserve the experience: houses—big and small, pastures where cows grazed lazily, the pines that seemed to whisper in the breeze, school yards filled with children, small towns with people milling about. He hadn't wanted to miss a thing.

When the sign announcing the town of Little Hope came into view, he took his foot off the gas and drove slowly through the main street. Even now, he could feel the disappointment he experienced on that day. It wasn't at all the place Jim Bob had described, and he wondered how on earth he had ended up there—of all places.

He had driven on, looking for the house number 302. Creeping along, he studied the numbers on each house as he approached: then a little farther 300 and farther still 301. All of them appeared abandoned, but there was no 302. He continued on for about a mile until there were no more houses, and the road came to a dead end.

Deciding that he had somehow missed it, he turned around and started back. This time he saw what had to be 302, but there was only rubble and the charred remains of what he assumed, had been a house.

He parked and got out of the car and walked toward the remains, kicking around in the ashes but finding no clues about the family who had lived there. He drove back to the little town's service station, hoping someone would have knowledge of his brother's whereabouts.

There had been no one in the office, so he followed the noise coming from the shop area. A man, wearing grease-covered coveralls that fit tightly over his large belly, was busy taking apart a motor. He was so absorbed in his work that he hadn't noticed him enter.

His conversation with the man was still etched in his brain.

"Excuse me," he had said.

The man looked up and said, "Sorry, I didn't hear you come in. I gotta have this motor up and running by this afternoon, or the guy said he won't pay me. Can I help you?"

"I hope so. I came here looking for my stepbrother, Jim Bob Thornhill. Would you happen to know him? I just came from the address he gave me and found only the charred remains of what, I assume, was his house."

"I'm just filling in while the owner's taking some time off. I remember that guy did work here a while back; strange thing about that house though, it burned down and nobody's seen them people since—they just up and vanished."

"And you don't know what caused the fire?" Eddie said.

"Nope, don't know no more than what I already told you. Sorry, I couldn't be of help."

"Thanks for your time," he had turned to leave.

"Hey, mister," the man called back, "you say that feller is your brother?"

"Yeah, stepbrother."

"I almost forgot about that woman that came in here a few days ago. Said she was Jim Bob's girlfriend, asking questions about him, same as you. Now, I don't get into other people's business, but I knew that man was married and had a kid or two. They kinda kept to themselves, especially after he got in all that trouble. Like I said, I don't meddle in folk's affairs, but the whole thing just didn't sit right with me," the man said.

Trouble? he had thought, but didn't ask. "So that was a couple of days ago, huh? Did she leave her name or a phone number for you to get in touch with her, just in case you got some information?"

He snapped his fingers. "Yeah, matter of fact, she did. I got it over here somewhere." He stood and walked to the front office and rummaged through the heap of papers on his cluttered desk. "Yep, got it right here," he said, handing him a small piece of paper.

Written on the paper was the name, Rita Reynolds, along with a phone number. "Do you need this back?"

"Nah, I figure you need it more than me, being his brother and all. I don't 'spect to have no more information than I got right now. Ain't nobody around here knows nothing. A whole lot of speculatin' about it, though," the man said.

He'd thanked the man for the information, and then he'd set out to make the call.

He'd stepped into the dingy phone booth that sat on the street corner, leaving the door open—the thought of being closed up in the small space had made him uneasy. He'd deposited coins in the slots, and after the last coin sounded a ding, he dialed her number. The conversation he'd had with her was still present in his memory. Even now, his face flushed as he remembered how he'd stumbled over his words. "Uh, hello ma'am, uh, I'm looking for a Rita Reynolds."

"Yes, this is Rita," she said, her voice silky.

"Well, uh, I got your name from, uh, the man at the gas station in Little Hope. Uh, he said you were in there a couple of days ago inquiring about Jim Bob Thornhill." he said, stuttering like a babbling idiot.

"Yes, that's right," she replied, keeping her answer brief.

"Uh, I'm his stepbrother, Eddie. Right now I'm in a phone booth in Little Hope. I had plans to drop in on Jim Bob and surprise him. Instead, I was the one surprised. I found his house burned to the ground, and nobody around here seems to know anything. Uh, I don't mean to pry, uh, I'm just going by what the man told me, but, he said, uh, that you're his girlfriend—is that right?"

There was no shame in her voice. "That's right," she said. Again, her short answers were not making his attempts for information easy. At least, she had admitted to being his girlfriend, that was a step in the right direction.

"Well then, I'm guessing you know I, uh, I was, uh,…I've been in prison. Jim Bob and I have stayed pretty close through the years. I'm hoping you might know where he's living now.

There was silence on the other end of the phone. Eddie had waited, assuming she was trying to decide if he was legit. Moments later, her sultry voice came across the line.

"Yes, Jim Bob mentioned you on several occasions. Especially lately, knowing your sentence was drawing near a close. Well, to tell you the truth, I'm glad to hear from you. I've been worried sick over his sudden disappearance. When he left here, he was supposed to bring me something when he returned—he never showed up."

Relieved that she had seemingly believed him, and that she was finally starting to talk, he pressed further. "Bring you something? Do you mind if I ask what that something might be?"

"Let's just say I've been here waiting with great anticipation. It's something I've wanted for a very long time. Jim Bob always wants to get me whatever my little heart desires. He's so sweet that way," she had said, her voice a soft purr.

He recalled fanning his flushed face with his hand and had wondered what it was about her—his mind was going places it shouldn't.

Forcing his mind back on the situation at hand, he wanted to know more about this thing that Jim Bob was supposed to bring to her, thinking it might have something to do with his disappearance. He sensed she was withholding this information for a reason.

Under his breath, he had cursed the operator when she came on the line asking him to deposit more coins. He only had enough for one additional minute.

"Look, like I told you, I'm calling from a phone booth, and I've run out of change. Is there any way we can meet in person to discuss our mutual matter?"

He'd been relieved when Rita agreed to meet at two o'clock the following afternoon—she gave him her address. He'd hung up the phone and taken a long deep breath to calm his nerves. This was his first interaction with a female in nine long years; he'd felt like a schoolboy asking a girl for a first date. He told himself that he needed to snap out of it before meeting with her. Otherwise, he'd never get the information he wanted. He had a strong feeling that Rita had withheld information about Jim Bob's disappearance.

****

Rita lived in Green Valley, Alabama, a town about the size of Little Hope, but the total opposite. On either side of Main Street, the buildings were painted in colors that coordinated perfectly, making the whole town appear pleasing and inviting. The pride the residents had for their town was on full display from the shiny glass windows to the tidy sidewalks and streets. People milled about greeting each other with smiling faces. This was the kind of town where he could see himself settling down. It made him wonder why Jim Bob had made his home in a place like Little Hope, where there truly was—little hope.

He had parked his car at the curb in front of Rita's house promptly at two. Her house was identical in appearance to those on either side, the only difference was the color. Hers was painted a pale green with white shutters. On the small front porch were two white wicker chairs with bright yellow cushions. Realistic looking flowers in pretty ceramic pots were scattered about, giving her home a welcoming appeal.

Standing at the door, he had raked his fingers through his unruly hair then knocked softly. Seconds later, the door opened, and a very attractive woman in her thirties appeared.

He took a quick evaluation. He estimated her height to be about five' six. Her hair was bleached blond and hung in loose curls across her shoulders. Her low-cut blouse revealed her rounded cleavage, and her skintight pants showed off her slim, shapely legs. Her eyelashes reached to her eyebrows—fake, he assumed.

"Uh, hello," he had said, extending a sweaty hand. Rita took his hand in hers, her soft touch sent flutters through his body.

"Hello, Eddie. It's very nice to meet you. Please, come inside where we can be more comfortable," she said.

He had followed her into her small living room. His gaze took in her overly ornate furnishings, not particularly tasteful but somewhat pleasing just the same. Her slender finger pointed to a chair where he'd tried to position his body among the multitude of pillows and ended up perched on the edge like a woman at a tea party.

"Would you care for something to drink?" Rita said.

"Yes, thank you. A glass of water would be nice, if it's not too much trouble."

When Rita left the room, he'd taken the pillows and placed them on the floor beside the chair. His eyes darted about the room, taking in the mishmash of trinkets and furniture. He'd never seen anything like it, but it told him a lot about this woman. She liked things, lots of things. He had wondered if the thing Jim Bob was to bring her could be something like the things in this room.

Rita returned with two tall glasses of ice water. She handed one to Eddie. He thanked her and took a long swallow. Her gaze fell on the pillows that lay on the floor beside his chair—she didn't comment.

He cleared his throat. He had rehearsed his speech, hoping to redeem himself from the blubbering fool he had made of himself the day before. "I know you're just as anxious as I am to learn of Jim Bob's whereabouts, so I hope we can trust each other enough to share any information that might lead us to him," he had said, pleased that he hadn't stuttered.

"I'm willing to share anything that will be of help," she said, with an endearing smile.

"When did you last see him? You weren't having any problems, were you? I mean, like any arguments that might have ended your relationship?"

"Certainly not," she said, raising her chin indignantly. "In fact, quite the opposite. We are deeply in love, and we're going to be married. He was here exactly one week ago. Then he left to tell his wife he was leaving her and her kid. She's a detestable person. Well, to be honest, I've never met her, but Jim Bob has told me horrible stories about her. Do you know her?" Rita said.

"I only met her a time or two when we were young. When my mother married my stepdad, Jim Bob's dad, we lived in the same town. Anyway, I only know she was a wild thing. Her parents were well off, and her dad spoiled her by giving her anything she wanted. He believed in free will and put no restrictions whatsoever on her behavior. An anything goes kind of parenting. I guess that's how she and Jim Bob ended up together. Two peas in a pod, you know."

"That fits the woman he described, but not my Jim Bob. My heart went out to him, married to that hell raiser and trapped in a marriage with a woman he didn't love and with kids he never wanted."

"Maybe Jim Bob has changed, but in his younger years, he was a hell-raiser, too."

"I've never seen that. He's sweet and as laid back as anybody I've ever known," Rita said.

"That's good to hear. I suppose he grew out of his wild ways. Oh, before you said Jim Bob was planning to leave his wife and kid, now you say he has kids, as in more than one."

"Well, that was my mistake. Yes, he has two children, two girls, one seven and one just about a month old. I would have thought you would know this since you stayed in contact with him," she said, eyeing him suspiciously.

"We didn't talk often, not like every week, not even every month. It was sporadic. I'd say twice a year would be about right. Thing is, he never talked about his family at all. Since he didn't bring it up, I didn't ask. I assumed he wanted to steer clear of the subject for fear our family's past would be brought into the conversation, and neither one of us wanted to go there."

"I see," she said. "Brothers would know what subjects to avoid."

He felt like they were playing a game of cat and mouse, neither one of them totally trusting the other, hoping to catch the other in a trap. So far, no red flags had been raised, but still he had a feeling she was withholding something big. He continued to play along.

"Yeah, when you've lived through some really bad stuff, the last thing you want is to relive it, so you avoid it altogether." He'd settled back in his chair to make his questioning appear more casual. "So, you said it was exactly a week ago when you last saw Jim Bob, when he left to get the thing you wanted?" More and more, he couldn't shake the feeling that the thing was an important piece of the puzzle.

Rita turned her focus to her water glass as if she were looking for answers inside it. "Yes, it's been a week since I last saw him. He was on kind of a double mission, all in one swoop, you might say."

Double mission, all in one swoop. What the heck did that mean? He had a strange feeling she was leading him somewhere, feeding him small bits of information to keep him playing along. He wasn't going anywhere. He'd play her game. "A double mission, all in one swoop, what does that even mean?"

She gave him a sly grin. "You know, kill two birds with one stone, two for the price of one—however you want to look at it," she said coyly.

He had stared at her as if she were speaking some foreign language. "If that's meant to be a hint, it's gone right over my head. If you want me to know something, I'd rather you just come right out and say it."

"Oh, alright. I can see that you're tiring of our little game. I was having so much fun. So, you're really interested in knowing the thing Jim Bob was supposed to bring me?"

He had moved to the edge of his chair and nodded, so sure that she was finally going to let him in on Jim Bob's important mission.

"Well, Eddie, maybe it's a personal matter between Jim Bob and me, and just maybe it's none of your business," Rita said, her eyes turning cool.

Up to this point, he had been quite entertained by her mysterious answers, but he feared that she was about to close the door on the subject. It was time to amp up his strategy.

"It's up to you. If it's that personal, maybe you shouldn't tell me, but if it will help us with our common goal of finding Jim Bob, then you might want to consider filling me in."

Rita had only glared at him. They seemed to be at a stand-off. The question was—who would win.

Chapter 18

Rita put on her poker face. Eddie didn't know it, but his showing up now was perfect. She began to set her trap.

Her eyes softened, and a sweet smile spread across her face. She studied Eddie. Like the words in a book, she could read people's faces. It was one of her many God-given talents. The deep-set lines embedded in his forehead made him appear rough, but it was the soft crinkles around his eyes that told her all she needed to know. This man, despite his criminal past, had a good heart, a trait that would serve her well as she spun her web. But she wouldn't count on that alone; she had other skills that had never failed to produce her desired results.

She'd seen how he looked at her, how his eyes were drawn to the fullness of her breasts. Like all the other men who had come before him, she would use her sexuality to get what she wanted. She'd convince him that she had only the best of intentions. She smiled devilishly. Soon she'd have him in the palm of her hand.

Alluringly, she batted her thick lashes and patted the space beside her on the small loveseat. As if mesmerized, Eddie rose from his chair and stumbled across the floor. He wedged himself into the teensy space, his thigh pressed firmly against hers. She shifted her body in his direction, using every move to her advantage.

She touched his knee and gazed deep into his eyes. Sighing heavily, she said, "I know this is going to sound bad, but I can assure you my heart was in the right place." She placed her hand over her generous breasts and paused as Eddie's gaze went there. "You see, Eddie, all I ever wanted was to do a good deed—make a bad situation better. Well, perhaps I should start at the beginning."

"Yeah, since I'm in the dark, that would be really helpful—I've got nowhere else to be."

"Okay, then I'll just start with how I met Jim Bob."

"I'm listening," Eddie said, with a slight shift of his body.

"Well, it started like this. I was filling in as a barmaid at The Bar None on Main Street. I do that on occasion. It's a way for me to get out and mingle a bit, make a little spending money. Anyway, this fellow shuffled in and took a seat at a booth in the far back corner. Rarely did anyone of interest come in, but right off the bat, he got my attention and the other gal, Sally Jane's, too. I was at his table before Sally Jane knew what hit her. The guy didn't bother to look up. I could tell he was in some kind of bad place, emotionally, I mean. I have that kind of sixth sense with men," she said, placing her hand on Eddie's thigh.

Again, she paused to explore Eddie's response. Seeing the tiny beads of sweat at his hairline, she grinned inwardly.

"It was a slow night, so I sat down beside him and asked if he was alright. He raised his gaze to me but didn't answer."

She paused again for effect.

"You see, I've always prided myself on my people skills." Looking into Eddie's, eyes she could see that he was falling under her spell, just as she had expected.

"I could see the guy needed some cheering up. I sat there jabbering on and on about nothing really. Without warning, he grabbed my arm and told me to shut up and leave him alone. Well, he could forget about me trying to help him out of his misery; he could rot in it for all I cared. I left him sitting there basking in his self-pity—wanting never to lay eyes on him again. But the next day, he showed up at my door with roses, saying he was sorry for the way he acted. Any other time, I'd have thrown the roses in his face and given him some real choice words, but to tell you the truth—I felt sorry for him. We sat on my porch and talked for hours. He asked if he could see me again, and I said yes. After that, he dropped by every day. I saw, despite his rude behavior in the bar that night, he was desperate for someone to talk to—I was willing to listen."

Rita drew in a deep breath and slowly released it while keeping her eyes fixed on Eddie's.

"He explained that he had come to town looking for work, but other than a random job here and there, he'd had no luck finding anything of a permanent nature. He was defeated in every way a man can be. He really was a train wreck."

Eddie grimaced. "I had no idea he was suffering like that. Our conversations had mostly been on world news, the weather, and such. Not that I could have done anything to help him, but hearing this makes me wish he had confided in me. After all—I am his brother."

Rita patted Eddie's knee. "I'm sure he was trying to keep things light and not burden you with his problems."

Eddie nodded, "I suppose so."

"Anyway, as we spent more time together, our friendly relationship grew into something more. He started spending most nights with me, sleeping beside me in my bed." She blushed and cast her eyes downward.

"Until this point, he hadn't revealed that he was married and had children, and by this time, I didn't really care. I couldn't see how it could be much of a marriage when he was never home. Then, he confided in me about the horrible ways his wife treated him. He said she was a slut, a drug addict, and unfit to be a mother. It had become impossible for him to live with her. And because he had no job options where they lived, he had to go from town to town looking for work. That's how he ended up here." She paused, placed her hand over her chest and exhaled deeply.

"Jim Bob's story just broke my heart. He deserved better, and his little children, the baby especially, needed to be properly cared for—in a loving home. I convinced Jim

Bob that the baby could be ours. We could take her and raise her. Since she was just weeks old nobody would suspect she wasn't mine. I was sure we could pull this off without anybody being the wiser. At first, Jim Bob wasn't thrilled about the idea. But finally he came around—after a little encouragement," she said, emphasizing the word encouragement.

Rita leaned in closer to Eddie, her breasts touching his arm. His body grew rigid, and she knew he understood the kind of encouragement she implied.

"So, you see, the thing I was so anxiously anticipating was the baby. The night Jim Bob went to get her was the last time I saw him. I haven't slept a wink or hardly eaten a bite since he's been gone. I'm desperate for information. All I really wanted was for us to be a family—it's what we both wanted."

Eddie scratched the stubble on his chin, mulling over this new revelation.

With the conversation stalled, thoughts were swirling around in Rita's mind as well. For years she had yearned for a child of her own, but that bubble had burst when she discovered she was infertile. Then along came Jim Bob. When he mentioned his baby daughter, the wheels started turning, and the baby became all she could think about.

That was when she devised her plan. Once the baby was hers, she'd send Jim Bob packing. He was baggage she didn't need. Then, it would just be her and her little bundle of joy—in her perfect house—living the perfect life.

Breaking away from her thoughts, Rita said, "You do see, don't you, that the baby would be so much better off with me than with a mother who cares so little for her? I'll love her with every ounce of my being."

Eddie squirmed in his seat—this didn't seem right—he had to discourage her. "I sense that your heart's in the right place, but I wonder if you and Jim Bob could be opening up a can of worms; this could turn into your worst nightmare. No mother, even a bad one, is going to let someone take her baby against her will."

Rita shifted her body, putting distance between them. She certainly hadn't expected this response from a common criminal, and she didn't like her decisions being challenged. But she needed Eddie's help. Taking a different approach, she pressed closer to him, so close she felt his body become tense. *Perfect.*

"Oh, Eddie, it's so sweet of you to think about the repercussions of such a thing, but we had already thought about that. Jim Bob assured me that he'd take care of any problems that arose. He told me not to worry my pretty little head, not for one little minute. But the thing that does worry me—it's been a week, and no word from him."

To seal the deal, she turned on the tears, a tactic that had never failed her. They flowed in tiny rivers down her cheeks and spilled onto her chest—she leaned into Eddie.

"Oh, Eddie, I just have to know what's happened to Jim Bob and the baby. If I don't find out soon—I'll just die." She covered her face with her hands and sniffled dramatically. Producing a tissue from her pocket, she dabbed between her breasts.

Inwardly, she beamed at her award-winning performance. The painful look in Eddie's eyes told her she had him—hook, line, and sinker.

"I can see how distressing this is for you," Eddie said, wiping the tears from her cheeks. I came here to find my brother, and that's what I aim to do. When I find him, I'll get to the bottom of all this. I promise I won't let you down. Got any ideas where to start looking?"

With big, sad eyes she looked at Eddie and said, "Jim Bob mentioned once that his wife has a sister. I think she lives somewhere in South Carolina. Maybe you should start with her—she might know something."

"Of course, I'd forgotten Lizzie has a twin. I vaguely remember her from when I lived there; hopefully, when I find her, she'll point me in the right direction. It'll be a start, anyway."

"There's one more thing I should mention. It's nothing concrete—more of a feeling. There is a chance that Jim Bob could be dead," Rita said, tears suddenly appearing.

A stunned look fell across Eddie's face—he couldn't believe his ears. "Dead? What on earth makes you think that?"

Rita twirled a section of hair around her finger and frowned. "Well, I didn't want to say in the beginning. It's just that Jim Bob was always so afraid of his wife, and what she would do to him if she ever found out about the two of us. He said she could go absolutely berserk when she was strung out on drugs; she'd even threatened to stab him in his sleep. He said he woke up one night with her standing over him with a large butcher knife. My gut feeling is that she finally followed through with her threat. I think it's possible that she killed him, burned the house, and got the heck out of Dodge."

Eddie was dumbstruck by this eye-opening revelation. He drew in a deep breath and exhaled slowly, willing his mind to clear. "Let's think this through. I was so distraught when I found Jim Bob's house burned to the ground that it didn't dawn on me until this very minute that there was a burned-up car in the front yard. So, how did Lizzie leave? A cab? A bus? Or did someone come and get them? The cab is probably out of the question, too much money, and that town didn't look like the kind that would have a need for one; besides, a cab driver would be a witness to her fleeing from a burning house.

"They could have taken a bus, but how would they would get to the bus station? And again, I'm certain that town didn't have one. No, I don't see that as an option either. I'm betting on the sister. I think she picked them up. Nobody saw them leave—gone like ghosts in the night."

"So, you believe it's possible that he could be…" she wiped away her fake tears, and her voice trailed off— "dead?"

"From what you've told me, I think it's the only conclusion. I suppose looking up the sister is a good idea. I'm guessing she still lives in Beau Ridge. It'll be a start anyway. I'm thinking that I won't approach her right off the bat. I'll just hang out, observe the layout, and watch who comes and goes from her house. I can learn a lot by talking to the townsfolk and doing some general snooping around. If the sisters are together, they don't know what they're in for. I can be downright intimidating when the situation calls for it."

"I just bet you can," Rita said. A pleased grin spread across her face. She had Eddie eating out of the palm of her hand. Her fingers tightened around Eddie's. "Why don't you stay for dinner, and we can talk more about your strategy." She put her hand on his shoulder and patted it tenderly. "With your keen mind, I think you'd make a first-rate detective."

Chapter 19

Day five had arrived with still no word from Lester. Every day Addie had expected him to come through the door bearing good news from the school board. The clock was ticking. At any time Bass could be at their door with his annoying knock. With Jessie's fate hanging in the balance, her body twitched nervously. Unable to sit still she began pacing the floor. *Lester, where are you?*

To settle her nerves, she busied herself in the kitchen, chopping onions and carrots into teeny-tiny pieces, for no particular reason—anything to push aside the thoughts of Mr. Bass and his ridiculous deadline from her mind.

From her place at the kitchen table, Lizzie took note of her sister's strange behavior. "What's got you all stirred up this morning?"

Addie had forgotten how easily they could read each other's emotions. "I wasn't going to say. I supposed that if I didn't, it would go away. Wishful thinking, huh? You know it's day five."

"Oh my... it is, isn't it? I wish that foolish Mr. Bass would drop off the face of the earth. He'll be here, though, waving his old legal documents in our faces, boasting about how he won. I'm assuming the school board didn't go for Lester's petition since we haven't heard from him."

"There's one thing I'm sure of—he gave it his best shot. We don't need to fault him if he didn't succeed," Addie said, in a sharp tone.

"Don't get touchy! The only person I blame is that Dumb-ass Bass," Lizzie said, scrunching up her nose at the thought of him.

Addie bent over double with laughter. "Dumb-ass Bass—I love it! The name suits him to a T! Oh, Lizzie, how I've missed you." Instantly, her worried thoughts returned, and her tone turned serious. "I guess I am a bit touchy. I was so sure all of this would all be resolved by now. Maybe it's best if we think positive. Dumb-ass Bass is probably too dumb to keep track of the days."

"People like him don't forget things like that. I bet he was bullied as a kid, and now he gets his kicks from pushing people like us around. It's a power thing. He'll be here—you can count on it," Lizzie said.

"You know, you're exactly right. He does have that bully attitude. He'll be here with bells on," Addie said, making a sour face like she'd just bit into a lemon.

"At least there's been no sighting of Eddie this morning, not yet anyway. Having him around is creepy. I wish we knew what he's really up to and what he knows," Lizzie said.

"We're sure to find out sooner or later. I think I can get him talking, but I still think until we know what's going on with him, you and the children should stay out of sight. We don't know what he's capable of, and we're better off safe than sorry. By the way, how are those booby traps coming along?" Addie said.

"I've been working on my strategy...the devil's in the details." Lizzie held up two fingers over the back of her head and gave her sister a wink.

"That sounds ominous. I can't wait to see what you dream up in that twisted mind of yours," Addie said, returning the wink.

****

It was just after eight o'clock when Addie and Lizzie looked out and saw the car from hell pull to the front of the house. Mr. Bass, carrying his worn black briefcase, got out and made his way to the front door. His knock, which was more of a pound, made the hairs on their arms stand straight up.

Addie opened the door just as his fist was raised to pound again. Flapping his arms to regain his balance he looked like an injured bird attempting to take flight. The sisters cast sideways glances at each other as they witnessed the comical scene. His usual pasty complexion had turned blood red. The sisters stood in the doorway giving him quizzical looks.

Shaking off the embarrassing incident, he took off his hat, revealing his greasy, bald head. He stammered out a cheeky greeting. "Mrs. Kent, Mrs. Thornhill, fine day, isn't it?"

His remark stung—today was anything but fine. With their bodies so close, Addie actually felt the anger building up in her sister. "Mr. Bass, we weren't expecting you so soon," Addie said. She felt the air grow thick around them.

"The early bird gets the worm, you know," he said, his wide grin showing his large, yellowed teeth.

The man had no filter—his words again hit a nerve—he might be a bird, but Jessie was no worm. The sisters glared at him.

"Now, where's my little girl?"

Bass had just ventured into very dangerous territory. Lizzie took a step toward him. Through blazing eyes and gritted teeth, she spoke, placing emphasis on every word, "Don't you dare refer to my daughter as your little girl—you dumb-ass."

Mr. Bass's head jerked back, his eyes popped open.

Lizzie's spontaneous remark took Addie by complete surprise. She covered her mouth to conceal her amusement. *Only Lizzie.*

Mr. Bass, having somewhat recovered from the insult, glared at Lizzie through his now pinched, beady black eyes. "Now, now, missy, there's no need for name calling. I'm just doing my job. Now, if you'll just bring the child here, we can be on our way. I've arranged for her teacher to have her desk and books ready—she can begin classes as soon as we arrive."

"Now, get this, mister," Lizzie said through clenched teeth, her anger obviously reaching a boiling point. "You will not be taking my daughter anywhere, you got that? I don't care what papers you have in that black case—you can take them and …."

Addie squeezed firmly on Lizzie's hand. She paid her no mind—her blazing eyes remained locked on Bass. If looks could kill—he'd be dead.

Mr. Bass nervously shifted his weight from one foot to the other. His demeanor told them that he wasn't going to let them get the best of him. He obviously considered himself a powerful man with a powerful position. Still standing in the doorway, he fumbled awkwardly to open his briefcase. He had not been invited inside or offered a seat.

Addie witnessed his awkwardness with a tinge of pity— tiny though it was. Apologizing for her poor manners, she ushered Mr. Bass into the kitchen and offered him a seat at the table. The repercussions of not cooperating with the law would only bring more trouble their way—they already had more than they could handle.

Mr. Bass took his seat and straightened his posture—his jaw set firm. Opening his briefcase, he pulled out the one-page document. "If you could just sign right here, Mrs. Thornhill," he said pointing his finger to a line at the bottom of the page, "then we'll be on our way."

By now, he knew better than to make specific reference to Jessie, but clearly that was what he meant. Lizzie glared at him with contempt.

"It's all legal, I can assure you. Your signature is all that's required," he said flatly.

Mr. Bass fidgeted in his seat. His eagerness to get the deed done and leave quickly was apparent. He couldn't leave fast enough to suit Lizzie, but she darn sure wasn't going to sign something she hadn't read.

Addie looked at Lizzie. Seeing that she was about to erupt again, she interjected, "Mr. Bass, it's highly unlikely that my sister is going to sign anything without reading it first."

Rising from her chair, Addie stepped to the counter, poured a steaming cup of coffee into a mug, and set it on the table in front of him. "Here, please enjoy some coffee while Lizzie and I look over this *legal* document."

Addie was actually stalling. She hadn't given up on Lester coming through for them. If he had been unsuccessful, he would have gotten word to her—she had no doubt. The document was riddled with legal jargon that was hard for a layperson to comprehend. Addie had no interest in what it said. She was more interested in seeing Lester come through the door.

Seated side by side, their heads bent over the document, Addie and Lizzie looked like two students studying for an exam. Mr. Bass continued to squirm in his seat while impatiently drumming his long, yellowed fingernails on the table.

"If you don't mind—I need to be going. Can we speed this up?" he said impatiently.

Neither of them responded or looked up, giving the impression that they were deeply engrossed. Under the table, the two elbowed each other relishing in the fact that, for now, the ball was in their court. They were thoroughly enjoying the game.

An hour passed and the two of them were still pouring over the document, occasionally asking Mr. Bass to interpret some term or other, that neither of them cared a hoot about. Mr. Bass gave his answers through tightly clenched teeth, which caused the sisters to clasp their fingers over their lips to hide their amused grins.

In a voice riddled with annoyance, he said, "Ladies, I simply must be going. You've had ample time to review every word," he emphasized word. "Now, if you would please sign here." He emphasized the word here and pushed his index finger hard on the designated line.

Lizzie rose from the table. With both hands to her mouth, she mumbled, "Excuse me, I'm going to be sick." She ran to the bathroom and closed the door, leaving Mr. Bass with a stunned and defeated look on his face.

"Perhaps you should come back later this afternoon," suggested Addie. "My sister is still suffering from the remains of that awful stomach virus. Not to worry though, this morning her fever is down considerably."

Mr. Bass must have forgotten all about Lizzie's virus. He suddenly turned white as a sheet, excused himself, and made a hasty beeline for the door.

Turning the doorknob, he looked back and said in a huff. "I expect Mrs. Thornhill will be feeling up to signing the document when I return. Rest assured—I will return, and the document will be signed."

"I hate that you had to make the trip all the way out here for nothing," Addie said, catching up with him at the door. When he didn't reply, she threw up her hand. "Toodeloo. Have a nice day."

Closing the door, Addie leaned against it. Lizzie appeared at her side. They held each other in a tight embrace, then broke out in hysterical laughter, finally falling into an exhausted heap on the floor.

"You deserve an Academy Award for that performance, Sis," Addie said. "Just when I was sure we had stalled all we could, your quick thinking bought us some time. Glory be!"

Lizzie took a bow. "Truthfully, just being in that repulsive man's presence made me want to throw up. That's when the idea struck me. Thank heavens he fell for it. I was seriously considering doing him bodily harm. If he had laid just one of his disgusting fingers on Jessie, I swear I would have!"

"Well, I'm glad it didn't come to that. It couldn't have worked out better if we had planned it. I'm so proud of you!" Addie said, giving her sister a high five.

"I sure did get a charge out of it. From here on out, if anybody wants to mess with us—I'm ready to take them on," Lizzie said, with a gleam in her eyes.

"I pity the person who tries," Addie said with a laugh. "Sounds like the old Lizzie is back—I've sure missed her."

****

Over breakfast, the two sisters giggled and reminisced over their childhood years, and all the fun they'd had together. They were making up for lost years.

With her spirits soaring high, Lizzie took Jessie's hand, turned on the radio and tuned it to a station playing a jivey pop song. As was one of the things she and Jessie loved to do, when Jim Bob wasn't around, they began dancing around the kitchen. When Addie didn't join in, Jessie took her by the hand and pulled her into the act. Jessie's laughter was contagious and soon the air filled with the most delightful sounds.

In that moment, Addie realized how mundane her life had been those years without her twin. Lizzie's gradual return to her old self was proof that her fire could never be extinguished. She'd always been the spark that gave life to her family—she was reigniting it once again.

****

Later that morning, Addie was in the yard dousing the vine with a double dose of The Formula, when she spied Lester coming around the corner of the house. Right away, she noticed his grim expression. "Uh-oh, must be bad news," she said.

Accustomed to the warmth of the sun, Addie welcomed it, but Lester, in his three-piece suit, wasn't faring as well. Noticing the beads of sweat gathering at his hairline and the way he was loosening his tie, she said, "Let's go inside. I'll fix us a nice glass of iced tea."

Lester was never one to turn down Addie's sweet tea. He took his usual place at the kitchen table and gazed blankly at the wall in front of him. His poker face wasn't giving her the slightest hint of what was on his mind, but his initial expression had made it clear that the news wasn't good.

Taking two glasses from the cabinet, Addie reached for the third but instead closed the door. She pushed aside her thought to involve Lizzie, knowing that her sister was all too likely to have a come-apart and take out her frustrations on poor Lester. *No, better if I hear the bad news first.*

Lester turned his attention to Addie, and noticed she had filled only two glasses. "I think it would be best if I relay this news to Lizzie as well," he said.

"Are you sure about that? Lizzie has a tendency to lash out without thinking, and I'd rather spare you that."

"I'm a tough old bird. I can take whatever she slings at me."

"Don't say I didn't warn you," Addie said.

Addie found Lizzie in the process of laying Lillie down in her crib for her morning nap. "Hey, Hon," Addie said in a hushed tone. "Lester's in the kitchen with news from the school board. He's not showing his hand, but from what I can tell, I think you should be prepared for bad news."

Moments later, the two entered the kitchen—Lizzie biting her bottom lip, Addie wringing her hands—their eyes locked on Lester's serious expression.

Lester stood, his good Southern manners ever-present, as the sisters took their seats. He brushed his hands down his pant legs before sitting again.

With eyes still locked on him, he remained silent—the tension grew. Opening his briefcase, he took out a file folder and riffled through the dozens of pages it held. This had been a hard-fought battle. He was good at taking his time, drawing out a final decision in dramatic fashion as his clients waited anxiously to learn of the outcome.

"Ah, here it is," he said. He pulled out a document consisting of multiple sheets of paper that had been stapled together and placed it on the table in front of him. He took a sip of tea, put on his reading glasses, then took them off again and wiped vigorously at a nonexistent smudge.

Lizzie's brows furrowed, her get-on-with-it look shot daggers at him.

Sighing deeply and shaking his head, he began reading it aloud.

"Dear Mrs. Thornhill,

Regarding the petition filed by your attorney, Mr. Lester Cobb, our board has given your request careful consideration. Your request for your school-age child to remain under your guidance and personal instruction has been viewed as highly abnormal..."

Lester paused, rubbing his forehead, his eyes lifting to study their reactions.

Pinched faces showed their disappointment.

"Hum, now where was I?" Lester said.

"Abnormal..." Lizzie said, her aggravation showing in her tone.

"Ah, yes," he said, continuing to read. "Has been viewed as highly abnormal and would be unacceptable under normal circumstances. However, due to Mr. Cobb's very thorough evaluation of the child's fragile emotional state, we have made an exception in her case with the following requirements that we insist be followed to the letter: ...."

"You scoundrel!" Lizzie sprang from her chair, wrapping both arms around Lester's neck and planting a grateful kiss on his cheek. "You really had me going!"

Smiling broadly, he said, "I couldn't resist. I hope you'll forgive me for having a little fun at your expense."

"I do, but I'll let you in on a little secret—I'd have done the same thing. I have to say, though, a couple of times I wanted to strangle you for making us sweat. The suspense was killing me!" Lizzie said.

"It was brutal!" Addie said, shaking her head. "So, it's a done deal?"

"Yes, once Lizzie's signature is on this document—the deal is done," Lester said. "Like the letter says... here you can read it for yourself," he said, handing the paper across the table to Lizzie. "There are some rather strict requirements you must agree to. It will also require a big commitment on your part."

"I'll agree to anything as long as Jessie can stay here with us," she said, taking the pen and scrolling her name across the dotted line. "What do I owe you? I don't have any money, but I can iron and mend like nobody's business," Lizzie said, her eyes glistening with tears of gratitude.

"Addie and I have an understanding. Now you and I should have one, too. We don't mention pay—ever. Addie is my longest and dearest friend, and friends do for friends. You are her sister, so that makes you part of our little clan—got it?" Lester said.

"Got it," Lizzie said. "Then I'll just say thank you from the very bottom of my heart. I'll never forget what you've done for us."

Lizzie kissed Lester on the cheek again and reached to take Addie's hand. She noticed that her sister's touch stiffened. She shook her head, dismissing her crazy notion.

"That's pay enough," Lester said. "Now, let me get this back to the committee before they change their minds."

"They could do that—change their minds?" Lizzie said, her body stiffening.

"Well, technically, no, it's all but set in stone, but you never know what measures Bass is willing to take when his authority has been threatened. At any rate, you won't be bothered by any future visits from him—I'll see to that," Lester said.

Addie caught sight of Lizzie's furrowed brows and narrowed eyes. She knew that look all too well. Her sister wasn't going for it.

"No, sir! I want to see him squirm," she said. "Nothing would please me more than to wave this paper in that disgusting little man's face and give him a dose of his own medicine. Seeing him leave without my daughter in his grubby grasp..."

Addie drew close to her sister and in a slightly lecturing tone said, "Okay, sweetie, we get the picture. Let's spare Lester our wicked thoughts, and let him get back to his paying clients. We've taken enough of his time."

"Uh, yes, of course," Lizzie's cheeks flushed crimson red. "You have been so kind, and here I am, carrying on like a mad woman." She squeezed his hand, her words becoming soft and sincere. "I truly couldn't be more grateful for what you've done for Jessie."

"It's my pleasure to be of assistance to you ladies. I want to hear all the details of this afternoon's meeting—should be entertaining, to say the least," Lester said, smiling broadly.

Addie took Lester's hand and walked him to the door. Looking deep into his eyes, she said, "Dear, sweet Lester, how on earth do I deserve a friend like you? Thank you from the very depths of my heart!"

"Anything for you," he said, in a wistful tone.

Before wrapping her arms around him, her lips briefly touched his. When she pulled away she gazed into his glistening eyes. "I love you with every ounce of my being. You'll always be my dearest and best friend." Addie said softly.

Lester only nodded and squeezed her hand.

She watched him as he slowly made his way to his car, his hands in his pockets, his head lowered.

What she had said was true: she loved him dearly—he would always have a special place in her heart.

****

Lizzie sat at the kitchen table, carefully studying the papers that Lester had left for her. The requirements weren't unreasonable, but they would require a lot of her time and Jessie's, too. Included was a lesson plan for each day. At the end of each week, she was to fill out a progress report and return it to the school board. There was only one hitch, if Jessie wasn't progressing to the point of the other students in her grade level, they would have the right to revoke their decision and require her to attend in-person classes.

She closed her eyes and shook her head. She had been such a poor student, never taking her classes seriously, and now she was expected to be a teacher; the thought of it sent shivers down her spine. For Jessie's sake, she had to get into the right mindset. She could do this, she told herself. She would learn right along with Jessie, and of course, she had Addie to encourage her and help in whatever way she was needed.

What a godsend Addie had been. She had no excuse for the despicable way she had treated her—her one and only sister—her twin. For Addie to have put their differences aside and rush to her aid was an act of genuine love. She lowered her head and sighed, wondering if her regrets would ever leave her—or would they weigh her down for the rest of her life.

Wrestling with her thoughts, she managed to put aside the unpleasant ones, deciding instead to focus on the good and caring people in her life.

When Addie came in from outside, Lizzie gave her a warm smile. "This isn't going to be easy, but it's wonderful news. I can't begin to tell you how grateful I am. Without you and Lester, what on earth would I do, and where on earth would I be now?"

"Sweetheart, all of this is just meant to be, and nobody does it alone. It takes a village, you know," Addie said.

"I'm learning that the hard way." She took Addie's hand in hers and held it tightly. "I want to make you a promise right here and now. I will never, ever let another man or anyone else come between you and me," Lizzie said, fighting back tears. She held up her pinky finger, and Addie wrapped hers around it like they had done many times in their youth. "Pinky promise," Lizzie said.

"Ditto that," Addie said with a grin. "Now, let's go give your sweet daughter the good news."

Jessie had been in her studio painting a picture of the green ivy that twined around the balcony railing. When her mother called to her, she bounded down the stairs and threw her arms around her. Tears of joy ran in green streaks down her face. "Oh, Mama! Isn't it great? When will I get my books?"

"Aren't you the little eavesdropper?" Lizzie said, smiling as she wiped away her green tears. "Before you get your books, you'll have to take a test to determine your grade level. Once that's been decided, we'll get the proper books and study sheets for your grade. We're to pick up the test at the school this afternoon."

Already making her way up the stairs with Copper on her heels, Jessie said, "I'm going to get my desk ready right now."

When she was out of ear range, Addie said, "I hope she'll still love the idea once she gets started. It appears it's going to require a whole lot of work."

"Believe me, she will. That child's like a sponge. She'll soak up every morsel and want more. It's me you need to worry about; I just hope I can keep up with her," Lizzie said, biting her nail.

"You'll both do fine, I have no doubt, but if you need me at any time, you know I'm right here for both of you," Addie said.

"I'm counting on that," Lizzie said, giving Addie's hand a quick squeeze.

Chapter 20

Thanks to Lester, the day they had been dreading had turned into a day of jubilation. Having no sightings of Eddie only added to their elation.

The results of their petition had them all in a good mood, especially Jessie. Addie smiled recalling the happy green tears that had streamed down her niece's sweet face upon hearing Lester's good news. All morning the child had been like a worm in hot ashes, her usual reserved behavior—gone out the window.

Jessie peeked around the door to Addie's bathroom where she was tugging her brush through her always unruly hair. "Aunt Addie, are you leaving soon—I can help you get ready—I'll brush your hair," Jessie said, all in one breath while hopping around on one foot.

A broad grin crossed Addie's face. It warmed her heart to see Jessie so excited over school work—of all things. "I could use some help with this crazy hair of mine." She knelt to Jessie's level and handed her the brush.

Starting at her crown, Jessie gently pulled the brush through the tangles. "You have pretty hair, Mama does, too, but not the same as yours. Yours is thick and curly. Mama has lots of hair, too, but hers is really straight," she said, while carefully pulling the brush through one section of hair at a time.

"You've done this before—I can tell," Addie said.

"Mama lets me brush hers, she says it makes her feel good all over."

"Well, she's right about that, I don't know when I've felt this relaxed." Closing her eyes, she felt the tension in her body melt away—so relaxed that she nodded off.

Jessie placed the brush on the vanity and said in a soft voice, "Do you want me to tie it back the way you usually wear it?"

Slowly coming out of her stupor, Addie stood and gazed into the mirror. The image looking back at her appeared so much younger. She did a double take. The tangled mess she had grown accustomed to seeing had been replaced by beautiful bouncy waves and loose curls. She bent and wrapped her arms around her tiny niece who never ceased to amaze her. "No, honey, I love it just like this. I'd forgotten my hair could look so good. From now on you've got a job," she said, with a twinkle in her eye.

The smile on Jessie's face went from ear to ear.

****

A short time later Addie arrived at Oakmont Elementary and pulled her truck into a parking space. She sat behind the wheel for several minutes, her gaze locked on the scene before her as cherished memories flooded back into her mind. *It looks exactly as I remember.*

The silvery Spanish moss still draped from the ancient live oaks, and children still took turns on the rope swings that hung from their massive branches. The same gay laughter filled the air as the children played the same games of her childhood: hopscotch, hide and seek, and kick-the-ball. She sighed deeply, realizing that Jessie wouldn't have this experience. *She'll be in a better place with people who love her. Besides, Magnolia Place is every bit as lovely,* she proudly reminded herself.

Finally, emerging from the truck, she strolled down the long walk leading to the impressive double doors. Once inside, she was taken aback by the transformation it had undergone. Brightly colored murals adorned every wall with illustrations of children playing gaily on the expansive lawn. The scenes were refreshing and for sure, a far cry from the stark white walls that she remembered.

She couldn't pull her eyes away from the masterful way the artist had duplicated the scenes she had just witnessed out on the lawn. It seemed as though the outside and the inside were fused together. She stood spellbound, amazed at how realistic it appeared. The silvery moss, the children's faces, the sky, and the lofty clouds—everything so perfectly rendered. The only thing missing was the joyful voices of the children.

A pecking noise caused her to turn her attention from the paintings and toward the sound. The pecking sound had come from behind the closed door with the word *Office* painted on the glass.

She tapped lightly on the door, stepped inside, and walked up to the long counter. The secretary, who had her back to her, was pecking away at the typewriter, obviously totally engrossed in her work. When she didn't look up, Addie cleared her throat.

Pollyanna Stroud, her hands still on the keys, slightly turned her head to gaze at Addie. "Oh my gosh, how long have you been standing there? I was so caught up in this letter that I didn't hear you come in. Please forgive me. How in the world are you, Addie?"

Addie waved her off. "Only a couple of minutes. If I had known it was you, Polly, I wouldn't have minded interrupting," she said with a laugh. "How are things with you?"

"I'll be better when your vegetables come in. My mouth waters just thinking about them. I found a new squash recipe in the Ladies' Home Journal; I'm itching to try it," Pollyanna said.

"Believe it or not, I've already been working in my garden. I've already begun to get the seeds started," Addie said.

"Well, I know you didn't come here just to talk about vegetables," Pollyanna said, with a questioning look on her face.

"You know I can go on forever when it comes to gardening, but actually, I'm here on an important mission. I came to pick up some test sheets for my niece. I think one of the teachers is expecting me," Addie said.

"Oh, yes. That would be Miss Brighton. I'll walk you to her room; heaven knows I could use a break."

She led Addie down the brightly colored hallway, flanked on either side by short lockers, and stopped when they got to Miss Brighton's classroom.

Standing in the doorway, Addie gazed around the cheery room that was sure to be the delight of any child. In one corner were shelves filled with books, and on the floor was a large rug where, she assumed, the children sat and listened to the teacher read to them. In another corner was a child-size kitchen with miniature cookware and brightly colored dishes. In the center of the room was a long table with chairs around it, obviously where learning took place. *Jessie would love this room*. The thought tugged at her heart.

A pretty young woman, who she estimated to be about her own age, stood and came around the corner of her desk to greet them.

"Please come in," the teacher said warmly.

She was tall and willowy, with wavy blond hair that fell to the middle of her back. Her clear blue eyes and sweet voice told of her gentle nature.

"Miss Brighton, this is Addie Kent. She's here to pick up some materials for her niece. By the way, if you haven't been to her vegetable stand, you've been missing out. I don't mean to rush off, but I promised Mr. Brown that I'd have this letter finished today—he'll have my head if I don't get back to it. Nice to see you, Addie," Polly said, rushing out the door.

Addie smiled to herself. Polly had never been much for small talk—she liked to keep it short and sweet. "Thank you, Polly. Nice to see you, too," Addie said.

After Pollyanna left the room, Miss Brighton stepped close to Addie and extended her hand. "Mrs. Kent, it's a pleasure to meet you," she said, her eyes showing her sincerity.

Addie smiled and shook her hand. "The pleasure is mine. I assume by Polly's remark about my stand that you're new to Beau Ridge."

"I moved here last fall, at the start of the school year. I fell head over heels in love with South Carolina years ago when my family visited the state one summer. The minute I learned of a teaching position at this school, I applied and the rest is history; I haven't regretted a single day. Now that I know about your stand, I have something to look forward to—I'm absolutely passionate about tomatoes."

"You've never had a tomato until you've tasted my heirloom Brandywines," Addie said with a wink. "Stop by and I'll treat you to some. I hope you're an early riser; folks come early, and those are the first to go."

"You're making me wish I had one right now. I'll be counting the days, but I may have to set my alarm clock; I have a tendency to sleep late in the summer," Miss Brighton said, with a cheerful laugh.

"Just so you know, I set up my stand starting in late April when my garden produces scallions, radishes, carrots, cabbage and lettuce. After that, I'll be adding other vegetables as they come in. And, if you like flowers, I'll have a lovely variety of them as well."

"I simply can't wait!" she said enthusiastically. She shook her head. "Where are my manners?" She pointed to a chair beside her desk. "Please have a seat."

Addie positioned herself on the chair as Miss Brighton took her seat behind her desk. Smiling warmly at the teacher, she started the conversation. "I really appreciate you taking the time to meet with me. First, I want you to know how eager my niece is to begin her studies. This is certainly an enticing environment and under normal circumstances, it would be the perfect place for her; I attended school here myself and know how special it is. But Jessie, although an exceptionally bright child, isn't like other children. She is a pure delight, but it pains me to say, her emotional state is fragile. You can be certain that her mother and I carefully considered every aspect before concluding that homeschooling is in her best interest."

"Of course, I understand completely. Homeschooling isn't a common path for students in our school system; in fact, Jessie is the first since I've been teaching here. It's quite an undertaking for a parent, but it can also be a rewarding experience for both parent and child—if it doesn't overwhelm. Of course, the option of in-person classes would be available for her at any time, if things should change," Miss Brighton said.

"Oh yes, certainly. We want only what's best for Jessie, and right now, I can assure you—this is the better option," Addie said.

"I don't mean to pry, but I gather that Jessie has had an unpleasant childhood; I understand she was abused by her father. Being the victim of abuse is never a healthy situation for a child, or anyone for that matter. So, the father is out of the picture?" Miss Brighton said.

Addie waited a few seconds before responding while she pondered why the teacher would be delving into such personal matters. *Could there be a legitimate reason for her asking?* Then it occurred to her. *If the father was still around, Jessie would be better off at school than having no relief from a hostile environment.* "I can assure you, he is completely out of the picture," Addie said emphatically.

"A loving home is what Jessie will benefit from the most, and it appears to me that she will have that with you," Miss Brighton said.

"That's very kind of you to say, and yes, she's adjusting to her new home amazingly well. She stole my heart from day one and continues to do so every day. She's a remarkable child. Kindhearted, loving, inquisitive, smart, and the sweetest child I've ever known."

"She sounds amazing. I hope I'll have the opportunity to meet her sometime," Miss Brighton said earnestly. "Now, let's see about those test sheets." She picked up an envelope from her desk and handed it to Addie. "Instructions are inside, but if I can be of any help at all, please don't hesitate to contact me. The children leave at noon, but I'm here until three every weekday. Oh, and please feel free to call me at home anytime."

She was writing the number on a piece of paper, and Addie almost stopped her but instead accepted it with a smile. "Thank you," she said, slipping the paper into her purse. "I can't begin to tell you how much I appreciate your kindness and your concern for Jessie's well-being. We had to do battle with the school board to get to this point, but I'm grateful that everything has worked out so well," she said.

Miss Brighton stood and extended her hand to Addie. "Good luck, and don't forget I'm here if you need me. You'll be seeing me at your stand. By the way, I love your hair. If you don't mind, I'd love to know the name of your hairdresser."

Addie touched a strand of her hair and a broad smile crossed her face. "I don't mind in the least. Her name is Jessie Thornhill," she said with a gleam in her eye. "Every day she surprises me with her unselfish gifts of love."

She took Miss Brighton's hand, thanked her warmly, then walked back toward the entrance. Before leaving the building, she tapped on the glass door and waved at Polly, who turned her head, gave Addie a quick wave and went back to pecking at the typewriter keys.

Once outside, Addie found the front lawn deserted of children and voices. She walked slowly back to her truck, taking in the tranquil beauty of the campus. Suddenly, she stopped dead in her tracks. Her body went rigid. Her vision blurred, and a shrill noise rang in her ears. She dropped her purse and the envelope and placed her hands over her ears. Standing still, she shivered violently. Moments later, the vision appeared. She saw a man wearing a red baseball cap with the letter A on the front of it. There was a house—her house. The man was speaking to someone, a young girl whose face was hidden from her. The girl turned her head; there was no mistaking her—it was Jessie.

She tensed, feeling the anger that was building inside her. "Leave her alone," Addie shouted. She could feel the blood pulsing in her temples. She rubbed her eyes in a desperate attempt to remove the vision from her sight. She had to find her truck, but her surroundings were out of focus. The man, the stalker, the convict, was at her house—with Jessie! Her mind screamed—***get to her, now!***

Miss Brighton emerged from the building headed to her car when she saw Addie standing in the walkway ahead of her. Something about her wasn't right. She ran to her side and guided her to a nearby bench. Alarmed by the faraway look on Addie's face, she said, "Mrs. Kent, are you alright?"

Addie stared blankly at her. Miss Brighton placed both hands on Addie's shoulders and shook them gently. When she didn't react, she shook more vigorously. "Mrs. Kent, is something wrong? Please tell me how I can help," she pleaded.

Addie cocked her head, a faint voice was calling her name. She tried to bring the face into focus. She blinked, then blinked again. Miss Brighton continued to shake her and call her name. As her vision began to clear, the teacher's face appeared, shrouded in a hazy fog.

Addie didn't respond, but the blank stare that had startled the teacher was gone, and her eyes appeared more normal.

"You gave me a fright," Miss Brighton said, tapping her hand over her heart. She bent, picked up the purse and the envelope and handed them to Addie.

"I have to go!" Addie said absently. She stood unsteadily and took a few shaky steps in the direction of her truck.

"I don't think you should drive–let me–"

Miss Brighton's unfinished sentence didn't reach Addie's ears. In that instant she fled toward her truck. When she reached it, she got in and sped away, leaving Miss Brighton shaking her head in bewilderment.

Chapter 21

The anticipation of being a real student had Jessie's heart skipping beats. Since she was going to be a schoolgirl, she wanted to dress like one. She put on the only dress she owned, brushed her long strawberry blond hair until it shone like silk and tied a ribbon into a loopy bow on top of her head. Looking in the mirror, she smiled seeing the studious-looking girl staring back at her.

"I'm going to be a real, true student, Copper!" she said, clapping her hands. She bent down and wrapped her arms around his neck, his tail thumping happily on the floor. Rising, she flinched. "It still hurts a little," she said, rubbing her hand over her wounded leg. "That's our secret, right?" She looked at Copper, he thumped his tail. "Good boy."

While she anxiously awaited her aunt's return, she used her boundless energy to convert her studio into a classroom. She gathered up her paints and brushes that filled the desktop and placed them neatly in a box. With the desk cleared, she had room for the items Addie had bought her. She placed the writing tablet directly in the center and the chunky-sized pencil to the left of it. In its usual spot at the back left corner, she placed her most cherished possession— her diary. On the opposite corner were the only two books she owned: *Charlotte's Web* and *The Secret Garden,* both treasured gifts from Mr. Lester.

Copper, as usual, lay comfortably on the floor, watching Jessie's every move as she scurried about. When her work was done, she returned her gaze to Copper, who looked up at her with his big sad eyes and moaned.

"Oh, I know what you want," Jessie said, patting his head. She began to sing some silly made-up song, and Copper moaned along to the tune. Abruptly, she stopped singing. "Shhh," she whispered.

Copper's ears perked up. Jessie turned her ear toward the window.

"Hey, little girl. Are you up there?" It was a man's voice. Stepping closer to the window, she peered out. It was him—the man in the red hat. He was standing right in front of the house and looking up at her window. She turned to leave, to tell her mother like she'd promised, but the man called out again.

"Please don't go. I just want to talk to you for a minute," the man said.

Jessie opened the window and leaned out. "What do you want to talk about?" Jessie said.

"I thought you and your dog could come out. I bet you've got some stories you could tell me about him," he said, knowing this was lame, but it was all he could come up with on the spot.

"He's not allowed outside," Jessie said.

"You can hold his leash so that he won't run off. Wouldn't that be okay?" Eddie said.

"Well, I guess that'll be okay. I'll ask my Mama," Jessie said.

That was the last thing he wanted; he had to think of something—quick. "Oh, I bet your mother is busy. I think she'd say it's okay," he said.

"Well, she is feeding baby Lillie," Jessie said.

He smiled slyly. Unknowingly, she had just given him a large piece of the puzzle—baby Lillie. All the pieces were coming together. The dog, the baby, everything except Jim Bob. He felt it in his bones—he was getting closer to solving the whole thing if he just played his cards right.

"In that case, you really shouldn't bother her. You and your puppy come on down. I like dogs, and I'd really like to hear your stories."

"Well, okay." She clipped Copper's leash to his collar and started down the stairs. Just as she reached the front door, she heard the sound of screeching brakes and flying gravel. She froze in her tracks. The next thing she heard was her aunt's loud, furious voice.

Arms swinging, fists clenched, Addie stomped angrily toward Eddie. "You leave my property this instant, or I'm calling the police," Addie threatened.

Eddie didn't flinch a muscle, but grinned devilishly, amused by her empty threat. "Don't get your dander up," he said casually. "I don't mean any harm."

"The heck you don't!" Addie said, her voice rising several decibels. "Get off my property!"

Eddie grimaced. His plan to entice the girl was working nicely until this raging witch showed up and spoiled it all. "Okay, okay, I'll go; no need to get so excited."

"Excited, you think I'm excited? You haven't seen excited yet!" Addie said, the veins in her temples pulsing, her face red with rage. "I'll have you put in jail if you even think about talking to that child again."

How did she know he'd been talking to the girl? This place and its occupants have something weird going on, but if she thinks she's getting rid of ole Eddie with her empty threats—she's got another thing coming. "Alright, alright, I'm leaving your property, but I'm not leaving town. I know you have my dog, and I intend to get him back. If I were you, I'd sleep with one eye open. Have a nice day, Ma'am." He tipped his hat to her in a gentlemanly fashion and slowly sauntered down the lane, hands in his pockets, whistling a merry tune.

The nerve of him! You'd think he was on an afternoon stroll in the park. She kept an eye on him until he was out of sight, then turned and went inside, slamming the door behind her. *That man is infuriating! He knows I can't go to the police. But using unscrupulous tactics to entice a helpless child was going too far—and now he's threatening us. We have to find a way to get rid of him—before things get out of hand.*

****

Later that night, when the children were tucked in their beds and fast asleep, Addie and Lizzie sat side by side, propped against the headboard of Addie's bed. The two were brainstorming how to rid their lives of Eddie. He had made it clear that he wasn't going anywhere until he found the dog. The dog that he hoped would find his brother's body, the dog that had become Jessie's best friend, the dog that belonged to neither of them. What a tangled mess they found themselves in.

Eddie had made a very disturbing threat. Whether he would actually break into the house at night was perhaps doubtful, but they couldn't take his threat lightly. They had to be prepared for anything.

Lizzie had come through with her booby traps—the whole house was an obstacle course. Tin cans were stacked at the front and back doors. Spoons dangled from strings in doorways, rugs had been upturned, and the furniture had been rearranged as stumbling blocks, all of which were meant to alert them of an intruder.

The room was quiet as the two racked their brains for a means of protecting themselves should Eddie show up in the dead of night. Suddenly, Lizzie clapped her hands, startling Addie so much that she fell halfway out of bed.

"I've got it! Copper and bats!" Lizzie said excitedly.

Addie scrambled back onto the bed and glared at Lizzie. "You scared me to death! What are you talking about?"

"Copper! He's our best defense—he'll protect us. And we need baseball bats. Two women swinging bats around would put the fear in any man," Lizzie said, her eyes shining devilishly.

"I'm not sure how much we can depend on Copper. I worry he might be glad to see ole Eddie," Addie said with a chuckle.

"It's a matter of loyalty," Lizzie said. "I have no doubt he'd tear into anybody who tried to mess with Jessie. And, for the next couple of days, I think we should all sleep in the same room. None of us should be alone if our worst fears are realized."

Obviously, Lizzie had given their predicament careful thought. It was all about survival, a lesson she'd learned the hard way. "Good thinking, Sis. The traps you've set are ingenious, and hopefully, Copper will come through for us if Eddie should break in—at least we won't be sitting ducks. And I love the bat idea; I'll round some up," Addie said, giving Lizzie a high five.

"I also have another idea. What if we get another dog, one that we can take outside that won't be attracted to the ivy and a different color than Copper? You told him you have a dog, and we know he'll be back here snooping around. We just make sure he sees this dog. It might just take him off our trail."

"Lizzie, I love the way you think! That's an excellent idea! My neighbor, Mr. McFarland, always has more dogs than he knows what to do with. He's offered to give me one on many occasions. I'll go see him tomorrow."

Satisfied that they had a good plan and were about to turn in for the night, Addie was reminded of their most troublesome problem. "What about the body? Even if Eddie gives up on the dog, he won't give up on finding Jim Bob. What do we do about that?" she said, yawning.

"Jim Bob!" Lizzie grumbled. "Even in death—he's nothing but trouble." She shook her head and released a long heavy sigh. "This train is on a never-ending track."

Chapter 22

The persistent rumbling noises in Eddie's stomach were growing louder, a reminder that he hadn't eaten a bite all day. He splashed some water on his face and ran a comb through his hair. Before leaving his room, he hung the *Do Not Disturb* sign on the door. He'd been trained to do his own cleaning—he preferred it that way.

The bell over the door jingled as he entered the diner. A young girl instantly appeared holding a menu to her chest. "This way, sir," she said, leading him to a table by the window.

"If you don't mind, I prefer a booth," Eddie said, pointing out the one in the back corner.

"Hiding out, huh?" she said, nudging him with her elbow.

"You could say that," he said dryly.

She laid the menu on the table. "I'll give you a few minutes to look it over, hon."

"Just give me a steak. Whatever you recommend will be fine. Make it well done, with some fries and water, please." He handed her the menu that he hadn't bothered to open.

Alone in the dark corner with his shoulders slumped and his eyes cast downward, he brooded over the episode he had just experienced with the witch sister. The show he'd put on for her as he left her property was the total opposite of his true feelings. On the drive back to town, he'd grown more and more depressed thinking about his continual defeats. How she had known that he'd been talking to the little girl had him believing she possessed some kind of sixth sense. He was even starting to second-guess his suspicions. *Could it be he had been barking up the wrong tree? That the dog and Jim Bob weren't on her property?*

Vigorously, he shook his head then slammed his fist on the table. *That witchy woman is messing with my mind. I have to get back on track, trust my instincts, and start playing hardball.* "We'll see who wins at this game!" Eddie said. His loud voice reverberated through the room.

He took a quick look around to see if anybody had heard his outburst and think that he had lost his mind—a thought that had recently crossed his own. Luckily, except for one other customer, who appeared oblivious, the place was empty. He assumed the waitress was on break. He hadn't seen her since she brought his food.

With his face set in a deep scowl, he drummed his fingers on the tabletop while considering other measures he could take. Then it occurred to him that if he was going to get anywhere near the dog, there was only one way to do it—he had to get inside that house.

He took his fork and stabbed the tough meat on his plate. It felt good. He stabbed it again and again and again. He was so caught up in his assault on the steak that he didn't notice the waitress standing over him.

"Sir!" she said, her voice trembling. "Are you alright?"

Suddenly, realizing he was in a public place and making a spectacle of himself, he came up with a quick excuse. "My dad taught me that little trick for tenderizing a tough piece of meat—works every time. I must admit it is a little extreme. Sorry if I alarmed you, ma'am," Eddie said.

"Sure," she said, keeping her distance. "I'll be happy to get you another steak," she offered, halfheartedly.

"That's not necessary, this one's fine now," he said. To ease her mind, he took the knife from the meat and placed it on the table

She walked away shaking her head and murmuring in a low voice. "I've seen all kinds of kooks come in here with all kinds of quirks, but this is the first time I've heard that crock of bull." She wondered if stabbing meat was symbolic of something more sinister. She decided she'd been reading too many crime novels and bustled off to wait on a new customer.

Even Eddie could see that he was getting out of control. He told himself to go to his room, get a good night's sleep, and see things with a fresh outlook in the morning. He settled up his bill and strode across the street toward the hotel. The phone booth on the street corner caught his eye, reminding him that he should call Rita and give her the latest report. Inside the booth he inserted coins in the slots and dialed her number. She answered on the first ring.

"Hello," she said, in her usual sultry voice.

"This is Eddie—just calling to give you an update."

"I was hoping it was you. I've been on pins and needles all day. I've hardly left the house for fear I'd miss your call."

"I'd have called sooner, but until today, I didn't have anything new to report," he said, yawning into the phone.

"You're not drunk, are you?" she said, annoyed at his lackluster tone.

"No, I'm not drunk, I'm beat," he said. I was headed to my room when I decided I'd call and give you a quick report."

"Okay, so what happened today? Any luck finding Jim Bob or the baby?" Rita didn't give a flip if he was tired, she'd waited all day for this.

"Well, I've been staking out the house, you know, watching their comings and goings. And the dog, I need to get that darn dog back..."

Rita interrupted him in mid-sentence. "Wait a minute, what dog? What does a dog have to do with this? I think you'd better start this tale from the beginning."

"Oh yeah, I forgot you didn't know about the dog. I'm not sure if I should tell the whole dog story over the phone. You know how ears listen in, so for now, let's just say an opportunity presented itself in the form of a dog, and I jumped on it. This dog is special. He can find things, you know, the kind of thing we're looking for..."

Rita interrupted him again. "You aren't making a lick of sense. Find things? What kind of things?" Then it suddenly dawned on her. "Oh, that thing and that kind of dog. Where on earth did you get a dog that can do that?"

I really shouldn't say, you know, the ears that could be listening," he reiterated.

"You're at a payphone, right? Sweetie, I really don't think anyone can listen in on those calls." His fragmented tale was trying her patience.

"You think not, huh? A phone line is a phone line. Have a little patience. I'll fill you in on all the details when we're face to face," Eddie said.

"Well, alright," she said, her voice showing her agitation. "So, what did you find out?" she asked again, hoping for a more sensible answer.

"So anyway, the first day I had the dog, he ran off, and I've been looking for him ever since..."

Eddie's way of giving information was killing her. She interrupted him again. "Where were you when you lost the dog?"

"At the sister's house. I had him with me the first day I went out there, and he took off. That's the last I've seen of him, but I know they have him. They always keep him inside—beats all I've ever seen. What kind of people keep a dog locked up inside a house and never let it out?" Eddie said.

"People who want to hide him, that's who," Rita said.

"Well, anyway, the sister says she's got a dog, says she's had him a long time. She says she hasn't seen my dog around her place, but I know she's lying like a dog." Eddie laughed at his clever play on words.

"Oh, for heaven's sake, could you please just get on with it?" Rita said gruffly.

Eddie cleared his throat. "Appears you don't appreciate a good sense of humor," he said.

Her response came through the receiver in the form of a heavy sigh.

"Well, I learned that the little girl spends most of the day in a room on the second floor of the house; it overlooks the front lawn. The dog stays up there with her, I know this because I've heard him growl. I've seen the girl watching me from the window, and that gave me an idea.

"Today I drove back out there and walked right up to the porch and called up to the girl. She was wary at first, but I finally persuaded her to come to the door with the dog. Just as she was about to come out, the witch sister came flying up the lane in her old pickup truck. She got out, ranting and raving, and shaking her finger at me. In all my born days I'd never seen a woman so mad. She ran me off, threatened to send me back to jail if I ever spoke to that little girl again. I tell you, she's got a mean streak a mile long," Eddie said. Just thinking about the incident made the hairs on his neck stand straight up.

"Wow, sounds like you're tangling with a wild cat," Rita said.

"You can say that again," Eddie said, rubbing his neck.

"Well, you're persistent, I'll give you that. But what did you find out?" Rita said, pushing him to cut to the chase.

"Sorry, I got carried away and left out that part. The girl said her mother was feeding baby Lillie, so you see, now we know for certain Lizzie is there with the baby, and the girl in the window is her other child," Eddie said.

A couple of minutes ago, Rita wanted to strangle him, but now she could kiss him. "Great detective work!" she said. "I don't guess the little girl mentioned her father."

"No, not a word, and after what happened today, I won't be talking to her again—the witch sister will make sure of it."

"So, Sweetie, now that we know they have the baby, you can get her and bring her to me," Rita said, her voice dripping with sweetness.

"That's not the plan. The plan, in case you've forgotten, is to find Jim Bob. Then we'll see about getting the baby," Eddie said.

Her hysteria had reached a crescendo. Eddie made it clear that he intended to stay on Jim Bob's trail. She had to keep him thinking that was what she wanted, too. She could be a real pain when things weren't going her way. In her opinion, Eddie was moving too slowly. His tactics were being thwarted at every turn. She had wanted to stay out of the picture, let Eddie do all the work, but if he couldn't get the job done, she might be forced to take matters into her own hands.

"What's your next move?" Rita said, the sweetness gone from her voice.

"Right now, all I want to do is shower and go to bed. Hopefully, something will come to me tomorrow. I'll let you know of any further developments."

The call ended on an abrupt and less than cordial tone, and without either of them saying goodbye. Eddie hung up the receiver and went straight to his room, glad that this day had finally come to an end. Unless he devised some remarkable scheme, he had no expectations that tomorrow would deliver any better results.

In the shower, he let the water run over his tense muscles. Only when the water began to go from hot to warm did he step out and dry off. He got into bed, positioned his head on the pillow just so, and closed his eyes. As dead tired as he was, sleep didn't come. As a last resort, he turned on the bedside lamp and pulled out the boring science book he referred to as his sleeping pill. Usually, a paragraph or two, and he was out like a light. Tonight, it wasn't working. He flipped off the light.

An annoying sliver of light was peeking through the drawn draperies that covered the window. Certain that this was the reason he couldn't get to sleep, he got out of bed, pulled the drapes close together then settled back in. With the room in total darkness, he rested his head back on the pillow and closed his eyes. Still sleep eluded him, his nerves quivering like live wires. To calm himself, he counted sheep jumping over a fence: a thousand forward, a thousand backward. Exasperated, he pushed off the covers and flung himself out of bed.

I can't just lie here all night staring into the darkness. I have to do something—anything would be better. Then the idea hit him. He'd been going to the house in the daytime. What if he changed things up and went out there tonight? It just seemed reasonable to check out the place while they were sleeping and weren't aware of his presence. He might just stumble onto something big.

****

Eddie walked the long lane to the house. Quietly, he made his way around the corner to the backyard. A voice took him by surprise. His heart beat wildly. Quickly, he ducked behind a bush and cautiously peeked around it. A woman he hadn't seen before was wrestling with a dog. She held his leash in a tight grip, but he overpowered her—pulling her this way and that.

"Behave! Just do your business so we can get back inside," the woman said, in an irritated tone. The dog kept pulling her to the ivy as she continued to pull him away. "Get away from there," she said gruffly.

It was a tit-for-tat. The dog pulled her one way, she pulled him the other. Eddie found the little scene quite fascinating. He stayed out of sight and watched it play out.

Over and over, the slightly built woman pulled on the dog's leash attempting to draw him toward the door only to have him pull her the other way. After several minutes had passed, the woman finally managed to wrangle him in the direction of the door.

Eddie sprang from behind the bush and ran toward the dog. Lizzie screamed. Copper pulled loose from her grasp and ran straight to the ivy.

Barking loudly, the dog jumped up and pulled away a mass of ropy vines. Lizzie ran to grab his leash that was trailing behind him. Eddie stepped in her path, preventing her from reaching it. He had no doubt that the dog, who had been trained to find dead bodies, was on the trail—he planned to make darn sure the dog accomplished his mission.

The commotion going on outside had awakened Addie and Jessie. Jessie was standing at the door, and was just about to go out when Addie stopped her. "Stay inside with Lillie while I see what's going on out here," she said, giving Jessie a pat on the shoulder. She reached for her bat and rushed out the door.

Something in the ivy caught Lizzie's attention—something that she hoped Eddie hadn't seen with the moon giving off only the tiniest sliver of light. Dangling amongst the ropy vines was a shoe.

With her bat in hand, Addie appeared at Lizzie's side. Lizzie tilted her head toward the wall, and Addie turned to look. Seeing the shoe, she responded by taking a few steps toward Eddie while wildly swinging the bat in all directions.

Eddie stumbled backward. A woman swinging a bat around was never a good thing. By nature, he wasn't a violent person, and he hadn't come to hurt anybody. He made a quick decision—he ran like hell.

Chapter 23

A new day had dawned, but the same old problems still haunted the sisters. They awakened early and were sitting shoulder to shoulder on the back porch steps, sipping coffee and wondering what in heaven's name had happened last night. Eddie had given no indication that he had seen the shoe, which relieved them greatly, but now there was no doubt—he knew they had his dog.

Addie stared into the blackish brew that matched her own dark mood. "One thing's for certain, Sis: this guy's not going to give up until he gets Copper—he proved that last night."

"He scared the living daylights out of me when he came out from behind that bush! Then you showed up swinging that bat around," Lizzie said, laughing at the absurdity of it.

At the sound of Lizzie's laughter, Addie's dark mood lifted, and she, too, burst out laughing. They giggled until they could hardly speak.

"When you get past the shock of it, it was a pretty hilarious scene. Wonder what ole Eddie's got up his sleeve after that fiasco?" Addie said, her voice raspy.

Lizzie shook her head. "I'm sure, as we speak, he's working on some outlandish plan—what that will be is anybody's guess."

"Now that he knows about the dog, that eliminates our need to get a second one. It hurts me to say it, but we both know it's true: at some point, Copper will have to be returned to the police. At that time we'll just have to find Jessie a nice puppy to help mend her broken heart," Addie said.

"I know," Lizzie sighed. "I've been racking my brain to come up with a way to keep him. Like you, I keep coming to the same conclusion."

"We'll work it out—if the good Lord's willing," Addie said.

"And the creeks don't rise," Lizzie said, adding the last line of the old saying.

****

Eddie was back in his room. His whole body still trembled from the ordeal he had just gone through with the witches. Propped against the headboard of his bed, he popped the top on the can of beer he'd bought at the joint down the street. He needed something to calm his nerves.

He tried to wrap his head around what had happened out there. His hand shook as he took a long sip, spilling some down his shirt. He breathed in several long breaths to steady his jitters. Never in all his days had he been so spooked.

It's true that the women had succeeded in running him off, but he'd gained some very valuable information from the process. As he suspected all along, they had lied about his dog, and he strongly suspicioned they were hiding something else. But he'd also learned that they don't scare easily and will do whatever is necessary to protect themselves—he felt outnumbered and outwitted.

If they think ole Eddie is giving up, they don't know who they're dealing with. He began to plot his next move, but his thoughts had become jumbled, and his eyelids had grown heavy. The beer had done its job. He set the empty can on the nightstand and rested his head on the pillow. Instantly, he fell into a deep sleep.

At half past ten, he woke up feeling as if he'd been hit by a fast-moving train and was unsure of his ability to move. With no new course of action, he considered whiling the day away in bed—it beat facing another failure. Then, he thought of Rita. He should call her and fill her in on his latest escapade—the thought of it made him cringe.

He closed his eyes, willing to sleep to return. It was useless. He winced as he pushed back the covers and groaned as he made his way to the bathroom. In the shower, he turned on the cold water and let it run over him. He emerged from the icy bath with a clearer head.

As he dressed, he gathered his thoughts. After nine long years in prison, he'd been given a new start. When he could be back in Tennessee enjoying his new life, he was stuck in this town, accomplishing absolutely nothing. It was time to get serious, no more fooling around—find Jim Bob and go home.

With renewed vigor, he left his room and made his way to the street corner. Entering the phone booth, he picked up the receiver and dialed Rita's number.

"Hello," she said, answering, as always, on the first ring.

"Hey—it's me, Eddie. Did you have a good night?"

"Question is, did you?" Rita said.

"No, not really. Though I do have some news for you," Eddie said.

"Well, don't keep me in suspense; I'm dying to know," she said, inspecting the polish on her nails.

Eddie took a long, deep breath. "So, after we talked last night, I was dead tired. All I wanted to do was go to my room and get some sleep, but that didn't go as planned. I had too many things on my mind—I was wide awake. I started thinking things over. I had only gone to the sister's house in the daytime. What if I went out there at night? What if I just hid out in the dark and watched? Maybe I'd discover something I'd been missing. I couldn't sleep anyway—why not?"

"I suppose that makes sense, so what happened?" Rita said.

"Well, I drove out there, walked up the lane to the house, and started around the corner. A woman's voice made me stop. I ducked behind a bush where I could watch and not be seen."

"Do you know who the woman was?" Rita said, her interest piqued.

"It was the other sister, Jim Bob's wife. She had the dog on a leash, taking him out to do his business. The dog kept pulling her to the side of the house that's covered in ivy. He was jumping, pawing, and pulling down clumps of the vine."

"That's odd," Rita said.

"Yeah, tell me about it. She and the dog were doing a tug of war; she kept pulling him away from the ivy, and he kept pulling her back to it. This back and forth went on until she finally managed to wrangle him back toward the door. That's when I came out from behind the bush. She screamed when she saw me and let go of the dog's leash."

"Oh my, what happened then?" Rita said, listening intently.

"Well, the dog immediately ran back to the ivy and began pawing and pulling at it like before. Then the woman moved in and grabbed for the dog's leash, but I managed to grab it first. That's when the other sister came tearing out of the house, swinging a baseball bat like woman gone crazy."

"Then what happened?" Rita said, her curiosity roused.

"I dropped the leash and ran like hell," Eddie said.

Rita sighed heavily into the receiver. "So, tell me, what exactly did you accomplish from this little escapade?"

"Don't you get it? The dog. I found my dog. You know, the dog that can find things—like the thing we're looking for."

"You mean the thing you're looking for," Rita said in disgust.

"I mean the thing that both of us should be looking for. I hope you're not saying that you've given up on finding Jim Bob. I'm thinking that whatever happened to him has a lot to do with you wanting that baby. And I'm beginning to think that you're so preoccupied with the baby that your priorities are all mixed up," Eddie said annoyedly.

Rita gritted her teeth. She couldn't believe this man was so hellbent on finding a brother that he hardly knew. He hadn't even laid eyes on him in years, they couldn't be that close. She took a deep breath to readjust her mindset. If she was going to get what she wanted, she had to keep Eddie on her side.

"Dear, dear Eddie," she said in her soft, sultry voice. "I think you've been working too hard and need a break from all of this. Why don't you come here for a day or two and let Rita give you some well-deserved pampering? I give a killer massage; I'd just bet your muscles are all tied up in knots."

His hand went instantly to his shoulder at the mere suggestion of a massage. His muscles were tight as a drum, and when he turned his neck from side to side, it sounded like Rice Krispies popping in a bowl of milk. *He couldn't turn down a good back rub.* "You've said the magic words," Eddie said. "I'll pack a few things and be there by late afternoon."

****

After hanging up the phone, Rita immediately began working on a plan that would get Eddie off the track of finding his stupid half-brother, and onto the one that would bring Lillie to her.

Men just need some encouragement, and I know how to give it. Her mind ticked off her strategical scheme: step one: a sensual massage; step two: some fabulous home-cooked meals; step three: would call for some of her more enticing talents.

Smiling wickedly, she thought of how she would set the mood: flickering candlelight, soft romantic music, erotic aromas, the table set with her best china, warmed scented oil for his massage, rose petals scattered on her bed. Soon, she'd have him eating out of the palm of her hand.

****

The sun was setting when Eddie parked his car along the curb in front of Rita's house. Retrieving his worn black suitcase from the back seat, he strode casually to the door and knocked. The door slowly opened. Eddie's eyes widened as he took in the lovely vision standing before him.

He gave her a quick up-down glance and grinned like a schoolboy.

Rita stood in the doorway wearing a long, flowing dress the color of lilac with a delicate lace trimmed neckline. Her hair was tied back loosely with a wide satin ribbon, and her high heels exposed her polished pink toes. Her makeup was minimal, only pale pink lip gloss on her perfectly shaped lips, and the tiniest amount of blush that accentuated her high cheekbones.

Eddie smiled inwardly at the transformation. The woman apparently had many sides to her—he found her mesmerizing. The way she looked tonight literally took his breath away.

She smiled slyly thinking that she should have been an actress with the way she could transform into whatever role best suited the situation. The current situation called for her to present herself as the perfect lady who would make the perfect mother—all the while seducing Eddie.

Taking his hand, she let him to her small loveseat. She settled in so close to him that she felt the tingle that pulsed through his body. "Did you have a pleasant drive?" she said, her face inches from his.

"Yeah, I did. I put everything out of my mind and just drove. Best thing I've done in days. Nothing but the road and the songs on the radio—just the way I like it."

"Well, that's nice. You deserve that, after all you've been through. Now, you just make yourself comfy while I go and pour us a nice glass of wine." She squeezed his hand and retreated to the kitchen.

The soft music playing, combined with the pleasant aromas, had such a calming effect that Eddie found himself drifting off a time or two before Rita returned.

She handed him a glass of red wine, took a seat beside him, and then clinked her glass to his. "Cheers," she said, her hand brushing lightly over his thigh.

Eddie squirmed nervously beside her.

This wasn't her first rodeo. She knew how to seduce a man, even married men, even this man who was obsessed with family loyalty. *Give him time, and he'll be completely under my spell.*

Tenderly, she took Eddie's hand in hers and looked deep into his eyes, as if she were looking into his very soul. "I hope you're not terribly hungry. I've got a lovely meal prepared for us, but I thought you might like a little time to unwind before we eat," she said, her voice low and sweet.

"That's kind of you," he said in a restrained tone, despite the tension building inside him.

Rita set her glass on the coffee table and walked to the back of the couch. Standing behind Eddie, she placed her cool hands on his shoulders and, with her slender fingers, began to massage his tense muscles. "Your muscles are in knots. Just relax, let Rita fix that," she said, in a voice oozing sexuality.

Rita's soft touch sent Eddie into another world. He pushed aside the cautionary voice in his head. He yielded to the pleasure of her hands working tenderly as he felt the tension in his muscles begin to subside.

Humming softly to the song playing on her stereo, She inched her hands farther down Eddie's back, her body leaning into his.

He sat trance-like under the spell of her magic hands. He told himself that he should make her stop, but he couldn't utter the words. He only moaned under the mastery of her touch. Never in his life had he been this relaxed. The combination of the soft music, the seductive aromas, her now warm hands on his tense body, and her soft hum close to his ear had him wondering: *had he died and gone to heaven?* For at this moment he could swear— Rita was an angel.

Her seduction of Eddie, not surprisingly, was going according to plan. Now, it was time to turn up the heat and seal the deal. She pressed her body into his and tenderly kissed his ear, allowing her lips to linger. Then, slowly, softly, she placed her lips on his.

Unable to suppress his burning desire for her another second, he drew her into him in a fevered embrace, his mouth pressing harder on hers, his body moving wantonly against her.

Rita took him by the hand and led him to her bedroom, where they feverishly tore off each other's clothes. Like a scene from a romance novel their bodies intertwined in steamy desire.

Rita had ignited a fire in Eddie that had long been denied. He was falling under her spell, like a sheep being led to slaughter. He submitted himself wholly to her will, disregarding all consequences of his actions and, worst of all, forgetting about his brother—the price for that would come later.

Having fallen into an exhausted sleep, they awoke famished. They dined by candlelight on the elegant meal Rita had prepared while romantic music filled the air.

A pleasured smile crossed Rita's face. She'd set her hook exactly as planned—Eddie was right where she wanted him.

In the dim light, Eddie studied Rita's face. She was exquisite. He wanted nothing more than to gaze upon her lovely face every hour of every day.

Rita reached across the table and tenderly took Eddie's hand in hers. "Darling," she said, the endearing term intended to set her hook deeper. "I know we hardly know each other, but I have a feeling about us—like we should be together."

A love-struck look fell over Eddie's face. Those words were all he needed to hear. "This is not at all what I expected when I came here looking for Jim Bob, and it happened so fast, but there's no denying how I feel—I love you," Eddie blurted out.

Rita smiled sweetly and placed a soft kiss on his lips. "Oh sweetheart, I love you, too." There was no doubt about it—he was putty in her hands.

With that was settled, there was no time to waste. She moved on to her main objective. "Sweetie, you know, we could be a family; you, me, and baby Lillie. You would make the most awesome daddy, and don't you think I'd be the most fantastic mommy? I'm a great cook; I keep a clean house; those things are very important for raising a child, don't you think?"

"A kid would be darn lucky to have you as a mother," Eddie said.

Rita conjured up some fake tears and looked into Eddie's eyes. "Why, my heart is so full of love, I could just explode. Everything would be complete, so perfect—if we just had Lillie. If I don't get her, I don't want to go on living," Rita said, wiping away a nonexistent tear.

Lifting her chin, Eddie looked into her eyes. "Sweetheart, don't you shed another tear. I promise— I'll get her for you."

Rita wrapped her arms around Eddie's neck and smothered him with kisses. "Oh, Eddie, really? when?"

His face turned glum. He wasn't prepared to leave her so soon—hoping for more blissful nights like last night. "Soon," he said, drawing her in close to him.

More tears emerged with tiny whimpers. Rita dabbed a tissue under her eyes, then blew her nose for added effect.

"Please don't cry," Eddie said, wiping her tears with his napkin. "I'll leave first thing in the morning. If all goes well, I should be back tomorrow night with the baby."

Just as he said those words—back with the baby—it suddenly struck him that he'd just agreed to steal someone's baby. He didn't know one earthly thing about babies, and how on earth was he going to manage this alone? Then it occurred to him. If Rita went with him, she could take care of Lillie—it was the perfect solution.

Eddie moved in closer to Rita and took her hand. "Darling, I think this is a job for both of us. I don't know anything about babies. And I can just imagine how terrified she'll be when a strange man snatches her from her mother—she's sure to be comforted in your arms."

This was not in her plan. It would only complicate things if she were to be seen. Right now, nobody but Eddie knew about her, or where he would be taking the baby. She had to make Eddie see it her way. "Honey, that's just not possible. Don't you see how this whole thing could be compromised if I should be seen? Those women have seen you; they even know who you are, but they don't know me. They don't even have a clue about me or where I live. Once I become known to them, that puts me in a very vulnerable position. You can see that, can't you, honey?" she said, her eyes sad and teary.

He shook his head. "Dumb me. It never occurred to me that your identity should be protected. I'll figure it out. Now don't you worry your pretty little head—I'll take care of everything."

Rita drew him into her arms and kissed him tenderly. "That makes me love you even more," she said, crossing her fingers behind his back.

Her words were like fuel on a fire. Now, he was more determined than ever to get her what she wanted. He made her a vow that he wouldn't disappoint her—not for all the tea in China.

Chapter 24

Lizzie and her children had been run through the wringer: physically and mentally. Sitting at the kitchen table, Addie racked her brain for a way to lift their spirits. She turned her ear to the sound of birds chirping happily outside the window. As if hearing her thoughts, they had provided the perfect answer. *Nothing cheers the soul like being outdoors, and everybody loves a picnic.* She made a mental note to fill the feeder with seeds as a thank you to her feathered friends.

From her cupboard, tucked behind a row of her homemade jams, she retrieved the metal can where she kept her mad money, as she called it. It had one purpose and one purpose only: to be spent in any frivolous way her heart desired—she knew just what to do with it.

She was putting on her coat and shoes when Lizzie came yawning into the room. Making quick excuses, she left through the back door. Lizzie, half awake, only nodded.

****

With spring just around the corner, it turned out to be the perfect time to shop for her girls. Betty's Boutique, to Addie's delight, was filled to the rafters with dresses for all ages in an array of beautiful spring colors.

With a keen eye, she rifled through the racks of dresses until she found the perfect ones for Lizzie, Jessie and Lillie. She even found ballet shoes that went perfectly with Jessie's dress.

On the drive home, she planned out every detail, wanting the day to be extra special, especially for Jessie. Luckily, the weather cooperated by bringing a near summer day with a clear blue sky and bright sunshine; everything was working out to perfection.

At breakfast, when they were all gathered around the kitchen table, she said, "I have a surprise for all of you, but I'm not telling you just yet what it is." There was a hint of mystery in her voice. The look on Jessie's face was just as she had expected—she beamed with delight.

Lizzie looked questioningly at her twin.

"I'll only give you one clue: dress like you're going to a party. That's all you need to know for now. Oh, one other thing—no looking out the windows," Addie said.

"What have you got up your sleeve, Sis?" Lizzie said, eyeing her curiously.

Addie only shrugged and walked out of the room, leaving them in total suspense.

****

The smile that had instantly lit up Jessie's face was worth a million dollars, but almost as quickly, it had faded. "Mama, I don't have party clothes," she said, obviously worried that she would disappoint her aunt.

"What we have will be just fine, sweetie. Believe me, you could never disappoint your aunt. Hurry up and get your lessons done, then we'll find you something nice to wear."

Jessie scampered up the stairs. At the threshold of her room, she froze. She stared in wonder at the dress draped over the back of her chair. Slowly, she ventured nearer, allowing her trembling fingers to explore every detail: the tiny embroidered rosebuds, the smooth satin ribbon, the soft and airy fabric. Carefully, as if it might break, she lifted it and held it to her body. It was the kind of dress made for twirling, and that's just what she did. She twirled around and around the room laughing gaily until something in the floor caused her to stumble. Looking down, she eyed the pair of pink ballerina slippers. She picked them up and held them to her chest, then slipped them on—they fit like they were made for her.

Quick as a wink, she stripped off her nightgown and stepped into the dress, then hurried to the kitchen where her mother sat holding Lillie in her lap. "Mama, look at my beautiful dress," she said, spinning around to show it off, her face glowing like sunlight.

Lizzie's eyes filled with tears at the sight of her little daughter. "Oh, sweetie, you look just like a fairy princess!"

"Thank you, Mama," Jessie said, running her hands lovingly over the front of her dress.

"No, sweetheart, you have your aunt to thank for it. I didn't know a thing about it. She must have bought it on one of her trips into town. You're a very special little girl, and your aunt loves you very much. You can thank her later. Right now, we need to get busy with your lessons. The sooner we do that, the sooner we'll find out about the big surprise," Lizzie said, rising up from the table.

In her own room, she found a lovely Chantilly lace dress in a pale shade of yellow. And in Lillie's crib was a velvety-soft white cotton dress with matching bonnet. *Addie, you never cease to amaze me.* Tears welled in her eyes that she didn't bother to wipe away.

****

Having finished the final touches, Addie stood back and observed her work. With loving care, she had transformed the front lawn into an enchanting fairyland.

Strips of pastel colored fabric, tied to the lowest tree branches, twirled gently in the light breeze. Spread out beneath a cluster of magnolias was a soft faded quilt upon which a delicate tea set and a large wicker basket were arranged in the center. The open basket, lined with white linen, was filled with finger sandwiches, fruit, and lemon cookies with sugar sprinkles on top. Three places were carefully set: a small china plate, a tea cup and saucer, tiny silver spoons and folded linen napkins. For Lillie, a pink satin ribbon was tied in a loopy bow around her bottle.

She exhaled a deep, approving sigh, then hurried indoors.

Wearing her favorite summer dress and her wide-brimmed straw hat, she called out to Lizzie, and Jessie. "Girls, are you ready? Meet me at the front door."

The words were barely out of her mouth when Jessie appeared at her side, hopping from one foot to the other. Moments later, Lizzie appeared with Lillie in her arms.

Addie nodded approvingly. "Ya'll look amazing! Now close your eyes." She opened the door wide. "Okay. You can open them now."

Lizzie gasped with delight. Jessie stood staring—her eyes wide as saucers. Seconds later she was bounding down the steps and onto the lawn, her hands held high as the streamers brushed the tips of her fingers. She twirled around and around giggling happily. The sweet sound brought tears of joy to the sister's eyes. Like a symphony— it was music to their ears.

Jessie ran to Addie and hugged her tightly. "Oh, Aunt Addie, I've never seen anything so beautiful, it's just like a fairytale. And, thank you for my pretty dress and my ballerina shoes." She held up one foot for her aunt to see. "They fit just right!" she said, hugging her again.

"Sweetheart, you are very welcome; I'm so glad you like them. In all my life, I've never seen anyone so pretty," Addie said, wrapping her arms around her niece. More than anything, Addie wanted Jessie to feel her worth; she hoped that today would begin that journey.

Hands joined, the three made their way to the quilt and took their places. Upon Addie's suggestion, they pretended to be of British royalty and sipped their tea from the dainty china tea cups while holding out their pinky fingers.

Addie, speaking in a most dreadful English accent, said, "My ladies, would you take some more tea?"

Lizzie replied, "Yes, my dame, thank you ever so much." She held up her cup and saucer as Addie poured.

Getting in on the fun, Jessie did as her mother had and held out her cup to be refilled. "Thank you most kindly, Auntie," she said, giggling with delight.

The rest of the day, all of their conversations were spoken in their terrible British accents, and every so often, they'd break out in laughter when the accent became tainted with their Southern drawl.

The day was intended to be an escape from the many problems that had plagued them, and it was proving to be just that, lifting their spirits to the heavens. Lizzie's face showed the joy she was feeling, especially in seeing how much Jessie was relishing in the sheer magic of it. Every now and then, she reached over and patted her hand or kissed her cheek.

After they had finished their lunch, Addie announced it was game time. Lillie had fallen asleep, and Lizzie gently laid her on the soft quilt, kissed her lightly on the cheek then went to join in the fun.

First, they had a sack race ending with the three of them in a pile, laughing joyfully. After that, Addie placed a can on the ground—the rules were simple: the first to kick the can across the line was the winner. On the count of five, all three ran to be first—pushing and shoving as their outrageous laughter filled the air.

Jessie insisted on playing the games over and over, and while the sisters obliged, they found it difficult to keep up with her youthful energy. When they could hardly muster the tiniest bit of stamina, to their great relief, Jessie finally tired. Retiring to the quilt they settled onto a spot near Lillie. Sprawled out on their backs, they watched the white clouds drift slowly across the bright blue sky.

The day was all about the four of them. Forgotten was Eddie; it had been a couple of days since they'd seen him. Little did they know that while they blissfully enjoyed the festive occasion—someone was watching their every move.

* * * * * * * * * * * * * *

Eddie sat in his car drumming his fingers nervously on the steering wheel. He had just left Rita's house and was already regretting the promise he'd made her. His head throbbed just thinking about the role he was to play in her kidnapping scheme. He felt sick. What she wanted him to do was a criminal act that could land him back in prison.

He rubbed his temples. How he could've been so stupid to agree to such a thing mystified him. It really wasn't that big of a mystery—he was head over heels in love. At the time, he would've agreed to anything Rita asked. Now he was having second thoughts, even questioning his ability to make moral decisions.

For one, Rita was the woman his brother was to marry. That fact alone was cause to rethink his involvement. Then, there was the kidnapping. Show him a car, and he could break in, hot-wire it, and be gone in less than sixty seconds. A baby was a whole different story. Babies cry. They need bottles and diaper changes. This job was definitely out of his league—and wrong to boot.

He sat frozen in the seat as he debated his predicament. His heart wasn't in it, but he'd made a promise, and he always kept his word. He was left with no choice—he'd do it for Rita.

With no plan in mind, he drove to the sister's property, parked his car in the usual place, and walked up the lane. The sound of voices on the front lawn caused him to stop in his tracks and dart behind a tree. While remaining hidden in the tree line he crept closer to the sounds until his eyes beheld the scene before him.

The lawn was decorated like something you'd see in a children's storybook. The sisters and the little girl, all wearing pretty dresses, sat atop a quilt and were having a picnic. He couldn't draw his eyes away from the fairytale scene.

Listening to their funny voices and seeing their happy faces made him smile. He observed how Lizzie interacted lovingly with her children. He frowned. This wasn't the horrible mother Rita had described. It was evident to him that she truly loved her children, and they loved her.

He rubbed his forehead as if this would clear his muddled thoughts. Maybe Lizzie was working on becoming a good mother and changing her ways, but this didn't seem to fit either. What he was witnessing couldn't be newly formed behavior. Lizzie and her children shared a deeply rooted bond. It didn't take a genius to see that.

Why was Lizzie described in such a malicious way when she's obviously a very good mother. The thought bewildered him.

Wanting further proof, he remained hidden, watching the scene play out. If Lizzie is the kind of mother Rita says she is, she would surely display her true character at some point.

Despite the doubt swirling around in his mind, he remained vigilant, waiting for the time to act. The perfect opportunity presented itself when they left the quilt to play their games—the baby had been left alone.

This is your chance, if you're going to do it, now's the time. He tried to take a step forward, but his feet stayed planted. Minutes ticked away. He still couldn't move. His heart wasn't in it—it was wrong—pure and simple. He couldn't take that baby from a mother who loved her; not today—not ever.

When the games had ended and the three of them retired to the quilt, Eddie saw no reason to linger. He left, leaving them in peace.

Back in his car, he sat slumped in the seat, considering his next move. Should he return the next day to observe this group—this mother? Truthfully, he didn't think anything new would come of that. Then, struck by the reason he had come there in the first place, he bolted upright in his seat.

He had come here to find his brother, and with the whole family on the front lawn there couldn't be a better time to snoop around. First, he had to get the dog—that meant getting inside the house. Once he had him, he'd put him to work uncovering whatever was behind that darn ivy. He gave himself two thumbs up for thinking of such a brilliant plan.

Hurriedly he made his way to the backyard, peering around the corner, making sure the ladies were still relaxing on the quilt. Seeing that they hadn't moved, he quickly ran up the steps and through the back door. Noisily, he tripped over the cans that were stacked just inside the door. He cursed, got to his feet, and weaved his way around the various pieces of furniture in his path. His head hit spoons that hung overhead, which started a series of loud jingling noises. Then, from out of nowhere, the dog appeared, barking maliciously as if he didn't know him.

"It's me, boy. You remember me." Eddie said in a hushed tone. He got his answer when Copper charged full force at him, knocking him to the floor and growling ferociously. Quick as a lightening, Eddie got to his feet and did what he does best—he ran like hell!

"Did you hear that?" Addie said, jumping up from the quilt.

Lizzie was already on her feet, running toward the house. She knew exactly what they had heard. She entered the back door only to find all the cans scattered across the floor and the spoons still jangling overhead. Addie came up behind her and pointed to a male figure in a red cap retreating into the trees.

The two of them sat on the porch steps and laughed uproariously. Maybe they should have been frightened by the intrusion, but they found Eddie much less of a threat than previously considered.

The day had turned out to be splendid in every way—absolute perfection. Their success at sending Eddie running for the hills again—was icing on the cake.

****

It seemed no day would be complete at Magnolia Place without multi-layers of drama and today proved to be no different. Soon after the incident with Eddie, Mr. Bass showed up. He parked his car at the front of the house, and with a swagger in his step, he approached the door.

Jessie was in her room and was the first to know of his arrival. "Mr. Bass is here!" she called out excitedly.

Five annoying knocks, to the tune of "Shave and a Haircut," told Addie he was feeling his oats and had not been told of the board's decision.

Addie pulled the door open before he could finish the last two beats of the tune, taking Bass by surprise. He looked ridiculous standing before her, his eyes wide and his fist raised in the air. He quickly extended his hand toward her, as if he had always intended to greet her with a handshake.

Poor little man. "Why, Mr. Bass, what a pleasure to see you again. Isn't it a glorious day? Come in, we were just relaxing in the parlor, won't you join us?"

Addie led him into the room and directed him to a chair across from the sofa where Lizzie was already seated. He was about to sit but instead took a couple of steps toward Lizzie and stretched out his hand.

Lizzie paused briefly before placing her hand in his. He didn't seem to notice the gap in time. When he turned his back to her, she frantically wiped her hand on her dress.

Addie glared at her and shook her head. She sensed that Mr. Bass hadn't expected a warm reception. After all, he'd come thinking he was leaving with Jessie. He also had to be thinking he had the upper hand. She and Lizzie planned to burst that little bubble, but first, they wanted to watch him squirm.

Lizzie, on her best behavior, directed her attention to Mr. Bass. "Oh my, Mr. Bass, we had the most wonderful day! Everything was absolutely perfect. Addie decorated the lawn, and you should have seen it—just like a fairyland," Lizzie said, her voice dripping with sweetness.

The sisters saw him roll his eyes. He shifted his body to the edge of his seat. "I'm certain it was all very nice, but..."

"Really, it was nothing, just some old rags I tied in the trees," Addie interrupted.

Mr. Bass cleared his throat, "Yes, ladies, could we..."

"It was nothing? Let me tell you, Mr. Bass, my sister has a knack for making things so lovely. And the food, oh—so delicious," Lizzie said, cutting him off again.

Addie cut her eyes to Mr. Bass and said, "Really, it was just some bread, cheese, and fruit—nothing special at all."

"I'm certain it was very good ladies, but let's get down to....."

"Well, you're just being modest," Lizzie said. "Everything was perfect, and the cookies were to die for."

The sister's conversation wasn't rehearsed, but was the kind of play acting they had done as kids. They kept up the tit-for-tat, meanwhile making it impossible for Mr. Bass to get a word in edgewise.

"The cookies turned out very well, I must admit," Addie said. "I have some left. Would you care for one, Mr. Bass?"

"Uh," was all he could utter before being cut off again.

"Where are my manners? Forgive me. I should have offered you refreshments right off the bat. Don't move a muscle, I'll be back in a jiffy." She was up and out of the room before he could blink.

With only the two of them left in the room, Mr. Bass set his gaze on Lizzie. "Well, Mrs. Thornhill, if we can get down to business..."

"If you'll pardon me, Mr. Bass, I need to check on my baby. It's about time for her to wake from her nap."

Before he could object, she was gone. An exasperated look spread across his face. He looked at his watch. "How long does it take to put a cookie on a plate?" He mumbled to himself in a low, agitated voice. He fidgeted restlessly, crossing one leg and then the other, his fingers drumming impatiently on the arm of the chair.

A number of minutes had passed when Addie returned with a tray of assorted goodies that were leftover from their picnic. Laying the tray on the coffee table in front of him, she handed Mr. Bass a plate and a napkin. "Please, help yourself. I'm sure you could use a little refreshment after driving all the way out here," she said warmly.

He hadn't come to eat, but he was always up for free food. Taking the plate, he pilled it high and tried to balance it on his lap while shoveling food into his mouth.

Addie waited until he had stuffed his mouth so full he wouldn't be able to speak, then directed the conversation to him. "I'm so sorry, but you had something you wanted to say. My sister and I didn't give you a chance, we were so caught up in telling you about our day. Now, please go ahead. You have my full attention."

He opened his mouth to speak, but instead of words, crumbs came tumbling out into his lap and onto the floor.

"How rude of me; of course, you can't talk with your mouth full of food. And I don't know what I was thinking asking for you to begin without my sister," Addie stalled.

Mr. Bass only nodded, still chewing on the huge amount of food in his mouth.

By the time Lizzie returned, Mr. Bass had swallowed his food and was just about to speak when Addie jumped up from her seat and threw up her hands. "I completely forgot to offer you something to drink."

Mr. Bass looked at Lizzie with a disgusted look on his face. Lizzie shrugged.

Addie made a quick departure and minutes later returned with a glass of tea which she handed Mr. Bass. She took her seat and turned to Lizzie. "Is Lillie still sleeping?"

"Yes, she's such a sweet little thing. She looked absolutely angelic in that pretty little dress you bought her. Wherever did you get it?" Lizzie said.

Addie opened her mouth to answer, but Mr. Bass interrupted.

"If you ladies don't mind. This conversation has been quite entertaining, and I appreciate the food, but I must be about my business. As you know, time has expired, leaving me no choice but to act on the order from the school board. If you would be so kind as to bring the girl here, we can be on our way," he said.

Fun and games were over. It was time to inform Dumb-ass Bass of the news, and Lizzie couldn't wait to lower the boom. She stood, walked over to where Mr. Bass was sitting, and held the paper close to his face. "This, Mr. Bass, is the decision of the board stating that our request for home-schooling has been granted." She thrust the paper into his hand.

His face turned as white as the sheet of paper he was holding. As he began to read the official document, his fury showed all over him. The veins in his temples throbbed, his nostrils flared, his eyes narrowed, and his whole body trembled. Clearly, he'd been taken off guard and furious that he hadn't been informed of this revelation.

He let the paper slip from his hand, his cold glare sweeping over them before he stormed from the room. In his hasty departure, he left the door standing wide open.

Lizzie and Addie stood in the doorway and waved as he sped away in a cloud of dust and flying gravel. The sisters celebrated with a high five.

"Another day, another conquest," Addie said—while wondering what crisis tomorrow would bring.

****

Later that afternoon, while Jessie was doing her homework and Lillie was napping, Addie and Lizzie went out onto the lawn. Lying on their backs atop the quilt, they basked in the warmth of the afternoon sun.

"This has been some kind of day, hasn't it, Sis?" Addie said.

"One of the best I've ever had. I have you to thank for everything; you and Lester, of course. You for the lovely picnic and all you've done for us, not to mention your involvement regarding Jessie's schooling. Lester, for his mastery in making it all possible. I'm indebted to you both," Lizzie said.

"I had only a small part in it, it's Lester who gets all the credit. Throughout my life, he's been the best friend I could ever hope to have. There's one thing I know for certain, through thick and thin, I can always count on him—he's never let me down," Addie said, her eyes glistening with tears.

"I've watched the two of you together. You have a great love for him, and I can see that he absolutely adores you, evidenced by his willingness to do anything in the world for you. I'm wondering why you haven't married him; I don't think it's because he hasn't asked."

Addie closed her eyes, then turned to look at her sister. "He has asked, many times, and he'd like nothing more—I know this. It's just that we've been such dear friends for so long. I'm afraid a marriage would ruin what we have, and I'd rather cut off my right arm than have that happen. I love Lester with all my heart.

"That's just like you to look at love in such a sensible way, but I think you're missing out on something that could be wonderful for both of you. Listen to me—like I know how to give advice about love. You know what an absolute disaster I've been regarding matters of the heart," Lizzie said.

Addie smiled and shook her head wistfully. "If only I had put love into the equation when I was young; instead, I looked at marriage as an opportunity. So, dear sister, it seems we both have warped values when it comes to love. I wonder if we are cursed—both of us widowed at such a young age. But, what I do know is that I treasure what Lester and I have more than life itself. I wouldn't jeopardize that for anything in the world."

"At any rate, what you and Lester have is something very special. You should consider yourself extremely lucky," Lizzie said.

Addie recalled the saying that went something like: if you have just one friend you can count on through thick and thin, you should count yourself lucky. She smiled, knowing how very lucky she was—Lester was that kind of friend.

Chapter 25

In his rented room, Eddie sprawled out across the dark brown bedspread. He wondered *why brown?* It wasn't a question that troubled him, nor did it particularly interest him. The arbitrary thought only served to delay the inevitable—Rita. She'd be waiting for his call, and the thought of telling her that he had failed again made his head throb. He thought about telling her some half-baked story, but he knew she'd see right through it.

No, skirting the issue wasn't his way; he always shot from the hip. Even when confronted by the cops about the car he had stolen and knowing what his punishment would be, he told them like it was. No cock-and-bull story—just the stone-cold facts.

A battle was going on in his head. Should he stick around and tell Rita the truth, or should he hightail it back to Tennessee and leave all this drama behind? There was only one way to decide. He took a coin from his pocket. "Heads, I call her—tails, I'm out of here." He flipped the coin into the air, and caught it on the back of his hand. "Heads! Darn it! Oh well, it's probably for the best—get it over with."

Inside the phone booth, Eddie dropped the coins in their appropriate slots and listened to the ding, ding, ding sound as each was deposited. He dialed Rita's number and waited for her to answer. Beads of cold sweat formed at his hairline, and he paced inside the small space.

"Hello," she answered sweetly.

"Hey, it's me, Eddie. How's it going?" Even to his own ears, it sounded lame. He was in a glum mood, and it showed in his choice of words.

"The question is, how's it going there?" Rita said, with a tad of irritation at his less than intimate greeting.

Eddie blurted out, "I couldn't do it!"

Rita's face turned blood red; her voice became edgy and shrill. "What do you mean you couldn't do it?"

The change in her was instantaneous. He grasped the receiver tight in his hand and spoke boldly. "I'm not a kidnapper. A thief, yes, but snatching babies is where I draw the line. At the sister's house, I watched the mother with her children. Either she's a fantastic actress, or she's a very good mother—I tend to believe the latter. I have no desire to take a child from a mother who displayed nothing but genuine love for her. If the situation was as you had said, that would be a different story—I didn't find it to be the case."

"You didn't find it to be the case?" Rita snarled. I cannot believe your simple-mindedness; those women have played you for the fool you are."

"Those women didn't know I was anywhere around. They were having a picnic and enjoying their day," Eddie said.

"You idiot, you stupid imbecile, you have no idea about women and how they can manipulate men," Rita said.

"Maybe not, but I'm beginning to see the light," he said.

Rita's temper flared. *Men!* A bitter taste formed in her mouth. *Never expect a man to do a woman's work—they'll botch it every time.* "I don't need your help. You can go back to your idiotic search for your idiotic brother. I'll get the job done myself," she hissed, then slammed down the receiver.

"Brother!" Eddie said. His ears rang from her piercing remarks. He hung up the receiver, feeling like the fool she had said he was.

Exiting the booth, he shuffled dejectedly, his eyes cast downward inspecting the cracks in the sidewalk. He knew Rita would be upset, but her response was totally unexpected.

In his room he stripped off his clothes and ran a hot bath. Laying his head on the back of the tub, he let his body sink into the scalding water. With each passing minute, he could feel his tight muscles begin to ease until all he felt was complete exhaustion. When he emerged from the tub, his legs were like limp noodles. In a zombie-like state, he staggered from the bathroom and fell upon the bed.

Since his release from prison, he hadn't experienced a single restful night. To relax, he'd resorted to counting sheep, reading passages from boring books, and counting the water rings on the ceiling, none of which brought the results he so desperately needed. Tonight was the exception—the instant his head hit the pillow, he was out like a light.

****

The clanking sound started low, then became louder as it drew nearer. His eyes flew open. He expected to see the prison guard, billy club in hand, rattling the iron bars of his cell. He sat up in bed and drew in a deep, ragged breath. Still groggy, his eyes surveyed his surroundings. Realizing he'd been dreaming, he slowly exhaled. He wondered if those memories would forever torment him.

For several minutes he sat motionless; the reminder of being locked up sent cold chills through his body. There were so many memories relating to his years in prison that he would like to erase from his mind, but the billy club was the worst of them. The guards were never without them, and the brutality he'd witnessed as a result of their use still made his blood curdle.

He shook his head in an attempt to rid his mind of the ghastly memories and reminded himself that he was a free man. He was free to come and go as he pleased and free from the sights and sounds contained within the prison walls. His heartbeat returned to a more steady rhythm, and he turned his thoughts to the situation at hand.

His conversation with Rita had him wondering how he could have been such an idiot. Thankfully, she'd shown her true colors before he did something really stupid.

Of all the things he'd learned in prison, the most important was to steer clear of the tough guys who wanted to control him. Eddie shook his head, realizing that was exactly what Rita had done. He'd fallen into her trap and allowed her to seduce him. He'd thrown the lessons he'd learned out the window and turned a deaf ear to his conscience. Although his involvement with Rita had been pretty much a one-night stand, she had him believing they could be happy together. She had played him like a fiddle, and he felt like a fool.

Another thing he'd learned in prison was to roll with the punches—get over it and move on. He was nothing to Rita; that was clear. He put her out of his mind and focused instead on the puzzle that he hadn't yet solved—*Where is Jim Bob?* His instinct was telling him that he was dead and buried somewhere at the sister's house. He resolved to do what he'd come to do—find him.

Later that night, he left his room and walked over to the diner. The townsfolk had gotten used to seeing him around. He was hard to miss in his red cap. He took a seat at the counter, where the waitress poured him a steaming cup of coffee and handed him a menu.

As he sipped the steaming brew, he scanned the room. At a nearby table, a man sat by himself, a half-eaten hamburger in one hand and a document in the other. In a booth across the room, a woman and a young boy were discussing an upcoming school project while waiting for their food. Wistfully, he thought how simple their lives seemed, and how he envied them.

He was finishing his second cup of coffee when a man and woman entered. The waitress guided them to a table near his seat at the counter. It was plain to see they were having a spat as the woman rejected the man's attempt to help her with her coat or to pull out her chair. Once seated, the woman began to talk in an angry voice that Eddie had no trouble overhearing.

"You didn't have to be so helpful," the woman said.

"I only gave her directions. Since when did that become a sin?" the man said.

"You're forgetting that I know how she came to ask you in the first place," the woman said.

"She just looked like she needed some help, so yes, I approached her and asked if I could be of assistance," he said, in a defensive tone.

The waitress interrupted their conversation.

"Good evening, folks. What can I get you to drink?" She laid two menus on the table and went off to get water for the woman and coffee with cream for the man.

"You're just a fool for a pretty face," the woman said, picking up where they'd left off. "You can't tell me you didn't have something more on your mind than offering a little assistance."

"You're making a mountain out of a molehill. That woman was pretty, I'll give you that. But you know, darlin', I don't have eyes for any woman but you," the man said, patting his wife on the shoulder.

The woman pushed his hand away. "Hogwash! I got the rundown from Pearl over at the bar. She said you were like putty in her hands, stammering and stuttering like a schoolboy."

"Now, hun, don't take offense at that. Sometimes I get a little too friendly, but that don't mean nothin'—you're the only one for me," he said, putting his arm around her again and pulling her close.

"Well, I guess since you gave her what she needed, the directions to that Kent woman's house, we can be done with her," the woman said, somewhat satisfied with her husband's explanation.

Eddie had been enjoying his meal with only half an ear to the man and woman's conversation until he heard the woman reference the Kent woman. He replayed their conversation in his mind: the pretty woman, her need for help, directions to the Kent woman's house. His voice rang out, "Rita!" His blood ran cold.

The couple gave him curious looks, then turned away. Paying them no mind, he jumped up from his chair, laid money on the counter and headed for the door.

Alarm bells sounded in his head. *Was Rita actually acting on her threat?* He couldn't take a chance—there was no time to waste!

Lester had just taken the last bite of his hamburger when he heard the mention of Addie's name and that someone had been given directions to her house. Troubling thoughts rang out in his mind. He was out of his chair and running for the door when he collided with the man in the red ball cap. He quickly apologized, then hurried to his car.

Neither man took note of the other's hasty departure, but both were rushing to the same destination—Magnolia Place.

When Lester reached Addie's driveway, the car that had been tailing him pulled in behind. His protection mode went into high gear. He stopped his car and went over to question the driver's intentions, only to find it was the man in the red ball cap again.

"I'm Mrs. Kent's attorney. I must ask your intentions, sir," Lester said.

"I'm the brother of Mrs. Kent's sister's husband. It's a long story, but I have reason to believe that that a woman has come here to steal Lizzie's baby—she'll stop at nothing to get what she wants. I fear she's out of control and could be dangerous." Eddie said breathlessly.

"I want to hear more about this later, but for now, it seems we're here for the same reason—to protect the women and children. We can be more productive if we work together," Lester said.

Leaving their cars behind, they walked quickly toward the house, forming a plan as they went.

Chapter 26

The afternoon sun was low against the horizon, bringing the amazing day to a close. The sisters, each in their own thoughts, were busily taking down the decorations and packing up the china.

Lizzie reached for a streamer and stopped to wipe tears from her eyes. The lovely time they had just experienced brought back memories of the sweet and carefree days of their childhood. The thought filled her with regret. This is the life she gave up, the life Jessie should have had. If it weren't for Addie, she wouldn't be here now. She'd be forever in her debt for bringing her here and showing her how good life could be again.

Addie was sitting on the quilt carefully packing the china into the basket. Lizzie moved in close beside her and tenderly placed her hand over hers. Her words stumbled out between ragged sobs. "You've made us feel at home...showered us with love...this is the life I want for my children....I can't thank you enough...for rescuing us and giving us a new start."

She paused to wipe her tears, then continued. "Today, it occurred to me why I had to go through ten long years of hell. I had some hard lessons to learn before I could truly appreciate what I'd given up and come to realize what really matters. I hate that Jessie had to go down that road with me, and I'll regret that till I die. I put myself and my desires above all else, but from now on—it's all about what's best for my girls and for you. As soon as things calm down, we'll find a place of our own, then your life can get back to normal.

Through her tears, Addie said, "Leave here? Why on earth would you do such a thing?"

"We've brought so much trouble into your peaceful existence—you don't need that. Besides, at some time, I'll need to establish a home for my girls," Lizzie said.

"Well, Sis, I can't deny that you've certainly made things interesting," she said with a laugh. "But you and your children have given me what I've longed for, too—a family. As for the girls, they breathe life into this place, and I'm enjoying being an auntie more than I can tell you. Now, no more talk of leaving, agreed?"

Lizzie nodded through her tears.

The sisters were rediscovering the connection that had been lost for far too long. There was a moment when they stopped working, turned to each other, and embraced. No words needed to be spoken—it was a gesture of the genuine love they had for each other.

Aware that her sister was dealing with far too much guilt, Addie attempted to comfort her. "Lizzie, I understand how you feel about subjecting Jessie to the horrible life you had with Jim Bob, but you shouldn't be so hard on yourself.

Jessie is a remarkable child, and you get all the credit for that. Even though she didn't get her father's love, you made up for it by giving her an abundance, and it shows. Though I do worry about the effect that terrible night might have on her. Unless there's a time she wants to talk about it, I think we should let sleeping dogs lie; at least we can spare her that memory."

"She's strong—stronger than me, if that's possible." She laughed. "But you're right, that subject should be put to rest—for good."

Back inside, Lizzie glanced at the clock: it was time for Lillie's bottle. She left the kitchen and made her way to her room. Reaching down into Lillie's, crib she realized, for the first time since she'd been there, her pain was gone. With Lillie in her arms and a skip in her step, she returned to the kitchen and took her seat at the table. Addie had retreated to her garden. The two had settled into a very comfortable existence.

✶✶✶✶✶✶✶✶✶✶✶✶✶✶

Night fell, and all had taken refuge in their comfortable beds, happily exhausted from the day's events. Amazingly, Jessie was the first to fall asleep, followed closely by Lillie, then Lizzie. Addie, back in her own bed, as usual, was slower to unwind. Although many of their problems had been resolved, Addie remained apprehensive about Eddie; she felt he wouldn't rest until his brother was found. Little did she know that tonight, Eddie was the least of her problems.

The wind-up clock on Addie's nightstand ticked off each second—*tick, tick, tick*—the steadiness of it having a soothing effect. Soon her eyelids grew heavy, and she fell fast asleep.

The house was dark and quiet. Even Copper was sleeping soundly in his usual spot on the floor beside Jessie. All was still. All was calm—for now.

****

Having coerced the information she needed from poor old what's-his-name, Rita wasted no time in hitting the road. Following the directions he'd given her, she easily found the property. The drive had given her time to plan her strategy, knowing the cover of darkness would be her friend. She parked her car in a thicket of trees several yards away from Addie's driveway and waited. By her calculations, full darkness wouldn't come for another hour or so. No matter, she could wait; what she wanted was far too important to get impatient.

She pulled the loaded pistol from her purse and checked it for about the tenth time. Then, rolling down the window partway, she used the glass to steady her aim. Her nerves were steady—her hand didn't shake. She smiled slyly to herself, convinced she could pull this off.

The night was moonless. It had grown so dark inside the car that she could barely make out the black bag that held the gun. Her hand fumbled for it; the cold steel was easy to identify, even in the darkness. With the gun in one hand she opened the door with her free hand and stepped out. The time was now. She had no second thoughts; she desperately wanted the baby, and she, not some imbecile, was going to make it happen.

The gun hung from her right hand as she walked with purpose down the road to Addie's drive. The lane was even darker than the road had been, and the tall trees that loomed eerily overhead caused Rita to shudder—only slightly. She lifted her head and trudged on—resolved to complete her mission.

When the house came into view, she stood still and assessed her surroundings, those that she could make out without the benefit of light. She proceeded with caution, aware that any misstep could draw attention to her presence and spoil her plan.

Stealthily, Rita maneuvered her way around the house to the backyard and climbed the steps leading to the door. Her hand reached for the knob, and she was surprised when it turned. *An omen.*

Entering the dark room, she felt her way along a line of hanging garments that led into another room filled with the aroma of herbs—the kitchen, she guessed.

Silently, she made her way from the kitchen into a long hallway. A loose floorboard creaked under her weight; she froze and listened for a reaction—there was none.

Proceeding on, she trod quietly over the wood floor, feeling her way along the wall. Her hand came to an opening into a room. She stood in the doorway, listening for sounds. Her ears perceived a soft coo, like that of a sleeping baby. Her pulse quickened. With the sound as her guide, she tiptoed in until she came to the crib. Standing over it, she peered inside, barely able to make out the tiny form. Aware that the slightest sound from the baby would wake the mother, she eased away.

She needed to account for everyone in the house. Her eyes searched the room. In the bed beside the baby's crib were two forms, which she assumed were the mother and the older child. Silently, she made her way back into the hallway where she located another room. Quietly, she stepped in and made a quick assessment. In the only bed, one person lay sleeping. All were accounted for; she crept back into the hallway.

Lifting the gun, she cautiously made her way back into the room where the baby lay sleeping. She stood mincingly over the mother's form and nudged her body with the cold barrel of the gun. Groggily, Lizzie pushed it away. Rita pulled back the hammer and positioned the barrel on Lizzie's temple. This time the cold steel against her skin caused her to jolt. Her eyes flew open.

Bewildered, Lizzie gazed at Rita and then at the gun. A frantic gasp escaped her lips.

"Do as I say, and nobody gets hurt," Rita said, her voice deep and gruff. She kept the gun aimed at Lizzie. "I've never killed anybody, but I'll do whatever I have to. I've waited too long to get what I came for; nobody's going to stop me, so don't get any foolish ideas. Get your child–the older one–but leave the baby in her bed. Don't utter a sound." Rita waved the gun around to show she meant business. "Get up and go to the room across the hall. Do it now, or I swear I'll shoot you both." She pointed the gun in the direction of the doorway.

Lizzie's mind was racing; she had no intention of leaving Lillie alone in the room with this crazed woman, but she had Jessie to think of, too. She followed instructions.

She reached over and gently shook Jessie awake and, in doing so, alerted Copper who immediately went into protection mode. Jumping onto the bed, his teeth bared, he growled ferociously, mere inches from Rita's face. The commotion brought a shrill cry from Lillie. With the gun still in her hand, Rita turned her attention to Jessie.

"Calm down that dog, or I'll shoot him," Rita said.

Jessie put her arms around Copper and spoke to him in a soft voice. He stopped growling—his ears stayed alert.

"What do you want?" Lizzie said. "If it's money you're after, you've come to the wrong place."

"Cute," Rita said. "I want something far more valuable than money."

"Well, don't keep us in suspense. What the hell do you want from us?" Lizzie said boldly.

"It's not only what I want. It's what I'm taking with me when I leave here." With the gun pointed to the floor, she moved beside the crib and cooed softly to Lillie. "My sweet baby, I've wanted you for so long. Don't cry. I promise I'll take good care of you; you'll be my little girl from now on."

"Like hell, she will!" Lizzie screamed. She had come up behind Rita and, with a slap of her hand, she knocked the gun from her grasp.

The gun slid across the bare floor. Lizzie and Rita scrambled to grab for it. Copper jumped on top of Rita, giving Lizzie a chance to go after the gun. Rita swore and kicked the dog hard in his side. Copper retaliated by biting into Rita's shin, her blood sprayed across the floor.

"You'll pay for this, you loathsome animal," Rita hissed.

Copper's growl grew more vicious.

Ignoring her excruciating pain, Rita dragged herself across the floor. Lizzie stood over her, hand trembling as she pointed the gun. Without a moments hesitation, Rita lunged at Lizzie and wrangled it from her grip, then turned it on Jessie.

"Take that dog and lock him in that closet. If you don't do as I say, I have a bullet with his name on it–don't think for one second I won't do it. After what he did to my leg, he's lucky he's still alive," Rita said, the open wound on her leg making a pool of blood on the floor.

Taking hold of Copper's collar, Jessie did as Rita instructed. She patted him tenderly on the head as she led him into the dark space and closed the door. On the other side, Copper whimpered softly.

Seeing that Rita's attention was elsewhere, Jessie slipped out of the room in search of Addie, only to find her rushing toward her. Addie didn't need an explanation. She knew trouble was just down the hall. Quietly, she took Jessie by the hand and led her to her room.

"Stay here," she whispered. She placed a kiss on the top of her head, then rushed down the hall to Lizzie's room, entering it cautiously. She surveyed the scene as best she could, given the minimal amount of light. Seeing Addie's form in the doorway, Rita took a step behind Lizzie and aimed the gun at her head.

"You, move over there." She pointed the gun at Addie and directed her to the corner of the room. "You, go with her," she said, giving Lizzie a push.

Rita wildly brandished the gun—clearly a deranged woman—totally out of control.

Jessie, normally an obedient child, had not stayed in her room as her aunt had instructed. She had returned to the room she shared with her mother and sister. She knew the woman had come to take Lillie, and she wasn't going to let that happen. Bravely, she walked right up to Rita. Rita turned the gun and leveled it at Jessie's heart.

Lizzie let out a deafening scream, but Addie didn't flinch a muscle; she had witnessed the scene that was about to play out and was aware of the outcome. Without uttering a word, she allowed her small niece to intervene on their behalf.

"Leave her alone," Lizzie shouted.

Rita kept the gun aimed at Jessie's heart.

The sound of the creaking floorboard alerted them that someone else was in the house. All eyes turned to see two male figures in the doorway. Even in the darkness, Addie recognized them instantly.

Rita snarled and waved the gun toward the corner. "You two, get over there with the women. I'll shoot anybody who gets in my way."

Addie looked at the men and held her index finger over her lips. They nodded. The four of them huddled together in the corner and watched as Jessie, the gun still pointed at her heart, stepped up to Rita and wrapped her small arms around Rita's waist.

A strange sensation surged through Rita's body, as foreign to her as a language she couldn't understand. In the dim light, she looked down into the tear-filled eyes staring up at her—her own filling with tears. This child, this incredible child, had touched her in a way no one ever had—not in her entire life. Feeling those little arms holding her tightly warmed her very soul. The gun she held in her hand suddenly seemed too heavy to hold. Tears began to fall in streams down her face, then turned into breathless sobs. She fell to her knees, the gun hanging loosely at her side.

Eddie quietly made his way across the room where Rita sat in a heap, her head bent in shame. Reaching down, he easily slipped the gun from her limp grasp. He patted her tenderly on her shoulder, then stepped away, leaving her to come to terms with the difficult situation she faced.

Lizzie ran to Jessie and threw her arms around her, telling her what a brave girl she was; tears of joy and relief spilled down her cheeks and onto her blouse. But, she had to know what had made her little daughter do such a thing. The woman was obviously unstable—she could have killed her.

Looking deep into her eyes, Lizzie said, "Honey, what made you do that? How did you know she wouldn't pull the trigger?"

Jessie simply replied, "Mama, I knew she needed to feel what love is."

Lizzie pulled her small daughter into her arms and held her tightly. She lifted her eyes upward. *Thank you, God, for giving me this precious child.*

★★★★★★★★★★★★★

It was Addie who stayed with Rita, helped her to her feet, then led her into the kitchen where the others were gathered around the table. With the lights now on, all eyes turned to Rita when she entered the room.

There was nothing she could say for herself—she couldn't look any of them in the eye. She felt exposed, as if she were standing stark naked in a room of strangers. She kept her eyes downcast as she walked toward the door. With blood still streaming down her leg, she limped out into the dark night. No one made an attempt to follow or dissuade her. She was all alone in the world—once more.

Chapter 27

Pairs of dazed and weary eyes stared at the closed door where Rita had just made her exit. All were thankful and relieved that the frightening ordeal was over and without a single shot fired—it was nothing short of a miracle. Minutes passed before any of them spoke.

Eddie, feeling awkward, given his previous encounters with the group, broke the silence. "I know you're all wondering why I'm here, and you deserve an honest answer."

Lizzie glared at him. "Well, yes, I think we'd all like to know the reason you showed up on the very night that woman came to steal my baby."

The shame of his relationship with Rita showed all over his reddened face; he fidgeted in his chair. "I don't know how much you know about Rita."

"I know absolutely nothing about her. I didn't even know her name until now. How about you fill us in?" Lizzie said, narrowing her eyes at him.

Lizzie turned to Jessie. "Honey, you look sleepy. Why don't you and Copper go on back to bed? I'll be there in just a bit." She kissed her cheek and waited until she heard her footsteps fade away. A nod to Eddie signaled him to proceed.

Eddie took a deep breath. "Some of what I'm going to tell you might be upsetting, I mean, in regard to your marriage to Jim Bob," he said.

"Don't worry about my feelings. There's absolutely nothing you can say about that man that will shock me," Lizzie said.

"Well, I suppose I'll start with my relationship with Jim Bob. We'd gotten to be pretty close in the brief time my mom was married to his dad. After the divorce we moved away, but Jim Bob and I stayed in touch, dropping each other a line a few times a year. His letters were the only ones I received while I was in prison; he was the only one who gave a darn. One of his letters included his address and he'd asked me to look him up when I got out. A few days ago I drove to the address he'd given me, only to find the house burned to the ground. Nobody in that town knew where he and his family had gone."

He turned his eyes to Lizzie who only stared at him. His eye twitched nervously. "I began my own little investigation. As it turned out, prior to my visit to Little Hope, Rita had also been there looking for Jim Bob. Fortunately, she'd left her name and phone number with the man at the gas station; I gave her a call. I learned that she'd been Jim Bob's mistress for a number of years. She said the last time she'd seen him was the day he'd left to rescue his infant child from her unfit mother."

"What!" Lizzie's face turned scarlet, her jaw dropped. Her eyes shot flaming darts at Eddie.

"Whoa, I'm only repeating what I was told," he said, holding up his hands in surrender.

Lizzie's stone cold eyes remained fixed on Eddie's.

He continued with caution. "Rita is a pro and she knows how to get what she wants. I'm terribly ashamed to admit this, but the reason I came here earlier today was to do what Jim Bob hadn't accomplished—I came to take your baby."

Lizzie was out of her chair, the veins in her temples pulsing. "I've heard all of I want to hear. Get out of this house this instant!"

Addie reached for Lizzie's hand and pulled her back into her chair. "Let's hear him out. I think there's more to his story we should hear—before we throw him out," Addie said.

Under the table, Eddie's knees knocked. "I'm sorry, truly I am. I know now what a fool I'd been to fall into Rita's trap. I had come here to take your baby, it's true. I hid among the trees, a distance away, and watched you interact with your children. I saw a much different mother than the one Rita had described; I knew then that everything she had said was just a pack of lies. I realized how she had manipulated me— she has her ways." He paused and looked to Lester for understanding.

Lester only shrugged.

Pulling at the collar of his shirt, Eddie took a deep breath. "Jim Bob and I were pawns in Rita's game—she used us both. After what I had seen with my own eyes—it was over. I had to tell her that I didn't take the baby—nor could I ever. She became enraged. She called me a fool, among other things, saying she'd take matters into her own hands. I didn't take her seriously. Then earlier this evening, I overheard a conversation that led me to believe she was going through with her threat. I had to stop her. That's when I ran into Lester, and that's how we both ended up here tonight."

"That's some story," Lizzie said, looking to Lester for confirmation of Eddie's account.

"It's true. I, too, overheard the man and woman's conversation about a woman asking for directions to Addie's house. Alarm bells went off in my head. I was racing to my car when I ran into Eddie. Neither of us knew we were headed to the same place. Once here, we realized we were on the same mission. We worked out a quick plan as we made our way to the house. Not that we were of any help, but that's why we came," Lester said, backing up Eddie's story.

"I never meant any of you any harm," Eddie said. "From the beginning, I only wanted to find my brother, and that hasn't changed. He obviously failed in his mission to get the baby for Rita, but his whereabouts are still a mystery that I remain determined to solve."

At least Eddie had provided the answer to Lizzie's most haunting question: the reason Jim Bob came for Lillie. She supposed she should be grateful to him for that. Now, she felt obligated to open his eyes to the real Jim Bob. She looked deep into Eddie's eyes and said, "Now that we're getting things out in the open, there are some things you should know as well. A few days ago Jim Bob came like a thief in the night—while we were sleeping. He took Lillie from my arms. When I realized what was happening, I was frantic. I fought to get her away from him. He showed no mercy, he brutally assaulted not only me but his little daughter, Jessie. He's not the person you remember. Life dealt him a bad hand and he'd become mean and full of hate. He made our lives a living hell. I suppose I should actually thank Rita. When he was with her, things were better—we had peace."

Eddie shook his head sorrowfully. "I didn't know; I'm so very sorry for what he put you through."

"Jim Bob was angry at the world but mostly at himself. Sadly, he took his bitterness out on his family," Lizzie said.

Eddie sat in silence for several minutes before speaking. "I guess the best I can hope for is that wherever Jim Bob is, he's made peace with himself. I think it's time for me to close this chapter and get on with my life," Eddie said, standing to leave. There was nothing left to say—no further information to divulge. Looking at the faces in the room, he sensed that his presence was no longer wanted or needed.

He said his goodbyes, wished them all a good life, and walked out into the dark night. With his hands in his pockets and his eyes to the ground, he sauntered aimlessly away.

Lester moved his chair close to Addie's and reached for her hand. Lizzie, noticing the gesture, thanked Lester for coming to their rescue, excused herself, and went off to be with her children.

Addie sat unmoving, reflecting on the revelations that had come to light. Like a scene from a sad movie, Lizzie's story had played out for all to see. Now it was time for her to let go of the past. Addie prayed that she could.

"Are you okay?" Lester said. "You're so quiet."

She squeezed his hand. "I'm just glad it's over and that nobody got shot." She laughed softly.

"I have to admit, I was shaking from head to toe when that woman started waving that gun around," he said with a laugh.

"There could be something terribly wrong with us, finding humor in such a horrifying ordeal," Addie said.

"At least we think alike; we look for the bright side of things. Speaking of which—you were amazing. All the credit for how it turned out goes to you and Jessie; you are both to be commended."

"I only knew how it would play out. Jessie's the one who deserves all the credit—she saved the day. I'm so very proud of her," Addie said.

"She's certainly amazing, but so are you," Lester said, taking Addie in his arms.

Addie breathed in his scent and laid her head on his shoulder. She whispered, "You're pretty amazing yourself."

Chapter 28

Months had passed since the horrifying incident at Magnolia Place; its occupants had comfortably settled into a peaceful, uneventful existence, busying themselves with their everyday tasks.

Addie tended to her lush and bountiful garden and sold her award-winning produce at the new farmers' market, appropriately named Earth's Bounty. Lizzie had finally taken an interest in the marvelous things the earth produced. She assisted Addie in the garden and delighted in learning things she'd never before cared about. Jessie had become quite the artist; in addition to her delightful pictures, she painted labels for the produce and canned goods they sold.

The beautiful way they had decorated their booth and, of course, the quality of the homegrown produce had people standing in line. And no one could resist playing with sweet Lillie, whose smile stole every heart. And, to no one's surprise, Jessie's paintings were as much in demand as the produce they sold.

****

Eddie hadn't returned to Tennessee but had remained in Beau Ridge. When posters started showing up around town announcing a reward for the missing police dog, he knew what he had to do.

He drove out early one morning, and while the sisters were working in the garden, he explained to them all about Copper and why he now needed to return him to his rightful owners—it was the right thing to do. Nobody wanted to be the one to tell Jessie, but it had to be done. The sisters turned their eyes to Eddie. He nodded, knowing it was his place to do so.

He sat on the floor beside Jessie and Copper and ran his hands through the dog's thick coat while he pondered how to break the news. "You love Copper, don't you?" he asked, keeping his eyes focused on the dog.

"Yes, he's my best friend," Jessie said.

"What would you say if I told you he belongs to somebody else, and that they've been looking for him?" Eddie said.

Jessie bit her bottom lip. Tears began to flow, and she buried her face in Copper's coat.

Tears, too, stung Eddie's eyes.

Several minutes passed before she lifted her head. Her voice quivered. "Who does he belong to?"

Eddie cleared his throat. "He's a very special dog who has been trained to do a very special job. He belongs to the police. I know this isn't going to be easy, but I think we have to give him back; it's the right thing to do," he said, looking into her sad eyes. He waited patiently for her reply.

As her tears fell on Copper's coat, she placed his leash in Eddie's hand.

****

The police were so grateful to get the dog back that they offered Eddie a sizable reward, which he couldn't accept, since he was the reason the dog was missing in the first place. But when they learned that a little girl had been keeping the dog safe, and how she'd grown attached to him, they made Eddie a deal. It seemed Copper had a brother who looked identical to him but hadn't made the grade as a cadaver dog. The police insisted that Eddie take the dog to the little girl as a replacement. Needless to say, Jessie was ecstatic; he was named Copper Two.

Little by little, Eddie was winning his way into their hearts.

****

Other than visits to town to shop and sell their goods, the family kept to themselves, with the exception of a chosen few. Picnics were a frequent affair, and everyone's birthday was celebrated in grand fashion.

Magnolia Place, at last, became a place where love and laughter abounded, and secrets remained hidden deep in the twisted vine.

Epilogue

One year later

Addie was in her garden when she heard the ringing sound coming from the house. Wiping her hands on her apron, she went up the back steps into the kitchen, where the phone was mounted on the wall. She lifted the receiver.

"Hello," Addie said.

When there was no reply, she said again, "Hello." Deciding it was a prank call, she was just about to hang up when a female voice spoke so faintly she could barely hear her.

"Please, don't hang up. This is Rita."

The hairs on Addie's neck prickled; she paused, unsure how to proceed. "Yes," she replied, not unpleasantly, but guardedly.

Rita took a deep breath and exhaled. "I know I'm the last person on the earth you and your family want to hear from, and I don't blame you for that. After all I put you through, I'm surprised you're still on the line.

"I'm listening," Addie said, her curiosity aroused.

Rita took a deep breath—this wasn't easy. "I wanted you and your sister to know that after that awful night, I went home and fell into deep despair." She swallowed hard before continuing.

"For the first time in my life, I wasn't able to control a situation. Control was the only thing I did well—this time I had lost. I stayed in that dark place for weeks on end, feeling sorry for myself. But something kept stirring inside me, pulling me up; it was that little girl's touch—her arms wrapped around me. Even when I had a gun to her head, she was unafraid. She embraced me, and something changed in me. I didn't know how to deal with what I was feeling. I reached out for help." She paused again.

Through the receiver, Addie heard her taking deep breaths.

"I've been in therapy for eight months. Initially, it was hard to admit that I needed help. But, through therapy, I learned that I'd been on a self-destructive path all my life. It was just a matter of time before it all blew up in my face, which, unfortunately, you witnessed.

"I had many hang-ups, but the biggest was my inability to love; your little Jessie turned that around for me. My therapist, through long, torturous sessions, made me see this. Anyway, I just wanted to call and tell you I'm sorry—so very sorry for all that I put you through. You could have called the police. I could be in prison right now, but you are all good and decent people. I know I didn't deserve any of the decency I was shown that night, but it was because of it that I have a better life now, and I have all of you to thank, especially Jessie. Would you please tell them this for me?"

Addie wiped away the tears that were streaming down her face. When she spoke, her voice was gravelly. "Why don't you tell them yourself? We're planning a big birthday surprise for Jessie in a couple of weeks. We'd be honored to have you as our guest."

Rita choked back tears. "I've come a long way, but I'm not sure I'm ready to come face to face with the people I held at gun point—but maybe someday," she said with a slight laugh.

"My therapist said I needed to face my demons and close those chapters of my life. Only then would I find true peace."

She sighed heavily into the receiver. "There's another matter that needs resolved—Jim Bob. Do you know where he is?"

Addie didn't hesitate. "Wherever he is, all I can say is— good riddance."

It seemed that Jim Bob's whereabouts would remain a mystery. At any rate, he was gone, and she could close that chapter of her life. "And, Eddie, do you know what's become of him?" He really is a good man, you know; I used him and treated him horribly."

Addie's gaze went to the kitchen window, to the four people in her backyard swaying peacefully in the glider under the canopy of the massive magnolia. Lizzie, holding

Lillie and beside them, Eddie, holding Jessie's hand. "He's amazingly well. I'll tell him you asked about him." It was an unexpected turn of events having Eddie as part of their family, but it seemed so right.

"And the other man who was present, unfortunately, I wasn't introduced," Rita said, her sharp wit still intact.

"Yes, that was unfortunate. That was Lester—the love of my life," Addie said, smiling. She fixed her gaze on her left hand, and the gold band that encircled her finger.

"Well, it sounds like everything has worked out well for all of you, despite all the harm I caused. I'm very grateful that you found it in your heart to speak with me today—I should go now," Rita said, her voice fading.

Addie told Rita she was glad she had gotten the help she needed and that she would give Jessie, Lizzie, and the others her heartfelt apologies. When she hung up the phone, she went to find Jessie—her love for her soaring to new heights.

Acknowledgement

As I think about the years it has taken me to write this, my first novel, I realize it is not my accomplishment alone—it truly takes a village.

First and foremost, I'm eternally thankful for God's gift of creativity—without it this book would never have come to be. To my precious husband and family, I give my love and gratitude for your amazing support and extreme patience. To my Steel Magnolias, my sisters and friends who have encouraged me every step of the way, thank you for believing in me and cheering me on.

And, as I reflect on the many people involved in this process, one person is at the top of the list—my dear friend, Lucy Majors. Without her help, I would still be struggling to discover the path forward. She guided me to Jody Dyer and Crippled Beagle Publishing where the wheels immediately began to turn. My endless gratitude goes to my team at CBP: Jody, Loysa, Kate and Brittany for their hard work, heart, and faith in me and my story.

To everyone involved, I give my love and devotion for helping to make this dream of mine come true.

Author's Note: I extend my heartfelt sympathy to Brittany's family and the team at CBP over her sudden and unexpected passing—she was a pleasure to work with.

About the Author

Jeanne Vaughn is a passionate storyteller drawing her inspiration from the rich culture, gracious people, and endearing charm of her beloved Southern roots. Woven into her fictional narratives are fragments from her own life's experiences, giving them a flair that is uniquely hers. In addition to her love for writing, she enjoys gardening, horseback riding, camping and spending time with family and friends. Jeanne lives with her husband on their family farm in Tennessee. This is her debut novel.